'I think we ought to tell somebody,' said Roy.

'I didn't hear . . .

'I think we o . . .

'Roy! You kn . . . . . . . . . . . . . . . . . rouble for leaving us! . . . . . . . . . . . . . . . get in trouble. . . ? We . . .

'What will th . . .

'I dunno. . . . Not exactly.'

'Put her in prison?'

'No, not that. But they will tell her off like anything, she said. And stick their noses in.'

'So why didn't she come home?'

# THE SECRET

Ruth Thomas

**RED FOX**

A Red Fox Book

Published by Random Century Children's Books
20 Vauxhall Bridge Road, London SW1V 2SA
A division of the Random Century Group

London Melbourne Sydney Auckland
Johannesburg and agencies throughout the world

Red Fox edition 1991

First published by Hutchinson Children's Books 1990

Photoset in Baskerville by Speedset Ltd, Ellesmere Port
Printed and bound in Great Britain by
Cox & Wyman Ltd, Reading

ISBN 0 09 984000 6

To Muriel and David,
remembering a very happy
childhood

# 1

## Before the accident

Mrs Mitchell's high heels went clatter clatter along the promenade. Her breath was coming in painful gasps because she was running, running, running. She didn't know what the time was, but it must be very late because it was getting dark – and darker and darker as she ran. And there might be a train to London or there might not, but let there be a train, she thought. Oh, please let there be a train so I can get back to Nicky and Roy tonight!

She should never have left them. It was mad and wicked to leave two children alone all night, and she saw that now; but when Tony came round, and said there was this caravan at Southbourne, and they could have it all weekend, just the two of them – well, there was this shining picture in her mind's eye of the funfair, and the lively seaside pubs, and the bright sea, all clean and sparkling in the sunlight. And Tony said the kids would be all right, they weren't babies; Nicky was turned eleven, for heaven's sake! And there wasn't time to ask somebody to keep an eye on them, and who would she have asked if there *had* been time?

Mrs Williams perhaps, next door – old Polly Pry. Oh yes, she'd have done it all right! She'd have loved the excuse to come in and poke her nose where it didn't belong. And then the whole of Gilbert Road would hear that Mrs Mitchell's bedroom was a tip, and there was no food in the house to speak of.

Or that fat frump the other side, with the dowdy

clothes and the glasses – Aunty Four-Eyes! Her name was Mrs Morris really, but Mrs Mitchell called her Aunty Four-Eyes once, when she was feeling specially bitchy, and the kids got a giggle out of it so the name stuck. Aunty Four-Eyes wasn't as bad as Polly Pry, but the trouble was, she was so *judging*. She'd be scandalized at the very idea of a mum leaving her kids all night just so she could go to the seaside with her boyfriend. And it was all very well for her! She had a good husband to look after her, with a good job so she didn't even need to go to work. How about if she had had the bad luck to marry a bully, how about that then? And had got left with two kids to bring up on her own?

True, Aunty Four-Eyes had her good points, and, fair's fair, she had minded Nicky and Roy with her own two a few times in the school holidays, and after school as well when they were younger. But Mrs Mitchell couldn't ask her to do it this time because they'd had a row, and they weren't speaking; and, come to think of it, Mrs Mitchell admitted to herself, come to think of it, she *had* used some rather strong language that time, when Aunty Four-Eyes opened her mouth about mothers who stayed out late at night, not because they were working, even, but just to enjoy themselves. And Four-Eyes had been shocked to bits by the language, or pretended to be, though she must have heard all the words before. So now when they met at their front doors, or passed each other going up the road, Four-Eyes turned her head away, as though there was a bad smell somewhere. And Mrs Mitchell laughed, because who cared what a dull cow like that thought?

But staying out late was one thing, and leaving the

kids all night was another, and she never should have done it, Mrs Mitchell knew. Tony had been very angry when she decided to go home after all; they had had a big row about it, and said some nasty things to each other. In the end, Tony had said she'd better take all her things, because he had no intention of bringing them back to her, or seeing her again, ever! Anyway, they were only her overnight things; they weren't important. She could run much better without her overnight things. And she didn't think she'd bother with boyfriends any more, after this. It was the kids that were important, wasn't it!

And it wasn't her fault what she did, you couldn't really say it was her fault. It was a big temptation, wasn't it – a whole weekend by the sea! Anybody could make a mistake. And anyway she was going home now, only please let there be a train, and she was running as fast as she could along the ill-lit seafront, with the black and silver water beyond the dark sands below. Across the road were the cafés and the amusement arcades, but Mrs Mitchell ran by the sea because there were fewer people that side; fewer people to get in her way, and slow her down, and make her miss the last train back to London.

Her bag swung from her hand; her everyday bag with all the everyday bits and pieces in it. All day she'd felt sore about that bag, when she'd stopped to think about it; but Tony had been so impatient, shouting up the stairs at her was she going to waste the whole day getting ready? And that made her nervous, so she just picked up her old bag, instead of stopping to change everything into one of the new ones. And the old bag didn't go so well with her seaside outfit; she was conscious of that even now, running so frantically to catch the train, swinging the old bag from her hand.

She did not notice the idle youth as she passed him; the youth who looked at the swinging bag, and at Mrs Mitchell's pretty, preoccupied face, and back at the bag again. She did not hear the boy's footsteps, as he ran on soft-soled shoes behind her. When she felt the tug she didn't, at first, grasp what was happening. Only when the tug came again, harder now and without mercy – only then did Mrs Mitchell realize she was being robbed.

She screamed. A powerful young arm tugged at the handle of Mrs Mitchell's bag, and Mrs Mitchell fought to hold on, though she felt her own hand was being torn right off. No one came to help. The strolling groups of people on the other side of the road did not seem to hear Mrs Mitchell's screams; and the cars streaked blindly past, their occupants not seeing, or not caring.

One last almighty wrench dragged Mrs Mitchell to the ground, and ripped the bag from her hand. Screaming with rage now, as well as fear, Mrs Mitchell pounded the ground with her fists, and yelled the worst words she could think of at the rapidly disappearing back of the thief. She sobbed and cried, and a young couple did stop then, to help her to her feet. 'What happened?' said the young man.

'He took my bag, he went that way!' said Mrs Mitchell.

'I'll get him for you,' said the young man, and he ploughed off gallantly, delighted at the chance to show off to his girl.

Mrs Mitchell was shaking, and her knees felt weak.

She was bruised, and the side of one leg was all grazed and bleeding. 'He's got all my money!' she wept. 'What am I going to do? I've got to get back to London, I've got to! And he's got all my money!'

'You poor thing,' said the girl – but she didn't offer to lend Mrs Mitchell enough for the fare.

The young man came back, puffing and disappointed. 'Disappeared,' he said. 'Couldn't catch up with him. Sorry.'

'He's got all my money,' wailed Mrs Mitchell. 'What am I going to do?'

'Find a copper,' the young man advised her – but he didn't offer to help.

'That's right,' said the girl. 'You find a copper.'

'Where?' said Mrs Mitchell, piteously. She was shaking so much now, she felt she could hardly stand.

'Oh – over there somewhere,' said the girl, pointing vaguely across the road. 'Sure to be one somewhere around.'

'You'll be all right,' said the young man, losing interest now he'd lost his chance of showing off.

'Yeah – you'll be all right,' said the girl, who didn't want to have to lend Mrs Mitchell any money.

They left her, and it was like a nightmare. Now she had stopped running, Mrs Mitchell could feel the cold night wind coming off the sea, and she shivered in her thin jacket. She was alone and cold, in a seaside town miles and miles from home, and no money to buy her train ticket. And the last train was going, going, going! She saw it in her imagination, chugging heartlessly out of the station.

Desperately, Mrs Mitchell's eyes scanned the pavement on the other side of the road. Was it. . . ? She thought so. 'Police, police!' she tried to call, but something had happened to her throat and she couldn't shout properly. She must get across the road! She must, she must, oh *quickly*, before she lost sight of this one last hope!

She heard the squeal of brakes, and that was the last thing she did hear, before the whole world went black.

# 2

# She'll be home tonight

Roy woke fuzzily, clawing his way out of a bad dream. He couldn't remember properly what the dream was about, but it was something to do with running; running in fear, and screaming. By the time he was fully awake he had forgotten even that much, and was just glad to be out of the horrible dream which wasn't true after all.

Then he felt it; the all-too-familiar coldness and clamminess, where the seat of his pyjamas stuck to him. With a sick heart, but hoping against hope, he put his hand down to feel the sheet – but this was no dream, there was no escaping this one. He had done it again.

Hot with shame, and quickly to get it over, he stumbled into his sister's room. 'I wet the bed,' he told her, miserably.

Nicky stirred, and muttered into the pillow, and humped herself over. 'What? What did you say?'

'You heard.' He had a habit of twisting his fingers, weaving them together like basketry. 'I can't help it. It comes when I'm asleep; I can't help it.'

Nicky sat up and glared. 'You're a nuisance, Roy Mitchell, that's what you are! Now you give me all the trouble to wash your sheets! You don't think of that, do you? What you want to wet the bed for, when Mum's away and *I* got to do everything?'

'She didn't ought to go away,' said Roy. 'It's not fair.'

7

'Don't be so selfish. She's got to have some fun.'

Roy knew he was selfish because Nicky was always telling him about it. But when you didn't have very much you had to hold on to things really tight. If you gave things away, or shared them, there wouldn't be enough left.

'Why couldn't she take me as well, then? I bet there's room in that caravan. Why couldn't they take me?'

'You're too young to understand,' said Nicky.

'I'm ten. Almost.'

'Well people would mostly think you're eight, to look at you. And if they know what you *do*,' she added cruelly, 'if they know what you do sometimes, they'd think you were *one*. . . . Anyway, you *are* going to the seaside, aren't you? You're going to Easthaven with the school, aren't you, we're all going. Don't be so greedy, to want to go to the seaside twice!'

Nicky pegged out the sheets and pyjamas on the line, watched through the garden fence by the disapproving eyes of old Mrs Williams. 'Washing on a Sunday!' said Mrs Williams, sniffing through her long thin nose. Her voice was harsh, and cracked, and not very pleasant.

'Don't you start,' said Nicky. 'We get enough of criticizing from over the other side.'

'I was talking to myself,' said Mrs Williams. 'You weren't supposed to be listening.'

'Am I supposed to be deaf then?' said Nicky.

'You're a very rude little girl,' said Mrs Williams.

'Good!' said Nicky. She hoisted the line and went indoors. 'Roy! Where are you? What you doing sneaking off to watch telly when you haven't finished the potatoes yet? All right, all right, I'll do them. You can go and get ready for Sunday School now, you know how long it takes you to do everything!'

'Oh, not *Sunday School*. Do we have to?'

'Yes.'

'It's not fair. I don't like Sunday School.'

'Bad luck,' said Nicky. She knew very well why Roy didn't like Sunday School, or ordinary school for that matter, but she pretended not to. 'Go on, go upstairs and put on your better clothes. It's nearly time to go.'

She opened the refrigerator, and took out the small joint of meat she had bought herself from Safeway, yesterday. They always had roast dinner on Sundays, it was the one good meal of the week. Sometimes they had it late in the day, because Mum wanted a lie-in, but they never missed it out. Mum had left twenty pounds, before she went off, for Saturday meals and Sunday roast, and something called 'emergencies'. It seemed an enormous amount of money at the time; but, amazingly, nearly ten pounds had disappeared already, so Nicky thought the other ten had better be kept for 'emergencies', whatever they were.

Nicky was delighted to have the chance of cooking roast dinner all by herself. Mum needn't think she was the only one who could do it properly. She put the meat in a roasting pan, arranged the peeled potatoes round it, and drenched the lot in oil, just as she'd seen Mum do. Easy peasy, nothing to it! She lit the oven, and set the meal to cook.

'And don't forget,' Nicky said to Roy, 'don't forget when we're in Sunday School, you haven't got to say one word that our mum is away! You haven't got to let anybody guess, else she's going to get in trouble.'

'I know, I know!' said Roy.

Outside the door they saw that Mrs Williams had moved from the back of her house to the front. Her thin bent figure was in its favourite position, leaning over the gate; her sharp eyes darted up and down the street, anxious not to miss anything.

'Bye, Mum!' called Nicky loudly. 'See you when we get back!'

'I'll bet she's not out of bed yet, even!' Mrs Williams muttered at her hedge.

'I heard that,' said Nicky.

Mrs Williams gave the hedge a malicious little smile.

'If you must know,' said Nicky, 'if you must know, our mum is cooking the dinner for us. She is busy cooking it now. Do you know what we're going to have for dinner? We're going to have roast beef, see? Roast beef, got it? Make sure you have it right because I'm sure it must be very interesting to you what we have to eat. We call you Polly Pry in our house, you know.'

'You're going to cut yourself with that tongue one of these days,' said Mrs Williams, going so red you could even see the flush on her scalp, through the skimpy fluffed-out hair.

Nicky shrieked with fiendish laughter.

Walking ahead of Nicky and Roy, going to Sunday School because their mother sent them, were Sonia and Eric Morris. Sonia was thirteen, and good all the time, and colourless. Eric was eleven, and overfed, and good when being watched by the grown-ups. He dropped back gleefully when he saw who was behind him. 'Who wet the bed last night, then?' he taunted.

Roy squirmed, and turned his head. 'Nobody,' said Nicky.

'Yes they did, I see the sheets on the line.'

'It was my sheets,' said Nicky. 'I spilled a cup of tea.'

'Don't lie. I see the pyjamas as well.'

'Leave it, Eric,' said Sonia.

'Roy Mitchell wets the bed, Roy Mitchell wets the bed!' jeered Eric.

'If you say that again,' said Nicky coolly, 'I'll punch your head in.'

'Not on the way to *Sunday School*!' said Sonia, shocked.

'What's that got to do with it?' said Nicky.

In Sunday school they sang 'Jesus wants me for a sunbeam', which was Nicky's favourite. She sang with gusto, oblivious of the fact that her strident voice was putting everyone's teeth on edge. 'A sunbeam, a sunbeam, I'll be a sunbeam for him,' sang Nicky. And there were several real sunbeams that morning, slanting through the tall windows; and Nicky thought it would indeed be lovely to be a sunbeam, all bright and free, and nothing to do but dance on the world for ever.

On the way home, Eric started again. 'Roy Mitchell wets the bed! Roy Mitchell wets the bed!'

'Have you forgot what I said?' Nicky warned him.

'Why can't he fight for himself anyway?'

'Roy can fight as good as anybody if he wants to,' said Nicky. 'Anybody says Roy can't fight is going to get their head punched in. Roy is a very good fighter, actually.'

Humiliated by the total lack of truth in this claim, Roy hung back, twisting his fingers and scraping the edge of the pavement with his foot. He scraped and scraped, and he would have liked it to be Eric's pudgy face he was scraping, instead of only the kerbstone.

'I can smell the lovely dinner our mum's cooking for us,' said Nicky. She sniffed the air ecstatically, wrinkling her nose and sucking through her teeth. 'Who can smell our roast then?'

The Sunday visitors were beginning to arrive. 'Oh look!' said Sonia. 'There's Uncle Bill and Aunty Mavis!' No uncles or grandmas ever visited the Mitchells' house. 'Who wants relations?' Mum said. Relations were more trouble than they were worth. 'Better off it's just the three of us,' Mum said. And they had fun sometimes, the three of them . . . games, and Mum telling funny stories so they rolled about on the floor with laughing.

A pity she had to spoil it just lately, with boyfriends, Nicky thought. Never mind, though, they still had fun *sometimes*.

'We're back!' Nicky called through the letter box. 'It's all right, Mum, you don't have to let us in. We got our key.'

In the dark little hall, Nicky turned on Roy. 'Ball up your fist,' she told him.

'What?'

'You heard, hit me!' She held up her hand. 'Hit my hand! Harder! Go on, that's right, *harder*! Ow!' Nicky doubled up, blowing on her stinging hand. 'You see? You see? You *can* do it!'

From somewhere in the region of Roy's stomach a small glow spread – up, up to the round baby-face where it appeared briefly as a bright little smile. Nicky said he could do it. All right then, he would do

12

it! Next time. Next time he would show them. He would fight them. He would fight Eric. . . . And then the smile and the glow died away, because he knew he would do no such thing really.

Nicky made gravy in the roasting pan. 'It's a bit lumpy,' she said, 'but it don't matter. Lumps are good for you.'

'The meat is too hard to chew,' said Roy, disappointed. Roy loved his food. It was one of the very few things he enjoyed.

'Don't grumble. It's a very good dinner, actually. Mm-m – delicious . . . chewing is good for you. Plenty starving children would be very glad to have a good dinner like this. . . . All right, if you're so critical I'll let you cook it next time. You ought to be able to. You're not much younger than me, you know.'

'Mum says I wasn't meant to be born, really. She says I was a mistake.'

'She didn't ought to say that,' said Nicky, frowning. 'Nobody's a mistake, actually. Everybody's meant to be here.'

'How do you know that?'

'Don't argue, I just know. . . . Anyway, you have to excuse Mum sometimes, she has a hard life.'

'I wish she would come back.'

'She *will* come back. She will come back tonight, she said. Don't be so impatient. We have all the afternoon first, and some very good things to do. I have, anyway.'

'I know what *you're* going to do,' said Roy, slyly.

'No you don't.'

'Yes I do then. You're going up in Mum's bedroom, and you're going to try on all her clothes.'

'No I'm not. I never thought of such a thing. What a peculiar idea!'

Nicky was flustered and embarrassed that Roy had caught her out wanting to make herself look nice. That was a very private pleasure, and one she had only recently discovered.

'You always try on Mum's clothes when she's not here, I know what you do. And you put on her lipstick as well, I seen you.'

'You sneak!' said Nicky, furiously. 'You creepy crawly *spy*!' She was so self-conscious now, she nearly didn't go after all. 'Creep!' she called, over her shoulder.

There were clothes everywhere, in Mum's bedroom; on the bed, over the chair, trailing on the floor. The wardrobe was crammed to bursting point. Nicky's eyes roamed happily over this tantalizing array, trying to decide. She picked up Mum's newest dress and held it in front of her. The dress was of emerald crêpe, and had a pattern of little glass beads all over the bodice. Nicky slipped the green dress over her head, and peered eagerly into the mirror.

The dress looked awful. On Mum it looked lovely, but on Nicky it was a disaster. The slinky material drooped and sagged over the thin body, only just beginning to develop, and the colour was too hard for the pale skin. It doesn't look quite right, she admitted to herself. I suppose that's because I'm not very pretty.

One day, Nicky would be beautiful. Her bones were all the right shape and one day the sharp, pinched little face would fill out and soften. The gingery frizz would be tamed by a good hairdresser, and the brilliant blue eyes would compel attention everywhere. Nicky would never be pretty, like her mother, but she would be beautiful. And she had no idea in the world that any of this was going to happen.

Tiring presently of the clothes and the make-up and the handbags, Nicky went down to the Back Room, where the television was, and the dining table; and the carpet with the stains and the worn patches; and the sofa with the broken springs. Roy covered something hastily, with his elbow.

'What you doing? Let me see!'

'No. It's mine.'

'Let me see.'

Reluctantly, Roy moved his arm. He had found some scissors, and some old copies of *Woman*. Using the coloured pages he was cutting out large letters, and spreading them over the table. So far he had made WELCUM. 'That's not how to spell "welcome",' said Nicky.

'How do you spell it then?'

'Give me the scissors, I'll do it.'

'It's mine, though.'

'I can do it better. Let me.'

Roy slouched over to the sofa and sat, slumped into a heap.

'Well come on, you can still help.'

'It's not mine any more,' said Roy.

'We can both do it.'

'But it's not *mine*.'

'Mum will like it better if we spell the words right. Like this, look – WELCOME HOME. . . . There, now we want something to stick the letters on.'

'I wanted it to be mine.'

'Don't be so selfish. . . . All right, I'll tell Mum it was your idea. . . . There! Satisfied?'

15

He twisted his fingers without answering. 'I wish she never went.'

'She'll be back soon.'

'What time, do you think?'

'I dunno. Eight, nine. Tony got to drive his car back from Southbourne, don't forget. It's a long way.'

'I don't like Tony,' said Roy.

'Neither do I, he's a creep! Don't worry, though, it won't last. She'll have a row with him soon, you'll see. Like she done with the others.'

'Remember when our dad was here?'

'Yes, but I rather forget.'

'I didn't like our dad.'

'Nor I didn't like our dad neither. And I'm glad he never comes to see us, aren't you? Aren't you glad about that, Roy? And I hope we never see him again.'

'Where shall we put the WELCOME HOME up?'

'Over the kitchen door, then she'll see it the minute she gets in. . . . And I'll tell her it was your idea.'

'You done it better than me though.'

'Only because I can spell.'

'Sometimes I think I can't do anything good,' said Roy.

'Stop saying bad things about yourself,' said Nicky.

After tea, Nicky brought the sheets and the pyjamas in from the line. They tried to watch the television, but it was only boring programmes. 'Let's go in the Front Room,' said Nicky. 'Let's watch out the window to see Mum when she comes.'

They knelt side by side on the red velvet sofa which stood across the bay window; the Front Room was where the best furniture was. They watched all the cars, because they didn't remember what Tony's car looked like, and really it was more exciting that way. Any car could be the one that would have Mum in it. Once a car did pull up, outside next door, but it was only the Morrises' Uncle Bill, bringing the grownups of the family back from church.

Restlessly, Nicky went back to the television. There was a James Bond film on now – that was better! 'Come and watch,' she called to Roy. But Roy would rather stay in the Front Room, watching for Mum.

He came in presently, twisting his fingers. 'What time is it?'

'Nine o'clock.'

'She's late.'

'Not really. You should go to bed, though. You're getting to look too tired.'

'I want to see Mum's face when she sees our WELCOME HOME. And you tell her it was me thought of it.'

'Just a bit longer then.'

Roy went back to the Front Room, and Nicky watched the end of the film. After that the programmes were boring again. Nicky fiddled with the buttons on the television, picked up a book, fiddled with the television once more. She looked at the clock. Half past ten, Mum *was* late. Nicky yawned. Roy was quiet – she went to see what he was doing.

Worn out with watching, Roy had fallen asleep. He was still kneeling on the sofa, his arms over its back, his head fallen on to his arms, and he was snoring softly. Nicky put an arm round his neck. 'Come on, wake up.'

'Is she here? Is she here?'

'Not yet, but we have to go to bed. Because of school tomorrow.'

'But Mum hasn't come! Where is she? She's *late*.'

'No she isn't,' said Nicky sharply. 'It's only half past ten, that's not late for grown-ups but it's late for us. Come on, Roy, we have to go to bed.'

'I want to wait for Mum.'

'Don't argue.'

They lay in their beds, but sleep would not come. A door banged, 'There she is!' Roy jumped out of bed and ran to the landing.

'It's only Uncle Bill and Aunty Mavis going home,' called Nicky. 'Why don't you go to sleep?'

'Why don't you?'

'How can I with you yelling at me? And running about all over the house?'

'Nicky. . .?'

'What?'

'Suppose she doesn't come tonight?'

'She will.'

She was nearly asleep when she found herself thinking it was lucky Mum always put her and Roy's dinner money in an envelope on Friday, so she wouldn't spend it by mistake over the weekend. Now why, Nicky thought, why did she have to think it was lucky they had their dinner money for next week? She must be getting as silly as Roy!

'But supposing—'

'Don't argue. Go to sleep. *Now!*'

He did presently, because he was tired out, but Nicky lay awake a long time, stifling unease, as she listened to the silence.

# 3

# A bad day

'You told a lie,' said Roy, reproachfully.

In the hall, Nicky shifted uncomfortably from one foot to the other. They had run through the house, and there was nowhere else to look. 'Well I didn't mean to, did I? I didn't know it was a lie, did I?'

The china-blue eyes blinked and glistened, and the lower lip began to tremble. Roy was going to cry and he mustn't, Nicky thought. If Roy cried it might make *her* start thinking there was something to cry about. 'She'll come today,' Nicky said firmly. 'When we get back from school she will be here.'

'You said she was going to come yesterday.'

'Well now I'm saying she'll come today. Don't go on and on. She might walk through that door any minute. Do you want her to see you crying when she comes through that door? Well then, pack it in! . . . Do you hear me, Roy Mitchell, *pack it in*!'

There was another reason Nicky didn't want Roy to cry. His crying could be quite desperate at times, and she didn't like to see it. She particularly didn't want to have to see it this morning, when she specially needed to be tough.

'Why didn't she c-come though?'

'I dunno, do I? Probably having such a good time. Don't you want our mum to have a good time? Are you so selfish you don't want our mum to enjoy herself? Well then.'

'She might have had a accident. They might have had a car smash.'

Nicky was ready for that one. 'She didn't have a accident. You want me to tell you how I know? All right, I'll tell you how I know. If there was a accident the police would come to tell us. They would come in the night and they didn't.'

A brief glittery smile lit up the baby-face. Roy laughed sometimes – quite hysterically when Mum was being funny; but he hardly ever smiled and when he did, Nicky found, she often could scarcely bear to look because the smile had so much hope in it. Too much hope. Dangerous hope, because Roy couldn't stand disappointment; he couldn't pick himself up when things went wrong. 'I wish we had a phone,' said Roy.

'You're always wishing things,' said Nicky. 'Phones cost money you know.'

'But Mum could ring us up, and tell us about she's having too much fun to come home.'

'Wash your face again,' said Nicky. 'It's not clean enough for school!'

On the way to school, Nicky bought some chewing gum. Chewing gum was not allowed in school, which was the reason Nicky bought it. She was just in the mood for doing something not allowed. She stood in the line in the playground, and chewed her gum aggressively.

'Nicky Mitchell, take that disgusting muck out of your mouth,' said Miss Powell, who was strict and short-tempered. Under cover of her hand, Nicky transferred the gum from one cheek to the other. 'Throw it in the bin, come along!'

The bin was behind Miss Powell, who was facing

the lines. Nicky pretended to throw away the gum, then blew an enormous bubble for the amusement of the assembled school. Miss Powell and the other teachers could not see the bubble, of course. 4P and 4H tittered, nudging one another, and Nicky blew a second bubble because the first one had burst. Miss Powell turned round and caught Nicky blowing bubbles. 'What a pain you are, Nicky Mitchell! I'm glad you're not in my class.'

Nicky was equally glad she was not in Miss Powell's class. Nicky was in Mr Hunt's class, and Mr Hunt was all right though nothing special. Where *was* Mr Hunt, by the way? Late, probably, as usual! Mr Hunt should not be so lazy, Nicky thought. He should get up early in the morning like other people, and come to school at the right time.

You could always tell the classes without a teacher, because of the noise. Mr Nelson, the headmaster, came limping along on his gammy leg and pretended to be very surprised that 4H were making all that noise just because their teacher was ill and hadn't been able to come that day. He would have thought that 4H, being practically secondary school children now, would have outgrown such infantile behaviour. Really, he was quite astonished at the infantile behaviour of a class at the top of the school.

However, there was an opportunity now for them to show how mature they were really, because here was Mrs Patel come to be their teacher for today. Who was going to be Mrs Patel's helper? Thank you, Joycelyn! And Nicky Mitchell could get off the windowsill, which had not been designed for people to sit on, and take that revolting stuff out of her mouth *please*!

Mrs Patel called the register. There was quite a bit of sniggering.

'Joycelyn Miles.'

Snigger, snigger.

'Yes, Miss.'

'Nicolette Mitchell.'

Silence.

'Nicolette Mitchell not present today?'

'Go on!' Eric Morris, who to Nicky's sorrow had been allocated a seat at her table, poked at Nicky with a ruler.

'Leave off, creep!'

'Nicolette Mitchell?' said Mrs Patel again, hopefully.

'Don't know anyone called Nicolette,' said Nicky. 'Anybody know anybody called Nicolette?' Jaws working again, the gum unpleasantly visible in the open mouth, Nicky directed her gaze in a sweep around the room. 'No, nobody here called Nicolette. Sorry.'

Mrs Patel looked confused. 'But it says it in the register. And she has been marked present last week.'

'It's Nicky, Miss.' 'She's joking, Miss.' 'She don't like her real name.' 'It's a joke.'

Mrs Patel looked puzzled, but she finished the register, and after that there was Assembly, and after that Mrs Patel started to write a lot of sums on the board.

'Do we have to do that, Miss?' 'Do we *all* have to do it?' 'We got our own maths, Miss, we all do different.' 'We do it different with Mr Hunt.'

'You will all do the same today,' said Mrs Patel, who could not possibly have coped with the complexities of individual work on her first day in a strange class.

Bored and restless, Nicky sprawled across her desk. She scribbled a few figures, fussed under her table for a rubber, rubbed out what she had done, dug her elbow into Joycelyn in the next seat, blew another gum bubble, and embarked on the spreading of a juicy piece of gossip, picked up that morning in the playground. 'Nicky won't let us get on with our work,' Eric complained.

'It's boring,' said Nicky.

'It is what you come to school for,' said Mrs Patel.

'I like your sari, Miss,' said Nicky. Mrs Patel's sari was deep pink and blue, with little tinselly bits that flashed and twinkled as she moved. 'You look like a princess out of a fairy story.'

'Thank you, Nicolette, now please get on with your work.'

'Indian ladies got lovely clothes,' said Nicky enviously. 'I wish I wore a sari, all lovely colours and shiny stuff.'

The class tittered. 'She look good, punching somebody's head in a sari,' said a boy called Marcus.

'Shut up, you!' said Nicky. 'You look like a sack of potatoes all the time. A sack of potatoes with a turnip on the top!'

Marcus flushed. He was lumpy and slow and he knew it. 'You didn't have to say that, Nicky,' said Joycelyn.

Joycelyn was big, and black, and kind. If Nicky could be said to have a friend, that friend would be Joycelyn, but they were not really close. Nicky didn't have any close friends, didn't seem to want to attach herself anywhere too permanently. She hung around

23

with this group or that, or just on her own if she felt like it. People tended to approach her with caution, wary of her moods. Even some of the teachers were a little bit afraid of her.

Across the yard at playtime, Nicky saw a crowd. There was jeering and booing; someone was being teased. The jeerers were mostly third years, but Eric Morris was there as well. Nicky ran.

Roy was closed against the playground wall by a half-circle of bullies. 'Cry-baby, wet the bed! Cry-baby, wet the bed!' Roy was not crying though, he was looking like a trapped animal instead; crossed arms hugging the thin chest, limp gingery curls damp with sweat, eyes wildly seeking escape. Nicky grabbed Eric by the hair and yanked him backwards. He staggered, losing his balance, and Nicky punched him in the back. 'Ow-w-w!' Eric rounded on her, and began flailing with his fists, but most of his punches missed. Nicky grabbed his hair again and slapped his face with her other hand. 'That's for picking on my brother! You want another one?'

'No-o-oh!'

'There's another one for you anyway. You want another one?'

'No-o-oh! Leave me!'

'You leave my brother alone then!'

'Break it up this minute!' said Miss Powell, on duty that morning and just arrived at the scene. 'All right, who started it?'

'She attacked me for nothing,' said Eric.

'When are you going to get civilized?' said Miss Powell to Nicky.

'He was making them all pick on my brother.'

24

'No I wasn't,' said Eric.

'Roy will never learn to stand up for himself with you babying him all the time,' said Miss Powell.

'It's not fair, though. It's too many of them, it's not fair!'

Roy was crying now, leaning on his arms against the playground wall, his small body racked with distraught sobs. 'He's just a cry-baby,' said Eric.

Nicky flew at him, and her scratching nails left three bright tramlines down the side of his face. 'That does it!' said Miss Powell. 'Nicky Mitchell, go in and report to Mr Nelson for fighting!'

'Who's going to look after Roy?'

'Do as you're told.'

'Not till I know who's going to look after Roy.'

'If Roy really needs a nanny he can come with me,' said Miss Powell, not at all kindly. 'And Nicky, if you don't go to Mr Nelson this minute, there'll be no more playtimes for you for a week!' There was unconcealed dislike in the eyes that followed Nicky's retreating back.

Mr Nelson was looking forward to his retirement at the end of the term. He had enjoyed his teaching life, but now he was tired, and it was all getting too much. He was not very well, he had lots of aches and pains, and this morning his arthritis was particularly bad. Mr Nelson's lined face was quite grey from the pain.

He was drinking his mid-morning tea and wondering if he could snatch a quick doze before the bell went, when Nicky Mitchell made her unwelcome appearance. 'Miss Powell said to come.'

Mr Nelson sighed, and ran a hand over the sparse strands of hair, plastered carefully across his head. 'Oh dear, what have you been doing now?'

'Nothing. . . . How is you arthritis today, Sir?'

'Come on, Nicky!'

'I can't remember.'

'Try. Force yourself.'

'. . . Only fighting a bit.'

'A good start to the week, wouldn't you say? And how many times last week?'

'They didn't ought to pick on Roy.'

'Children can be very cruel, I know, but Roy has to learn to stand up for himself. What's going to happen next term when you're at your new school?'

'Don't *you* start!'

'Nicky!'

'Sorry, Mr Nelson! But you don't know what it's like for him. They tease him to death. You want to try it some time.'

'Come on, Nicky, you know the old saying – "Sticks and stones will break my bones but names will never hurt me."'

'The one that said that told a lie,' said Nicky.

'I believe you've got a point there,' said Mr Nelson, thoughtfully. 'You're a funny mixture, aren't you?'

'*I* don't think so,' said Nicky.

'Look, we'll make a bargain,' said Mr Nelson. 'I'll have a word with Roy's teacher and see if we can do something to stop this teasing. It *is* only teasing, isn't it? He's not getting knocked about in any way? . . . I thought so. Right. I'll have a word with Mrs Blake and *you*, *you*, Nicky Mitchell, keep your fists to yourself in the playground for a week. Done?'

'Done!' said Nicky.

Only the playground, Nicky told herself. Sir only said

in the playground. And Eric Morris was sitting there looking just a bit too pleased with himself, in spite of the scarlet scratches down his cheek. Perhaps *because* of the scratches. Looking forward to the story he was going to tell his mum, probably, all about that evil witch Nicky, who went about clawing lines down people's faces, and pulling their hair nearly out. But he wouldn't bother to mention what he did first, oh no!

The class was working an English exercise in their best books; listlessly, but with only a few muttered complaints. Mrs Patel, straight and composed with folded hands, watched them from the front. Her eyes moved serenely from right to left and back from left to right. When Mrs Patel's eyes focused right, they covered Nicky's group. When they moved left, Nicky's arm shot out and pushed Eric's elbow so his ball-point pen made an ugly score across the page. 'You jogged me!' Eric was deeply aggrieved. He took a pride in having neat books, and now his book was spoiled.

'Who jogged you? I never jogged you!'

'Yes you did, Nicky Mitchell! Look what you done to my book!'

'I never! I never, did I, Joycelyn? I never touched his book, did I?'

'What is the matter?' said Mrs Patel.

'Look what that hell-cat done to my book. *And* to my face!'

'Do you think that is a nice name to call someone?' said Mrs Patel.

'Nicky ain't a nice person,' said Marcus.

Nicky grinned, enjoying herself.

'Please do not let there be any more trouble,' said

Mrs Patel. But next time her eyes travelled to the left, Nicky's arm shot out again, and now there was a jagged tear, as well as a black score, on Eric's page.

'Tell her, Miss!'

'Nicolette, please come and sit at this desk by yourself,' said Mrs Patel.

The desk in question was a spare one, against the wall at the front of the room. Sitting in it, Nicky was behind Mrs Patel and her calm searchlight eyes. It was a small desk, belonging to the younger classes really, and Nicky had difficulty fitting her long legs under it. She fidgetted, and knocked her knees against the desk, and sat sideways. She was *nearly* under the board. Nicky picked up a piece of yellow chalk and stretched across the little desk to draw on the board.

She drew a fat boy, with bloated cheeks and a great rolling belly. The class began to giggle. Nicky was no artist, but the fat boy was clearly meant to be Eric. To leave no possible room for doubt, Nicky added three lines down the side of his face. Then she drew a great balloon, coming from the fat boy's mouth. Inside the balloon she printed the words I AM A FAT PIG. It was not very funny really but the class, bored to tears with the English exercise, found it quite hilarious. Eric, sensitive about his curves, began to cry. 'Who's a cry-baby now?' said Nicky, scornfully.

Mrs Patel was very much put out. 'I think you are a very naughty girl,' she said to Nicky. 'Are you always a naughty girl like this?'

'Yes,' said Nicky, grinning.

'Please use my name when you speak to me,' said Mrs Patel, who was not used to rudeness from eleven-year-olds.

'Yes, Mrs – Whatsyournameagain?' said Nicky. The maddening grin was still on her face.

The class giggled when Nicky called Mrs Patel Mrs Whatsyournameagain. 'My name is Mrs Patel, and that is a very ordinary name, so it is easy to remember. In fact, I notice that there are two children already in this very class with that name.'

Nicky shrugged.

'Please get on with your work now, all of you.'

Nicky looked at the clock. Only half past eleven, three quarters of an hour before dinner time, and *how* this day was dragging! What did Mr Hunt want to be ill for? Probably he wasn't ill really. Probably he just had too much beer at the pub last night, so he didn't feel like coming to school. So the whole class had to put up with boring Mrs Patel, and the morning that was never going to end. What about doing a magic spell, to make the time go by, so it would be home time, and she could know for certain that Mum was really back? Nicky experimented with making up a few spells, and chanting them under her breath, but they didn't work. So there was nothing for it, she would have to liven up the morning instead. She would bait Mrs Patel a bit. That would stir things and amuse the class.

'Mrs Whatsyournameagain,' said Nicky. 'Mrs Whatsyournameagain, can you help me, please, Mrs Whatsyournameagain?'

Under the light brown skin, Mrs Patel's cheeks went a dusky red. 'You are being rude on purpose,' she said, hurt and puzzled by this behaviour.

'She can't help it, Miss,' said Marcus. 'She's always like that. She can't help it.'

'That's right,' Nicky agreed with him. 'I can't help it, see? I was born like it.'

Mrs Patel must have wished very much to be allowed to slap Nicky's grinning face. 'If you cannot control your insolence, I do not want you any more in my class,' she said. 'You will have to go to the headmaster, to Mr – er – Mr. . . .' It was very embarrassing for Mrs Patel; in the stress of the moment she had forgotten *his* name.

'It's quite a ordinary name,' said Nicky, goading her. 'It begins with a N.'

'Take your books and GO,' said Mrs Patel.

Nicky sat outside Mr Nelson's room for the rest of the morning, because his ulcer was playing him up now, as well as his arthritis, and he couldn't think of anything else to do with her. From time to time she called companionable remarks through his open door, because really she didn't like being bad friends with Mr Nelson. But Mr Nelson firmly ignored her. He even made her eat her school dinner all by herself, which was hard on her, and Mr Nelson didn't like doing it, but the child mustn't be allowed to get away with everything. And after dinner she had to go to Miss Powell's class, because Mrs Patel still wouldn't have her back. Miss Powell was not pleased to have Nicky Mitchell dumped on her.

Miss Powell was nursing another grievance as well. She was a conscientious teacher and an ambitious one. She worked very hard with her class – for instance there was always lots of fabulous art work on display in her room. Although she was young, she was already Deputy Head of the school, and she had thought she was going to be made Head when Mr

Nelson retired. But there had been a meeting to choose the new Head, and the meeting didn't choose Miss Powell, they chose someone from another school altogether. Perhaps the meeting thought it would be nice to have someone kinder than Miss Powell. Anyway, Miss Powell was still sore about it, and even snappier than she used to be before the meeting.

'Sit there!' she said to Nicky. 'No, not *there*, stupid child, THERE!'

She had a face like an old-fashioned Christmas card, Nicky thought, with a little pink mouth, and shiny-gold hair like a rippling waterfall, down her back. Quite pretty, really. What a shame, to have such a pretty face, and be so cross-tempered! 'If I knew where THERE was,' said Nicky, 'I could sit in it.'

'If you were as smart as you like people to think,' said Miss Powell, 'you'd know very well I didn't mean you to sit next to Jason. No one in their right mind would put Nicky Mitchell within spitting distance of Jason Charles. And let me assure you,' she added bitterly, 'that in spite of a good many thankless years of beating my head against a brick wall over people like you, I'm not actually certifiable yet!'

'I don't know what all that was about,' said Nicky. 'Where am I supposed to sit?'

'Sit by Karen, you rude little madam. And try not to do anything to annoy her. And don't move, and don't open your mouth. I want to be able to pretend you're not here.'

Nicky sat meekly by dull, good Karen; she had quite lost interest in being naughty. She felt spiritless all of a sudden, and tired. She had slept only half the night, and her eyelids were heavy. Her head nodded over the book she was supposed to be reading, and presently dropped forward on to the table in front of her.

She slept soundly through the afternoon.

Roy was already at the house when Nicky arrived. She found him peering forlornly through the letter box, and calling 'M-u-um! Mu-u-um!' There was only one latch key and one mortice key between the children, and Nicky carried them both. 'She's not answering,' said Roy.

'Shut up!' said Nicky. 'Do you want everybody to hear? She's not supposed to be here this time of day, remember? She's supposed to be at work. . . . Perhaps she *is* at work. Perhaps she came home and went out again.'

The house was silent, empty of presence. The WELCOME HOME banner was still a bright splash of colour over the kitchen door, but the house did not feel as though it had welcomed anybody today. The children rushed through the downstairs rooms, looking for signs. 'She hasn't made a cup of tea,' Nicky admitted. 'But perhaps she didn't have time.'

'Her stuff isn't here.'

'Her stuff will be upstairs, in the bedroom,' said Nicky. She bounded up the stairs and was quiet for a long time. When she came down she was smiling and singing 'Jesus wants me for a sunbeam', to show she wasn't worried really.

'Her stuff ain't there, is it?' said Roy.

'Don't say "ain't",' said Nicky. 'It's bad manners.'

'She hasn't come home, has she?' said Roy. He was

sitting in a dejected heap on the sofa with the broken springs, twisting his fingers.

'Well no, she hasn't *come*. As a matter of fact she hasn't actually come yet, but she will.'

'When?'

'Tonight. You know what I think it is? You know what I thought of when I was upstairs? She came back from the seaside and went straight to work! There, now we know why she hasn't been home yet.'

'I want Mum!'

'Well, you're going to *have* Mum. Tonight. When she comes back from work. . . . So you can stop moaning now and help me. Let's think what we're going to have for tea.'

'Can we have baked beans?' said Roy, cheering up a bit.

'If there is any.'

There was one tin of baked beans in the cupboard, two tins of peas, one of spaghetti hoops and one of rice pudding.

'Shall we wait for Mum to come before we have it?' said Roy.

'She might be late, so we might as well have it soon,' said Nicky. 'And it will be just like ordinary times when Mum is late home from work. It will be just like that, Roy, no different. And after tea we will watch at the window again, to see her come.'

They watched at the window, and the minutes crawled. 'She's not coming from work,' said Roy. 'It's got too late!'

'I know what it is then,' said Nicky. 'I just thought. She's having another whole day by the sea. In the lovely weather.' In fact, the day was rather chilly. 'She will come home when it's dark, you'll see!'

'I don't think she's going to come at all,' said Roy.

'Let's play Rough Games,' said Nicky.

They rampaged round the house, shrieking with laughter and pelting one another with cushions. Mrs Williams banged on the party wall to stop them, and they banged back. 'Suppose Mum's dead!' said Roy, suddenly.

'Don't say things like that!'

'But supposing she is?'

'You're silly. How could she be dead?'

'Like I said . . . there might have been a accident in the car.'

'The police would have come. Remember the police?'

'How would they know where to come, though, if Mum's dead?'

'Tony would tell them, of course. You are *silly*, Roy.'

'Supposing Tony's dead as well?'

'. . . In the car accident?'

'Yes.'

There was a terrible silence for a moment. 'I know though,' said Nicky, 'I know, her handbag!'

'What about her handbag?'

'The police can find people's address from their handbag. They always do that. You know – like on the telly.'

'How?'

'How what?'

'How can they find people's address from their handbag?'

'You *know*. Letters and things.'

'Mum doesn't have any letters.'

She didn't – or hardly ever. She had bills, but they

always went behind the clock in the Back Room. 'I know, I know – her Benefit Book!' said Nicky, triumphantly. 'You know, that she gets money with every week. From the post office. You know that book! It's got our address on it and she always keeps it in her handbag, always!'

'I think she didn't take that bag.'

'Yes she did, yes she did, I remember! That pig was shouting at her to hurry up, and she come down with her old bag, I remember. . . . And anyway her new ones are all in the bedroom, because I saw them.'

'So the police would know where to come!' said Roy, eagerly. 'They would know where to come because of her bag!'

'Yes.'

'So she isn't dead!'

'I told you already, why don't you listen? And mind you put on a clean shirt tomorrow! That one's got all messy.'

Pamela and Pandora, who lived by the sea at Southbourne, were playing in their back garden. They were eight years old, and twins, and exactly like each other, and rather awful. Their mother had a new baby to look after, so she was pleased to have the twins amusing each other in the garden, and not getting under her feet – and she didn't very often get round to asking them what they were doing.

On this sunny summer evening, Pamela and Pandora were playing at crawling behind the shed. The hedge which bordered the road had grown and thickened since the shed was built, and now there was only a small space between it and the shed, just big enough for an eight-year-old to squeeze through.

'I've found something,' said Pandora, emerging first at the other end.

'Show me,' said Pamela.

'No,' said Pandora. 'It's mine. I found it.'

'You're a mean stinking pig!'

'And you're a smelly cow! All right, you can just look. It's a handbag.'

'That's a funny thing to be behind our shed. Who put a handbag behind our shed?'

'I don't know, do I? I don't know everything in the world. It's only an old one anyway, so they probably threw it away. They probably didn't want it any more.'

'We can have it for our dressing up,' said Pamela.

'You mean *I* can have it for *my* dressing up,' said Pandora. 'I was the one that found it.'

'You're a stingy sausage!'

'And you're a greedy gobble gobble turkey!'

'What's inside it?' said Pamela.

Pandora opened the bag, and tipped the assorted contents on to the ground. 'Lipstick!' said Pamela, in delight. 'And keys!'

'I might just let you put the lipstick on sometimes,' said Pandora. 'If you are polite to me.'

'What's this?' said Pamela.

'It's a cheque book,' said Pandora. 'You know, for getting money out of the bank. They must have not wanted that any more as well.'

'That's not a cheque book, you silly stupid fool! Cheque books are blue.'

'Not always.'

'All right then, prove it. Prove that's a cheque book. See, clever-clogs? You can't prove it!'

'Yes I can then, it's got pages you can tear out.

36

When you go to the bank to get the money. There's one, see?'

'Don't tear out any more,' said Pamela. 'We can play at going to the bank with it. When we do our dressing up. And lock our door first with the keys.'

'And we can put on the lipstick,' said Pandora. 'And this lovely eye stuff.'

'Wash it off before Mummy sees, though.'

'Oh *she* won't see,' said Pandora. 'She's too busy to see anything! She won't see if we lipstick ourselves all over! She will just say, "Run away for now, darlings, I have to change Richard's nappy, I think he's done a poo!"'

'We have a lot more fun now, don't we?' said Pamela. 'Since Richard came.'

The garden shed was also the twins' playhouse. Daddy had painted it for them in bright colours, one Saturday. They hardly saw Daddy during the week, because he worked in London and didn't get home till late. The twins didn't mind about not seeing Daddy much, because they had their red, yellow and blue playhouse, with lots of lovely secrets inside. And now this! The cheque book and the make-up and all the other odds and ends were scraped off the ground and put back into the handbag, so the grown-ups wouldn't know the twins had found it. Because grown-ups were funny about things that got found, and so fussy they might even take it all away.

Pamela and Pandora put Mrs Mitchell's handbag into their playhouse and hid it under a jumble of dressing-up things. There was no money to be put back in the bag, of course. The thief had taken the money before he threw the bag away; before he stuffed the bag between the hedge and the little shed,

37

leaping on to the wall outside for a moment to make himself tall enough to do it. He would have taken the keys and the Benefit book as well if he had been a proper thief and known what to do with them. But he wasn't a proper thief. This was only the second bag he had ever snatched in his life, and once he had the money all he wanted to do was get rid of everything else, hopefully where nobody would find it.

In the middle of the night Roy woke, cold inside and desolate. He slipped out of bed, and stood forlornly in the doorway of his sister's room. 'Nicky. . . .'

'What's the matter? Did you wet the bed?'

'No. . . . She didn't come, did she?'

'No.'

'Nicky. . . .'

'What?'

'I know she's not dead, but suppose she's ill?'

'Tony would bring her home.'

'Suppose she had to go to hospital?'

'Tony would tell us.'

'Suppose Tony had to go to hospital as well?'

'Well *someone* would tell us. Stop supposing bad things and go back to bed.'

'I'm not only supposing she didn't come! I'm not only supposing that. It's real!'

'Well it's nothing to worry about. She's probably having such a good time she forgot what day it is.'

'Will she come tomorrow, then?'

'Yes.'

'Are you sure?'

'*Yes!*'

# 4

## Covering up

'I think we ought to tell somebody,' said Roy.

'I didn't hear that!' said Nicky, sternly.

'I think we ought to, though.'

'Roy! You know Mum's going to get in trouble for leaving us! Do you want our mum to get in trouble. . . ? Well, then!'

'What will they do to her?'

'I dunno. . . . Not exactly.'

'Put her in prison?'

'No, not that. But they will tell her off like anything, she said. And stick their noses in.'

'So why didn't she come home?'

'Actually, I don't understand it,' Nicky admitted. 'But I expect it is something quite ordinary really. Anyway Mum will explain it to us when she comes.'

'She better come today! She better!'

'Let's think about good things now,' said Nicky. 'Let's think about the Outing. And we can take our letters back, that Mum had to sign for us to go. We forgot them yesterday.'

At school, Roy lurked behind the toilets, wishing the bell would go. Every second in the playground was one more second of danger. At any moment some of them might start – carelessly, calling names for fun, with no idea of how terrible they made him feel. But once in the classroom he was reasonably safe, because they couldn't do much with Mrs Blake there.

39

He thought about Mum not coming home, and it was like looking into a dark tunnel you couldn't see the end of. It was frightening; there was something wrong about it, whatever Nicky said! Mums didn't do things like that, did they? Anyway, he never heard of it before.

The bell at last! Roy dawdled to 3B's line, hoping to be at the end. If he was at the end there would be nobody behind him to hiss nasty things into his ear.

There was some commotion going on in 4H's line – Nicky scuffling with Eric Morris again. Then Nicky was being hauled out of the line, and was arguing with Miss Powell about whether she was supposed to be in 4H or 4P that day. She finally accepted Miss Powell's judgement with a bad grace, and stood behind Jason Charles, whispering uncomplimentary things about Miss Powell over his shoulder. Then Miss Powell was leading her class into school, and Roy saw his sister mimicking Miss Powell's walk. It was not difficult to make fun of Miss Powell's walk because, although her face was pretty, she was unfortunate enough to have a long body and short legs like a duck, so her bottom stuck out and wiggled as she went. Roy saw that most of Class 4P were turning round to watch Nicky's performance, and he dreaded that Miss Powell would turn round and catch her at it, and she would be in even more trouble.

Mrs Blake had noticed, of course, that Roy Mitchell had no friends. She had also noticed that Sharon, Jennifer and Claudette, a trio of black chatter-boxes, were prepared to be kind to Roy up to a point, when they could spare the time. So Mrs

Blake, who was kind herself in a limited sort of way, had Roy sitting at the same table as Sharon, Jennifer and Claudette. This left two vacant seats at that table, however, and since there was a fair sprinkling of naughty children in Class 3B, and since Mrs Blake very definitely didn't want all the naughty ones sitting together, the last two seats of that table were occupied by Gary and Sanjay, two of the worst by anybody's standards, and the cause of daily misery to poor Roy. Not as bad as his sufferings in the playground, of course, but bad enough.

They wouldn't start anything while Mrs Blake was watching, but Mrs Blake couldn't be watching all the time. She moved from group to group, and as soon as her back was turned this morning, Gary began. 'Roy Mitchell wets the bed!' Gary had bulging eyes and buck teeth, and his voice, even his whisper, was rasping and cruel. Sanjay echoed him, his mean little ferret-face alight with malice. Roy blushed.

'Shut up,' said Sharon, whispering.

'Yeah, shut up,' said Jennifer, out loud. 'You get on our nerves, keeping on the same thing all the time.'

'Pencils down!' said Mrs Blake.

She had just remembered that Nellie (Mr Nelson) had asked her to have a word with her class about everyone picking on Roy Mitchell; and being a bit tactless, as well as kind, it didn't occur to her that she should arrange for Roy not to be there. She went on and on about how ashamed she was to think that people in her class were guilty of persecuting, which was a despicable thing to do. And Roy Mitchell had done nothing to them first, so there was absolutely no excuse. Well – yes – he *had* been known to hide people's rubbers once or twice, that was true, but only after they had driven him to it with their teasing. As she said, the behaviour of the class in general towards poor Roy was really despicable, and she wanted to see no more of it. . . . And now back to work!

Roy's scarlet face was buried in his arms. He dared not lift it. Everyone must be looking at him. Mrs Blake had only made it all worse.

Gary, deeply resentful at being called 'despic-', whatever it was Mrs Blake said, whispered in Claudette's ear. Roy couldn't hear what he said, but it must be something rude because Claudette sniggered and said, 'Don't be nasty!' And Claudette whispered to the other two, cupping her hand over her mouth to keep Roy out of it, so he knew it must be about him. And then the girls were all sniggering, not looking at him. There was a sick feeling in Roy's stomach. They were all against him now, all of them!

Anguished already because Mum hadn't come home, Roy twisted his fingers and felt the bitterness and the anger surging inside him. He swallowed it down because there was nothing he could do about it; he knew he was too scared to have a go at his tormentors. It wasn't fair, it wasn't fair! Why couldn't he be the same as everybody else? Other people just lashed out with their fists when things upset them. They didn't think about it, they just did it. Other people didn't wet the bed. So why couldn't he be like other people, then? He was unlucky, that's what it was. He was unlucky and it wasn't fair! The helpless rage went on boiling and boiling inside him, till he felt he was going to explode.

He tried to think about getting his maths right and

42

making Mrs Blake praise him, so there would be one good thing at least about this day. He was quite good at maths; it was his best lesson. Not *very* good; there wasn't anything he was *very* good at. And today he wasn't even being a bit good, because his mind was filled up with pictures of grinning faces. He could see them grinning, all around him, even though he wasn't looking at them. Even though, as a matter of fact, they had tired of the rude joke and gone back to their work. In his head, Roy could still hear their sniggers, even though they weren't actually laughing at him any more. The grins in his mind's eye grew wider, the sniggers in his head grew louder, till the grins and the sniggers filled the whole world.

At playtime, Roy took Gary's plimsolls and put them down the toilet.

It wasn't the first time he had thought about putting someone's plimsolls down the toilet, but it was the first time he had actually done it. No one saw him. He was quite cunning, he lingered in his seat until everyone else had left the classroom, and when Mrs Blake told him to hurry up and get downstairs, he took Gary's P.E. bag, which was over the back of Gary's chair. Then he carried it out casually, swinging it from his wrist as though it were his own. He had meant to put Gary's shorts down the toilet as well, but found he was too frightened after all. Instead, he stuffed the shorts and the bag behind the cistern, and ran down to the playground.

At first, Roy was quite exultant about what he had done, but satisfaction soon changed to guilt and fear. What about when Mrs Blake found out? He remembered the few occasions when Mrs Blake had caught him out in little tricks before; those tiny, weak things he did sometimes, like hiding people's rubbers. He remembered what a fuss she always made about that!

Roy imagined Mrs Blake's long, mournful face bending over him, when she found out about the plimsolls. The beads round her ridgy throat wobbled up and down, and her voice went higher and higher as she squealed like a squeaky gate all about how ashamed of him she was, and how ashamed he ought to be. She did the same to anyone who was naughty, of course, not just him, but it was all right for them because they were the same as each other, and didn't feel like a piece of rubbish already. When Mrs Blake found out about the plimsolls she was going to make him feel all shrunk up, like an insect. She was going to make him feel like an insect and she was going to squash him, right into the ground.

'Where's my P.E. bag?' said Gary, indignant and aggressive immediately. 'Someone's took my P.E. bag! Come on, who's took it?'

'Don't look at me,' said Sanjay.

'One of you girls! Come on!'

'Don't accuse people of things they didn't do,' said Claudette. 'We don't want your smelly old bag.'

'You left it in the cloakroom, I expect,' said Mrs Blake.

'I didn't. It was on my chair. Didn't I leave it on my chair? Who saw it on my chair before play? See, Mrs Blake, it was on my chair and somebody took it!'

'Roy's gone all red,' said someone on the other side of the class.

He had to go to Mr Nelson, and Mr Nelson was quite a bit more understanding than Mrs Blake, who could excuse the rubbers on reflection, but not the plimsolls. Mr Nelson understood that people didn't actually *want* to do horrible disgusting things to other people's property, it was just that people were so horrible themselves, sometimes, it made it so other people couldn't bear it without doing something horrible back. Mr Nelson understood how it was, but he still wouldn't let Roy go back to his class just yet because he thought it was important for Roy to have some time to himself, he said, to consider how putting people's plimsolls down the toilet only made a bad situation worse. That was what Mr Nelson *said*.

So Roy had to sit outside Mr Nelson's room, where Nicky had sat the day before, and everyone saw him there in disgrace, so he felt like an insect after all.

When 4P passed by, on their way down to the hall for P.E., Nicky saw Roy sitting outside Mr Nelson's room. 'What you there for?' she hissed at him. She was surprised, because he was quiet in class, and sitting outside Mr Nelson's room was mostly for the disruptive ones.

'Put Gary's plimsolls down the toilet, didn't I?'

'You did *what*? You silly stupid baby, that's a thing that Infants do!'

'He said bad things about me.'

'So? Why didn't you just smash his face in?'

'Nicky Mitchell, get back into line!' said Miss Powell's cross voice.

At dinner time, Mr Nelson judged it was safe to let Roy back to his class. 'Come and sit with us,' said Claudette. 'We're on *your* side.' Like twittering birds, the girls closed round him.

'Gary *deserve* it,' said Jennifer.

45

'*I* put someone's plimsolls down the toilet once,' said Sharon. 'When I was five.'

'Poor Roy!' said Claudette, with an arm round his neck.

They were trying to be nice, but they were treating him like a baby, and it wasn't what he wanted, it wasn't what he wanted! Nothing happened like he wanted it to happen. He wasn't enjoying himself in the world, and he didn't *like* the world! With downcast eyes, Roy stared morosely at his plate. 'You're not eating your dinner, Roy,' scolded Claudette, who hadn't tasted hers yet.

'It's horrible,' said Roy.

School dinner was, indeed, a singularly unappetizing mess that day. It was meant to be a savoury mince, but something had gone wrong. The cook had been too heavy-handed with the stock cubes, and the meat had burned on the bottom of the pan as well. All over the hall were sounds of protest and rejection, and from the fourth year table, shrieks of fiendish laughter; Nicky's laughter. She was sitting next to Jason Charles, a boy with magnificent dreadlocks and a terrible reputation, and their heads were together, and they were plotting something.

Roy watched, nervously. Nicky was going to do something bad, he could feel it. He didn't understand why Nicky did outrageous things for fun, in school. She made the teachers so angry with her sometimes that it was like all the anger in the school came raining like hailstones down on Nicky's head. Roy didn't understand how anyone could *enjoy* trouble. But Nicky thrived on it; the hailstones bounced off her somehow, and she came up grinning every time.

46

Although he didn't understand her, Roy thought it must be quite nice to *be* her.

They were nudging one another, Nicky and Jason, exploding now and again with little bursts of malicious glee. They were nudging people around them, and pointing at Eric Morris, who was sitting further down the long table. Eric loved his food, even more than Roy did. And whereas Roy was choosy, Eric would eat anything. Eric was gobbling up the savoury mince with relish, quite oblivious of the fact that he was practically the only one eating it.

Jason was egging Nicky on to something. Roy couldn't hear what he was saying, there was too much noise in the hall and the fourth year table was too far away, but he could see Jason's mouth making the words, and he thought it was something like 'fat pig', and 'serve him right', and 'I dare you'. Then Nicky was getting up from her place. She was picking up her dinner. Oh no, what was she going to do with it? She was going to get in trouble, she was going to get in trouble! She was walking round the table. What was she going to do? Mrs Blake was on duty; why didn't Mrs Blake make Nicky sit down? 'Sit down, Nicky Mitchell!' Mrs Blake's voice shrilled, much too late.

'There!' said Nicky to Eric Morris. 'There's a second helping for you!' And she threw her savoury mince right into Eric Morris's face.

It stuck in his hair, and dribbled over his shirt. He gulped and spluttered, and everyone was so shocked they didn't even laugh, at first. Only Nicky, cackling like a demon, broke the silence which had suddenly come over the hall.

So then she had to go to Mr Nelson, and what with

one thing and another, and his arthritis having such cruel fun with him this afternoon, Mr Nelson was quite a bit tetchy with Nicky. 'It won't do, Nicky,' he said, wincing at a particularly vicious twinge.

'Is your leg hurting you, Sir?'

'How did you guess?'

'You're making funny faces.'

'That's enough!' said Mr Nelson, sharply. 'Look here, Nicky. Twice yesterday and now today, and your brother was a nuisance as well this morning. That's too much aggravation from one family, and I'm not going to have it.'

'Sorry, Sir. Sorry about your bad knee as well, Sir.'

'Both knees today, if you must know. It must be going to rain. And sorry isn't good enough. One more piece of nonsense, just *one* more, Nicky, and I shall have to ask your mother to come up to the school. Again.'

'Oh.'

'What does "oh" mean?'

'It means Roy won't do no more wrong things, which is easy. And I won't do no more wrong things, neither.'

'Which is much, much harder.'

'Oh I mean it! Cross my heart and hope to die! And you can forget all about asking our mum to come up to school. You can forget all about that because me and Roy will not think about giving you the trouble when you are so busy, and you have a bad leg. *Two* bad legs. Which makes me very sad for you.'

'All right, don't overdo it.'

Nicky told Roy on the way home. 'We got to be good, so Mr Nelson doesn't fetch our mum up to school and find out she isn't there.'

48

'You said she *will* be there. Today.'

'I mean in case. Just in case.'

'But you *said*.'

She *had* said it, but it was getting harder and harder to believe it. 'Oh Roy, I don't know, do I? We'll see in a minute. . . . I know – if we don't step on any lines on the pavement, Mum will be home when we get there! Careful, it will be all your fault if you spoil it!'

Mrs Williams was standing at her gate. 'If you make that racket again, like you done last night, I'm coming in to see your mum.'

'You're not the boss of our house,' said Nicky.

'If you're going to be cheeky, I'm coming in to see her *now*.'

'She's at work.'

'I didn't see her go.'

'You don't see everything. Even you don't see *everything*.'

Mrs Williams sniffed.

The WELCOME HOME banner still smiled mockingly, over the kitchen door. Some of the letters were beginning to peel off. 'She didn't come,' said Roy.

'I know. . . . What shall we have for tea?'

'She didn't *come*!'

'All right, all right, I can see! I'm not blind, you know. I said, what shall we have for tea?'

Roy was crying. He twisted his fingers and licked one salty tear as it rolled down his cheek. 'Stop that!' Nicky turned away and rummaged fiercely in the cupboard. 'Spaghetti hoops. We can have the spaghetti hoops. D'you fancy spaghetti hoops, then?' Suddenly her arm went up to cover her eyes, and her shoulders began to heave.

'You're *crying*!'

'No I'm not, I just got something in my eye. . . . A-all right, I am! What about it? I *am* crying. I'm s-scared! I d-don't know what to d-*do*!'

Roy held his breath, silent with shock. Nicky never cried, never! Then his terrified sobs shook the little kitchen. Hysterically, he pounded on the unit top, and kicked at the cupboard doors. His grief was an unleashed monster, raging through the empty house.

Nicky thumped him on the back, hard.

'Leave me!'

She thumped him again, harder. 'You got to stop it! Now! Come on, Roy, I'm not joking!' The desperate crying subsided. 'We got to think. We got to think together.'

They went into the Back Room, and sat on the sofa with the broken springs. 'Isn't she coming back at all?' said Roy.

'Of course she's coming back,' said Nicky. 'The only thing is, we don't know when.'

'I think she's dead,' said Roy.

'If you say that again I'll hit you,' said Nicky. 'She can't be dead because her handbag, remember? It's got our address inside, remember? And about the police? And she can't be ill because Tony would bring her home, or tell us anyway. Or someone would.'

'So why didn't she come?'

'Maybe she's in some trouble.'

'What trouble?'

'*I* don't know, do I? Some grown-up trouble, *I* don't know. . . . The thing is, the thing is, Roy, we have to not tell of her like she said. You don't want our mum to get in trouble, do you? Well then!'

'You just now said she *is* in trouble.'

'No I didn't. I said maybe . . . I said . . . I don't know what I said, you're muddling me up!'

'I'm scared.'

'Don't be silly, there's nothing to be scared of.'

'You were scared just now, you said.'

'Well I'm not scared now. I finished being scared. We just have to keep the secret, that's all. You have to promise to keep the secret, Roy. I promise you, and you promise me, right? Right?'

'I want Mum!'

'I want Mum too but we can't have her till she comes home, and in the meanwhile we have to keep the secret.'

'There's nothing to eat though, only spaghetti.'

'No there isn't, we got the rest of the emergencies money.'

'What's emergencies?'

'I think this is. We can buy food with the emergencies money because I think that's what it's for. We don't have to have that yucky old spaghetti if we don't want to, we can choose. What do you choose to have for tea, Roy?'

'Fish fingers!'

'All right, we'll have fish fingers. You see, we can have anything we like. You choose today, and I'll choose tomorrow . . . if Mum isn't home by then.'

'Can we have chips as well? From the chippie?'

'Well – just for today.' Uneasily, Nicky was remembering how quickly the first ten pounds disappeared.

'And Coke?'

'I'll buy a big bottle, but we got to make it last.'

'Only till Mum comes back.'

'Well that's right, that's right. And if Mum is enjoying herself at the seaside, we can be enjoying ourself here. That's fair, isn't it?'

'You said she isn't enjoying herself, you said she's in trouble.'

'I didn't, I didn't, I said she *might* be in trouble. Don't go on about I said she's in trouble! Most likely she's enjoying herself, and good because she has a hard life.'

'She's supposed to come home, and look after us,' said Roy.

'You're always thinking about yourself,' said Nicky.

There were things to be bought, as well as fish fingers and the chips and the Coke. There was a new packet of cornflakes, for instance, because the old one was running out; and some biscuits for after the fish fingers because Roy would ask for something sweet, and he would probably turn his nose up at the rice pudding. Nicky put the change away carefully.

'Perhaps she'll come tonight after all,' said Roy, after tea.

'Perhaps,' said Nicky.

'Shall we watch at the window again?'

'No,' said Nicky. 'Watching's silly, it doesn't make her come.'

But Roy sneaked into the Front Room anyway, when Nicky was watching television, and he opened the window with the special key, which he wasn't supposed to do; the Front Room window was *always* kept locked. Roy leaned over the back of the best sofa, and as far out of the window as he could, as though the effort of straining might make Mum come after all.

And someone was coming up the path, but it wasn't Mum. Roy slammed the window down and scuttled into the Back Room. 'There's somebody at the door.' He couldn't say who it was, because he wasn't supposed to have been watching.

'Who is it?' called Nicky through the letter box. Mum always said they must be very careful about who they opened the door to.

It was Mrs Morris from next door, and Mrs Morris was not welcome, but there was no excuse for not opening the door to her. 'Oh hullo, Aunty Four-Eyes,' said Nicky.

Mrs Morris flushed; she did not like Mum's rude name for her. 'I want to see your mother,' she said.

'What about?'

'I want to see your mother, Nicky, not you.'

'She's not in.'

'It's past seven o'clock!'

'She's not in, she's working late.'

'At seven *o'clock*?'

'Don't you believe me?'

Mrs Morris sniffed. 'Anyway she ought to be home, minding you.'

'That's her business,' said Nicky.

Mrs Morris swallowed. She was a dull, whiny sort of person, middle-aged looking already, although she was only a year or two older than Mrs Mitchell. She knew she was too fond of judging people; she knew it wasn't really Christian to do that, and from time to time she made a real effort to be better. 'I wouldn't come if I didn't have to,' she said.

'Is it important then?' said Nicky.

'As if you didn't know!' Mrs Morris burst out.

53

'Two days running! First his face all scratched, and now his shirt ruined. Gravy stains all over it!'

'Oh *that*!' said Nicky.

'Yes, that! And you can take that smile off your face, it's not funny!'

'Can't you wash Eric's shirt?'

'That's as much as you care, isn't it! You don't care his shirt is ruined and no good for school any more. You had your fun, and that's all you can think about. I want to see your mother.'

'She's not in, I said.'

'What time's she coming back?'

'*I* don't know.' A sudden terrible thought struck Nicky – the WELCOME HOME, over the kitchen door! Could Mrs Morris see the WELCOME HOME? Nicky pushed the front door quickly, and Mrs Morris stepped back, thinking it was going to be shut in her face.

'All right, I'll just go and see the headmaster tomorrow then! He'll get on to your mum, he'll have to! I'm not the only mother's getting sick of your carryings on up that school.'

Nicky opened the door a fraction more, and squeezed herself into the porch. 'Don't do that, Mrs Morris! *Dear* Mrs Morris, please don't do that!'

'What are you trying on now?' said Mrs Morris, suspiciously.

'Mum isn't very well.'

'Huh!'

'She isn't, she isn't, she's very brave about it, she doesn't tell many people.'

'She's well enough to stop out.'

'She's got a terrible pain though. She's not

54

supposed to have people worry her. I'm sorry about Eric's shirt, I won't do it again.'

Mrs Morris hesitated. She knew it was right to forgive people when they said they were sorry. She knew it was right to help people if they were ill. 'What sort of a pain has your mother got?'

'Just a pain. She's had it for weeks, it comes and goes.'

'What does the doctor say?'

'He says it's just a pain.'

'Are you *sure* that's all he says?'

'Oh yes. But he says she mustn't have nothing to worry her. She has a hard life, you know.'

'You should have thought of that before, shouldn't you?'

'Yes I should, I'm a terrible person, I know! But I won't do it again, I promise. See this wet, see this dry, cross my heart and hope to die!'

'It's all very well—'

'*Please*, Mrs Morris. *Please*. Don't go up to school about me, please!'

Mrs Morris hesitated. 'I'll think about it.'

'Think about my mum with her pain, that she is so brave about. Think about that.'

'All right, all right! Is there anything I can do, then, to help?'

'No, thank you,' said Nicky. 'We're fine.'

'Well tell your mum she knows where I am if she wants me.' Mrs Morris thought she ought to say that, even though she felt awkward, and not at all sure she really wanted to help that woman.

'Goodbye,' said Nicky, firmly.

Back in the house, Nicky ripped down the WEL-COME HOME banner. 'Thank goodness Aunty

Four-Eyes didn't see this! Thank goodness, eh Roy? That would make her ask questions for certain, if she saw this.'

'I think she's going to come again anyway,' said Roy nervously. 'To spy on us.'

'Don't worry,' said Nicky. 'I'll get rid of her if she does.' She scrumpled up the banner, so carefully made, and stuffed the sad remains into the waste-bin, in the kitchen.

'I think other people are going to come and spy on us,' said Roy, twisting his fingers. 'I think Polly Pry is going to come, and I think the people at Mum's work are going to come. I think they're going to come here soon, to find out why she is stopping away all this time.'

'Oh *they* won't come,' said Nicky. '*They* don't care. You know what Mum told us! They just want a laugh and a joke. And the boss only cares if they all finish a load of dresses to make money for him! Nobody cares about Mum, and she rather have it like that, because then they don't poke their noses in. Did you hear what I said?'

'What about?'

'About the people at Mum's work don't care.'

'Don't they?'

'You weren't listening!'

'I was thinking something else.' His face was turned from her, his thoughts a secret yet.

'What?'

'Just something.'

'*What?*'

'Well . . . I was thinking it's my birthday on Thursday.'

'So?'

'Well . . . so Mum will come home then, won't she! She won't miss my birthday, will she?'

He looked round then, and his eyes were alight with hope. Too much hope. Troubled and confused, Nicky tried to be realistic for him. 'Do you know what I think? I think we didn't ought to say a exact time for Mum to come. I know I said before . . . I mean I know I *said*, but that was when it wasn't so long. . . . It's different now, it's all different, so we didn't ought to think the same.'

But Roy looked the other way again, not wanting to hear.

Miles away in Southbourne, a woman opened her eyes and blinked. She felt very muddled. Everything looked strange and there were parts of her that hurt, but it was confusing trying to decide which parts they were. 'What?' she muttered. 'What? . . . What? . . . What?' She seemed only able to say one word, and even that was not very clear, so the nurse had to bend over to catch what it was.

'You're all right,' said the nurse. 'You're quite safe. You're in hospital.'

'What? . . . Why?'

'Don't you remember the accident?'

'Accident? . . . No . . . no . . . what?'

'Hush,' said the nurse. 'You're all right. You were knocked down by a car, and you've got a few broken bones but they'll mend. The main thing is – you've been asleep rather a long time. Everyone is going to be very pleased that you've wakened up at last.'

The woman in the bed did not actually hear the last bit of that, because she had drifted down, down, down into sleep again. She floated nearly to the surface, sank again, rose once more, and opened her eyes. 'Oh,' she said.

The nurse was still there. 'We've been trying to find out who you are.'

'Oh.'

'Your name?' said the nurse, hopefully.

'Yes . . . what?'

'Your name!' said the nurse.

The woman struggled to remember. 'Yes. . . . What? . . . I don't know.' The room was blurring and tipping about. 'Does it matter?'

'Well yes,' said the nurse. 'It does, rather.'

'Ask somebody else,' said the woman, indistinctly; and she dropped back into the warm darkness.

# 5

# The birthday party

Nicky had not forgotten Roy's birthday; only which day it was she was supposed to give him his present. She'd had the present for a week, and it was quite hard to keep hidden, because it was two goldfish in a bowl. Nicky knew Roy would be pleased with his present, because he was always hanging around the goldfish in the hall at school. Of course the goldfish at school were in a proper tank. Nicky would have liked to get a proper tank for Roy, but they cost too much money. The bowl was in a junk shop. Nicky often looked in the junk shop window, because there were old and beautiful things there as well as rubbish, and that was how she came to see the goldfish bowl. And the lady let her have it for a pound, because there was a chip in the rim.

She had a card for Roy, as well as a present. The card had rabbits on it (she couldn't find one with goldfish) and a lot of tinselly stuff, and it said TO A DEAR BROTHER.

She wondered if Mum had a present for Roy, and she thought of going to look, but then she thought it was best not to know. She didn't want to have to tell Roy Mum hadn't thought about his birthday yet. She also didn't want to have to see his disappointment if Mum didn't turn up, like he was making himself expect. He was building his hopes in a wobbly tower, like babies' bricks piled one on top of the other. And she wished he wouldn't do it because the bricks would fall, they would fall if Mum didn't come, and Roy would be all in pieces like the wobbly tower.

It hurt her to think about that, it really hurt. Because honestly, honestly, Nicky didn't think you could count on Mum coming just because it was Roy's birthday. Whatever was keeping her was not going to stop keeping her just because Roy had a birthday on Thursday. Maybe she forgot all about it was Roy's birthday! She did that once before, until Nicky reminded her. She was sorry after, but she could do it again perhaps, Nicky thought.

And Nicky had to admit she didn't know what to make of this funny thing about Mum staying away so long. It really was getting very hard to think of a good explanation. Or to know what to expect any more. Or to know what to say to Roy – so he wouldn't hope too much, or go the other way and give up hoping altogether.

Just two things stood out clearly. To keep the secret so Mum wouldn't get in trouble; and make a good birthday for Roy, whatever!

Nicky counted her little store of money. There was seven pounds forty-seven pence left out of Mum's twenty pounds, and one pound thirteen pence in her own private purse. She usually had more than that, but the goldfish and the goldfish food and the card had taken up the biggest part of her savings. She put the five-pound note from Mum's seven pounds forty-seven into the pocket of her school dress. She hoped she wouldn't have to spend it all.

In school there was one good thing, and that was Mr Hunt was back. Nicky put her arm round his neck in the playground and gave him a kiss. 'What have I done to deserve this?' said Mr Hunt, who was good-natured but lazy, and made no special effort to make himself liked.

'Now you're here, can I come back to my own class?' said Nicky.

'Nicky was bad while you was away, Sir,' said Marcus.

'So what's new?' said Mr Hunt.

'I'll tell you what's new,' said Nicky, warmly. 'What's new is I'm not going to be bad any more! I'm different, I'm changed.'

'You're frightening me!' said Mr Hunt, pretending to cower behind his hands.

She was as good as her word, though. Miraculously, her good resolution lasted all day! She even helped Joycelyn, who was a bit slow, patiently explaining the maths to her, long after Mr Hunt had given up trying.

'While I was on my bed of sickness,' said Mr Hunt in the staff room, 'something has happened to Nicky Mitchell.'

'She's seen the light, I think,' said Miss Powell.

'Meaning?'

'Meaning that Nellie threatened to have her mother up to school.' (Nellie was the teachers' nickname for Mr Nelson.)

'Nicky's mother's been called up at least five hundred times,' said Mr Hunt. 'That never bothered Nicky before!'

'Nellie probably threatened her she'd get left out of Easthaven as well, if she didn't mend her evil ways.'

'*That's* more like it,' said Mrs Blake.

'Don't remind me!' groaned someone else. 'All our horrible lot at the seaside, imagine!'

'Getting lost!'

'Being sick!'

'Drowning themselves!'

'Oh, a few lost, a few drowned, what's the difference?' said Miss Powell.

'Well I'm looking forward to it,' said Miss Greenwood, who was new and innocent. She fluttered her eyelashes at Mr Hunt, hoping he would notice how fresh and sweet she was. She thought Mr Hunt had the most fascinating moustache she had ever seen, but so far he hadn't shown any interest in her.

'We're all looking forward to it, really,' said Mr Hunt, still not showing any particular interest in Miss Greenwood. 'Don't take any notice of what we *say*. It's better than the classroom any day. And some of those kids never see the sea.'

'Roy and Nicky Mitchell, for instance,' said Mrs Blake.

'Poor little devils, they don't have much of a life, do they?'

'Can't have, can they, with that scatty mother!'

'You can say that again! Defends 'em like a she-cat when there's trouble, and then neglects them half the time. The last eighteen months or so, anyway.'

'Spends enough money on her own back, from what I can see, and Nicky's still in last year's summer dresses!'

'Have you heard she goes out late at night? Well that's what I've been told. Leaves the kids on their own till goodness knows what time!'

'Where did that piece of information come from?'

'One of Eric Morris's little titbits,' said Mr Hunt.

'And you know what a tattle-tale that boy is! Still – he does live next door.'

'I must say they seem very fond of her,' said Mrs Blake. 'Roy and Nicky, I mean. Fond of their mother.'

'Well of course,' said Mr Hunt. 'She's all they've got!'

At home time, Nicky deliberately gave Roy the slip; she had some important shopping to do that she didn't want him to see. After she had done the shopping there was only six pence left out of the five pounds she had put in her dress pocket. She was a bit frightened to have spent so much, but she stamped on the fear hard. Today she had to think about making a good birthday for Roy. She would think about money tomorrow. Or the next day.

'We'll have the spaghetti for tea tonight,' said Nicky. That would save spending.

'You don't like spaghetti,' said Roy.

'I changed my mind,' said Nicky.

'The telly's gone wrong,' said Roy, peevishly. He was still sulking because she had been so long coming home and he couldn't get in.

Nicky fiddled with the knobs, but the picture refused to come back. 'Well all right, the telly's gone wrong! So what? Haven't you got anything else to do except watch telly?'

'No.'

'Homework?'

'No.'

'How about your toys?'

'They're all broke.'

'Mend them then.'

'I can't.'

'I wouldn't like to be you,' said Nicky, exasperated.

'*I* don't like being me.'

'All right, wait till tomorrow! You'll like being you then!'

'Because Mum's coming home.'

'Perhaps. But other things, other things, Roy. You just wait!'

After the spaghetti, the children ate the rice pudding. Roy would have preferred biscuits, but Nicky said it was still her turn to choose. And after tea there was that nuisance Aunty Four-Eyes at the door again.

'Told you!' said Roy.

'I – er – I was wondering about your mum,' said Mrs Morris. It cost her quite a bit to come and say that. They had quarrelled, she and Mrs Mitchell, and there had been harsh words, and unpleasant language. But Mrs Morris had been counting her blessings, and noticing how many more blessings she had than Mrs Mitchell, and thinking that as a Christian she really ought to try to make it up. Even though it wasn't her fault in the first place, it was Mrs Mitchell's.

'What about my mum?' said Nicky. 'Aunty Four-Eyes!' She'd been so good all day, she really couldn't resist that one.

Mrs Morris swallowed. It was hard to be a Christian in the face of deliberate rudeness. 'You know. What you said yesterday. The pain.'

'Oh that – it's better.'

'Are you sure?'

'Of course I'm sure. I said so, didn't I? Goodbye.'

Mrs Morris swallowed again, and made one more effort. 'You don't have to talk to me like that. Actually, I brought something for your mother if you'll give me a chance to say it.' She was carrying a dish-sized object wrapped in a plastic bag. 'Something I made to help out, in case she wasn't up to cooking.'

'I'll take it,' said Nicky, stretching out her hand.

'Give it to your mother, and say I'd like to speak to her,' said Mrs Morris, determined to see it through now she had got this far. 'Say I know we had words that time, but I was thinking we are neighbours and we didn't ought to be bad friends.'

'Oh . . . you want to make up,' said Nicky.

'Yes.'

'I'll see what she says,' said Nicky. She disappeared into the Back Room and counted to ten, slowly. She knew what she had to do, but it was very, very hard. She went back to the front door, still carrying the dish-sized object, wrapped in the plastic bag.

'She doesn't want to see you,' said Nicky to Mrs Morris. 'She doesn't want to make up and she doesn't want this.' Regretfully, she handed back the casserole, which would have made a good meal for her and Roy. 'She said some rude things about you which I rather not repeat,' she added, to make sure that Mrs Morris would go away.

Mrs Morris's pudgy cheeks went very pale. '*Well!*'

'It's not my fault,' said Nicky. 'I can't help what she said.'

Mrs Morris's cheeks turned to fiery red, and she stumped down the short front path without another word. Her indignation burst at the Mitchells' gate, all over Mrs Williams who had been listening at *her* front gate while pretending to be very much interested in something down the road. The two women spent the next ten minutes, quite enjoyably, exchanging complaints about that unspeakably dreadful Mrs Mitchell.

Nicky gave Roy the goldfish and the card, and he was thrilled as she knew he would be. He put the goldfish in his room, and watched them swimming round and round; and they were beautiful, and they were *his*. He said nothing about Mum, but his eyes were shining still, and avoiding hers, so Nicky knew he hadn't changed his mind about his hope. And then the thought struck her that if Mum didn't actually come, she might at least have remembered Roy's birthday. Suppose she sent him a card – now *that* would be exciting!

The post came when they were getting ready for school, and Nicky ran to get it; the postman didn't often call at their house so it might be, it might be! It wasn't a card from mum though, it was only the electricity bill, she put it behind the clock with the other odds and ends, just in front of the rent book. The rent book! What about not paying the rent? But Mum was often behind with the rent; no one would start fussing about that for a while. Much more interesting than the rent book was the paper Mum had left with her seaside address on it. 'For emergencies,' Mum said. What *were* emergencies exactly? It was hard to know, Mum didn't explain it properly, she was in too much hurry. The only thing she explained was, she was going to get in trouble if anybody found out she left them on their own all night.

Roy knew why Nicky ran to get the post, and he

was disappointed for a moment that there wasn't a card from Mum. But it didn't matter, did it? It didn't matter because Mum was going to be back tonight, she was going to be back tonight, she *was* going to be back tonight, she *was*! And meanwhile he had his goldfish.

Roy thought about his goldfish all morning. His goldfish make him feel safe; they came between him and all the horrible things in the world. 'It's my birthday today,' he told Claudette, when it was nearly dinner time. 'And my sister gave me two goldfish.'

'What did your mum give you?' said Claudette.

Roy hesitated; he was not good at making up lies, his thoughts moved too slowly. 'A bicycle,' he said at last. Before he had the goldfish, he used to think a bicycle would be the most wonderful thing in the world to have.

'A bicycle?' said Gary, impressed. 'Why didn't you say that first?'

'I like the goldfish best,' said Roy.

'I bet you can't ride the bike,' said Sanjay.

'I bet I can,' said Roy.

'Prove it. Ride to school tomorrow.'

'My mum might not let me.'

'Can I come round and see your bike then?' said Gary. 'Can I have a go?'

'Can I?' said Sanjay.

'Can we come too?' said Claudette. 'Me and Sharon and Jennifer?'

All of a sudden Roy found he was embarrassingly popular because he had a new bicycle. 'My mum said I mustn't let anybody ride it, only me.'

'Are you having a party?' said Sharon. 'For your birthday?'

'Nah!' said Roy. 'Don't like parties.'

Gary whispered something to Sanjay, and Sanjay sniggered. Roy blushed. 'Shut up, Gary,' said Claudette. 'Don't be horrible.'

'He don't like people coming to his house in case they see—' Gary whispered again.

'We'll come this afternoon then, all right?' said Sanjay, taunting him. 'All right, Roy? Me and Sanjay's coming round your house to see your bike. And see you ride it. After school, all right?'

'And see—' Sanjay whispered to Gary, and the boys exploded with not-very-nice laughter.

'Don't take no notice of them, Roy,' said Jennifer. 'They don't mean it.'

But Roy was very much afraid they did, and he tried to forget about Gary and Sanjay, and think about his goldfish again instead. In the afternoon his class were writing stories, and often Roy had no ideas for stories at all, but today he wrote happily, 'There was wuns a boy called Roy who had to goldfish for his berthday he dident no if they were boy goldfish or girl goldfish so he called them fishy and goldy.' After that he sucked his pencil and thought about what he would do at home time, because Gary and Sanjay were clearly plotting something, and he would have to be a bit cunning to give them the slip.

He was pretty sure they didn't know where he lived. Well – they might know it was Gilbert Road, but they wouldn't know which house it was unless they followed him. Roy decided to hide in the toilets until they had gone. Slowly, carefully, he began to plan how he would do it.

Coming into school the classes were nearly always escorted by their teachers, and sometimes going out as well. But at home time things were more haphazard, with some people going to the cloak-room, and some having nothing to go there for, and some staying behind to chat to Mrs Blake, or help tidy the classroom. Roy dawdled down the stairs, aware that Gary and Sanjay were keeping close behind him. He bent to tie the laces of his plimsolls and they passed him, giggling and nudging one another. Roy could hear the muffled sniggers coming from where they lingered round the corner on the next landing of the winding stone staircase. Swiftly, Roy ran back up the stairs and along the corridor to the boys' toilets. He passed his own classroom as he went, and heard Mrs Blake's mournful voice exhort-ing her helpers to hurry up and finish clearing, because there was a staff meeting and she was supposed to be there.

Roy was tempted to lock himself in one of the cubicles; but he didn't, because he had already thought out that would be wrong. That way he could get trapped. If Gary and Sanjay came back to look for him, they would be sure to notice that one of the cubicles was locked, and they wouldn't rest until they found out who was inside. A better idea was to squeeze behind the main door into the toilets, which stood open. They might not think to look there.

As a matter of fact, one of the cubicles *was* locked, because someone from the other third year class had a tummy-ache. Roy heard the pounding footsteps of his enemies, and Mrs Blake shouting, 'Stop running,' and Sanjay's voice calling, 'Here he is! Locked in, so he thinks we won't find him!'

'Come on out!' said Gary. 'We know you're in there!'

69

'Leave me!' said the muffled voice of the person with the tummy-ache. Sanjay was in the next cubicle, climbing to look over the partition. Roy could hear his grunts, and the hollow-sounding thump of his knees. Then there was a shriek of outrage from the person with the tummy-ache, and Mrs Blake coming to see what all the noise was about, and one of the teachers from the staff meeting as well, despatched by Mr Nelson to sort out the trouble. Gary and Sanjay were sent packing, the person with the tummy-ache was comforted, and after everything had died down, Roy crept out of his hiding place. No one noticed him slinking down the stairs by himself; for once, just for once, things had gone right for him!

They were waiting for him round the corner; he might have known they would be! He ran, of course, but it was hopeless. They caught up with him, and pinned his arms on either side. 'Come on then, take us to your house!'

Roy began to cry.

'Cry-baby!'

'Cry-baby wet the bed!'

'Cry-baby can't ride a bike!'

'Leave me!' In desperation, Roy began to struggle, but they only held him tighter.

'Temper, temper, naughty, naughty!'

Roy gave in, and went limp. This wasn't happening to him, it was happening to someone else. And he wasn't here, being frogmarched down the road by two nasty bullies; he was somewhere else altogether, in a dark secret world inside himself, where they couldn't get at him.

'Come on, then, which way?'

'I'm not telling you,' said Roy's voice, from

somewhere in that outside world where the bullies were.

'It's Gilbert Road, isn't it?'

'What do you ask for, if you know?'

'Is it this house?'

'No.'

'This one?'

'No.'

'I can see where it is,' said Gary. 'It's the one with Nicky Mitchell standing by the gate!'

She was waiting for Roy, impatient for him to come home. 'Let go my brother! Creeps!'

'We come to see Roy's bike,' said Gary, dropping Roy's arm. There was no point holding him now, anyway.

'What bike?'

'Didn't he get a bike? Did he make it up?' Gary doubled up with mirth.

'Push off!' said Nicky, furiously.

'Didn't he get a bike for his birthday, then?' said Sanjay, the small eyes mocking.

'None of your business,' said Nicky. 'I told you to push off.'

'It's a free country.'

'No it's not, not this bit of it. This bit is ours. Get lost!'

They lingered, nudging one another and grinning.

'Go on then, what you waiting for?'

'Can't Roy have some mates in on his birthday?' said Gary.

'Roy got plenty of mates coming,' said Nicky. 'Roy got mates you don't know nothing about. A lot better'n you!'

'You're a liar,' said Sanjay.

'Shut your mouth,' said Nicky.

'Liar, liar, liar!' said Sanjay.

Nicky punched him. 'That's for opening your mouth when I told you to shut it.'

Sanjay made a feeble attempt at punching back, but he wasn't much of a fighter, and he was quite a bit afraid of Nicky really. Nicky pummelled him, contemptuously, and he turned to run. Nicky aimed a kick at his backside, to help him on his way.

'I saw that!' said Polly Pry, calling out of her window. 'Poor little boy!'

'Mind your own business!' said Nicky.

'Wait till I see your mum!'

'My mum says you're a nosy old bag,' said Nicky. 'She won't listen to you whatever you say. She only makes fun of you behind your back.'

Mrs Williams's mouth opened and shut a few times, but only strangled sounds came out because she was actually too angry to speak. The red colour was all over her face and her neck and her scalp. Nicky thought, with mild interest, that if she got any redder she might burst into flames. 'All the time!' she added. 'She makes fun of you all the time!' The window banged shut. 'Yes?' Nicky said to Gary, who still hovered. 'Looking at something?'

She pushed Roy into the house. 'Where's Mum?' he said.

'I've got a surprise,' said Nicky. 'For your birthday.'

'Where's Mum though?'

'Come and see the surprise.'

'I don't *want* the surprise,' said Roy. 'I want Mum.' The china-blue eyes filled with tears and then, as reality dawned, the hysterical crying began.

72

'I want Mum! I want Mum!' He rampaged through the house, kicking doors, thumping walls, and finally banging his head against the sofa with the broken springs again, and again, and again.

'Finished?' said Nicky.

'I want Mum,' said Roy.

'*I want, I want, I want!*' said Nicky, disgustedly. 'That's all you can say, isn't it! Only what *you* want. You don't think about me, do you? You don't think about what I want, do you? And I got a surprise for you for your birthday, and I wanted you to be pleased, and all you can do is go on about *I want Mum.*'

Roy buried his face in his arms and said nothing. His shoulders still quivered but he was calm now, the anguish spent.

'Well?' said Nicky. 'Are you going to say something or what?'

'What have I got to say?' The sound was muffled against his arm, the words ending in one last sob.

'Say, "Thank you, Nicky, for my surprise. What is it?"'

'Thank you, Nicky, for my surprise. What is it?'

'Don't strain yourself saying it like you're the least bit interested!' said Nicky. 'All right, it's on the table! It was on the table all the time only you were so busy hollering you didn't see it! Wait a minute, though, wait a minute, keep your eyes covered! *And* your ears. Just a minute. . . . Now! De-dah!'

Roy turned round slowly and saw what she had bought—a large cream gateau, with HAPPY BIRTHDAY on a red and gold band round the edge. Nicky had just lit the ten candles on the top. It was the best birthday cake he had ever had; Mum usually bought a small chocolate sponge and stuck candles in that. 'Well?' said Nicky.

Roy struggled to cope with having opposite feelings both at the same time. 'Happy birthday to you-u-u, Happy birthday to you-u-u!' sang Nicky in her strident voice. 'Well?'

He swallowed. He didn't know what to say, because the thoughts and feelings were too jumbled up, inside him.

'Say you like it then! Just say you like it!' Her face was so eager, and he did like it, he did! He tried to say 'Yes,' but the sound wouldn't come. 'Blow the candles out anyway,' said Nicky, disappointed. He blew them and then, unexpectedly, threw an arm round Nicky's neck. 'We'll have Rough Games after tea,' said Nicky with a radiant face.

Once again they wreaked havoc in the house, everywhere except the Front Room, which was always treated with respect, thumping and banging and shrieking with boisterous laughter. Exhausted finally, they rolled on the threadbare carpet in the Back Room, panting for breath. 'It's the best birthday I had up to yet,' said Roy.

'See?' said Nicky, triumphantly. 'I told you!'

'And Polly Pry didn't even bang on the wall,' he marvelled.

'That's because I told her where to go.'

'Like you told Aunty Four-Eyes.'

'Yeah! I told her an 'all, didn't I?'

'Nicky. . .'

'What?'

'Do you think Aunty Four-Eyes might go up to the school after all now? Now you said Mum wants to go on with the quarrel?'

'Oh cripes, I forgot about that!' Nicky admitted. She had been rude to Mrs Morris to stop her coming into the house; but she needed to be polite to Mrs Morris to stop her going to Mr Nelson. How complicated things were getting to be! It was like trying to juggle a lot of little balls, and keep them all in the air at the same time.

'Nicky,' said Roy. 'About Mum.'

'Let's not talk about Mum tonight.'

'I won't cry!'

'All right then.'

'I'm not going to cry about that any more. . . . Only I had a idea.'

'What?'

'Do you think Mum quarrelled with *Tony*?'

'So they split up, you mean?'

'Perhaps he come back in his car without her. Perhaps he just left her there.'

'She would come by the train.'

'Oh yeah!'

'I wish we knew where Tony lives in London though,' said Nicky. 'Then we could go and see if he's there. I know, she put the caravan address behind the clock. Perhaps she put Tony's address behind there too. She must have writ it down somewhere.'

'Perhaps he's got a telephone as well,' said Roy.

'Oh yeah, that's a good idea.'

They searched behind the clock, and behind the bills and so on. There were several addresses on bits of paper, because Mum wasn't organized enough to have a proper address book; there was nothing about Tony, though. The children looked at the caravan address again. 'I wonder what we supposed to do with this,' said Nicky.

'I wish it had a telephone.'

'I don't think caravans have telephones.'

'So what's the use of the address?'

'I don't know,' said Nicky. 'She didn't explain it.'

'Perhaps we supposed to tell somebody.'

'NO! Don't let me hear you say that again. . . . Perhaps we supposed to go there!'

'To Southbourne?'

'Yeah. Perhaps.'

'All by ourselves?' said Roy, alarmed. 'It's too far! It's too far, Nicky.'

'There's a train.'

'What about the money for the ticket?'

'Yeah, that is the problem.'

'We can't go then, can we? We can't go because we haven't got enough money.'

'I wish I had a hundred pounds,' said Nicky.

'I rather have my goldfish,' said Roy. '*Much* rather!'

Pamela and Pandora were in their playhouse, in their garden by the seaside. It was past their bed-time really, and they were rather hoping Mummy had forgotten them, because they were having an interesting game of going to the bank with their 'cheque book'. They were going to get a hundred pounds and buy a pony, who would live in the playhouse, and eat the grass on their lawn. Pamela tried to tear out the page, but had trouble with the perforations.

'You poor weak twit-nit, give it here!' said Pandora impatiently. She wrenched at the page, and it wouldn't tear for her either. She slapped the 'cheque book', and shook it, to punish it for being so awkward – and a piece of paper fell out. The piece of paper said

TONY on it, in printed letters, and underneath there was an address. The address said 12 BRUTON AVE, LONDON NW10

'There's a telephone number as well,' said Pamela.

'It might be the lady who owns the handbag's friend,' said Pandora. 'Shall we ring him up?'

'It's in *London*,' said Pamela.

'I bet you don't know how to telephone to London,' said Pandora.

'I bet I do,' said Pamela. 'Why do you always think you are the only one who knows things? Anyway, what will we say to him?'

'We'll ask him to give us a reward, for finding the bag.'

'You stupid egg-brain! They didn't *want* the bag, they threw it away!'

'They might have changed their mind.'

'Then we could really buy our pony. With the reward. . . . All right then, we'll ring him up.'

'We more or less finished with the silly old bag anyway.'

'Yeah, we don't want their stupid bag any more, do we? They can have it back now, and we'll have the reward.'

Pamela regarded the torn 'cheque book', and the depleted make-up. 'We tore the cheque book though,' she said, thoughtfully.

'And used the lipstick.'

'We might get into trouble.'

'Let's *not* phone up Tony.'

'All right, let's not.'

# 6

# A watery grave

Roy fed his goldfish, sprinkling the delicate flakes over the surface of the water. He watched with delight as Fishy and Goldy rose so gracefully to receive their meal. They were beautiful, and they were his. He was not going to think about Mum any more; thinking about Mum hurt too much, like thinking about how he was going to be all alone next term, when Nicky went to her new school. From now on he was going to think only about Goldy and Fishy.

He said goodbye, then changed his mind and picked up the bowl instead. It was heavy, and the water sloshed about as he moved. He held the bowl against his chest, and went to the head of the stairs. 'You go on to school without me,' he called to Nicky. 'I'll come on in a minute.'

'You hurry up and come now!' said Nicky. 'You're going to be late, else.'

'Only a minute. I'll come in a minute.'

'You've got something there,' said Nicky. 'I can see! What is that thing you are covering up?' She came up the stairs a few steps and Roy turned, hiding the bowl with his body. 'You're not taking your fish to school!' she scolded.

'I can if I want to. I want to show them to Mrs Blake.'

'Mrs Blake seen goldfish before.'

'She hasn't seen mine.'

'You're silly!' said Nicky.

Roy flinched from her scorn, but held his ground. 'I don't care if you say I'm silly. I'm taking my goldfish to school, so there!'

'All right then, *be* silly. Do that silly thing and have everybody laugh at you, *I* don't care. But don't blame me if you drop the bowl and break it. And don't expect me to carry it for you when it gets too heavy. Because I'm going to school like a sensible person, and I'm not going to help you at all.'

Nicky pranced ahead, and Roy lagged farther and farther behind. His arms ached intolerably, and the front of his shirt was all wet, from where the water had sloshed on it. He sat on someone's garden wall, and rested the goldfish bowl on his knees. Gary passed, scuffling an old tin along the pavement. He turned back to jeer. 'Is that what you keep your goldfish in? That old cracked bowl?'

'You're just jealous,' said Roy, bravely.

He felt worth something, today. Not a mistake, not an insect; ten years old and the owner of two goldfish! Almost as good as anybody else.

'Jealous? Ha, ha, ha! Jealous about *goldfish*? What is there to be jealous about goldfish?'

But Mrs Blake was in a good mood that morning, and made quite a fuss of Fishy and Goldy. She put them on her table where everyone could see and the class had an impromptu lesson about goldfish. Mrs Blake said the fish ought to be in a tank, really. And Roy said he was going to start saving his pocket money to buy one. Roy was sent to the library to see if he could find any books about tanks and goldfish. He was allowed to choose one person to go with him, and he chose Claudette. Gary found himself very resentful that the person who put his plimsolls down the toilet only on Tuesday was getting so much attention and privilege now.

When they were supposed to be writing about goldfish, Gary began to whisper with Sanjay, behind his hand. Little bursts of sniggery laughter began to explode from their shielded mouths. 'Gary and Sanjay, you're annoying me,' said Mrs Blake. 'I suppose it's too much to hope you've done a stroke of work between you. . . . I thought as much! What's this rubbish? What is it, Gary? When you can write something other people can actually read, then you may be forgiven for wasting your time occasionally!'

Gary's face went a sullen red, and his eyes bulged like gobstoppers. People were supposed to laugh at Roy, not him. Angry at being held up to ridicule, he plotted with Sanjay when Mrs Blake wasn't looking. And when the children came back from play, the goldfish bowl was empty.

Roy stared in stricken horror, unable to speak or cry. 'Mrs Blake, Mrs Blake, look!' Everyone else was very excited. 'Look, Mrs Blake, Roy's goldfish has gone!' There was much indignation, some of it pleasurable.

Mrs Blake was very angry indeed. 'Who knows anything about this?' she said, her gaze sweeping the room. There was nudging, and names were being whispered. 'Sanjay and Gary come into school, playtime,' said one voice out loud.

The two culprits were giggling a bit, but nervously now they saw they weren't going to get away with it. 'It was only a joke,' said Sanjay.

'We didn't hurt them,' said Gary. 'They can still swim.'

'Swim *where*?' said Mrs Blake, her voice going so high it cracked on the top note.

'In the toilet,' said Gary, faintly.

But when Mrs Blake went striding on her long thin legs to look, followed by half the class, Fishy and Goldy were, alas, no longer swimming in the toilet bowl. 'You wicked boys!' said Mrs Blake.

'Somebody must have pulled the flush,' said Sanjay. It had seemed a good way of getting back at Nicky for yesterday but he was frightened now, and wishing he hadn't done it.

'That is the cruellest trick I've ever come across in all my years of teaching,' said Mrs Blake.

'Nicky Mitchell's going to kill Gary,' said someone, in an audible whisper.

'We didn't think nobody would pull the flush,' said Gary, who had actually rather hoped that somebody would, and said as much to Sanjay who had hoped the same.

'Didn't think was made to think!' said Mrs Blake.

They had to go to Mr Nelson, and Mr Nelson was very angry as well, and not at all convinced that Gary and Sanjay hadn't *really* meant harm to Fishy and Goldy. Mr Nelson was so angry and upset that for the moment he forgot all about his arthritis and his ulcer. 'You took something from Roy that was very precious to him,' he told the boys. 'Probably the most precious thing in the world at this moment. And to make you understand just a little bit what that feels like, I am going to take away something precious to *you*. You won't be coming with us to Easthaven, either of you. You can come to school; one of the teachers will be staying behind, probably Miss Powell. She will make sure you don't waste your

81

time! You can tell your parents that you will be having extra tuition on Wednesday . . . all day.'

Mr Nelson sent for Nicky. 'I'm sorry to say that Roy is just a little bit upset,' he told her carefully. 'And I don't want you to get any silly ideas.'

'Me? I don't get silly ideas!'

'No, of course not. My mistake.'

'What is Roy upset about?'

'Well – I'm afraid his goldfish have gone down the drain. Literally. I understand you gave them to him.'

'Who done it?'

'The school will replace the fish. Roy can have two from the tank in the hall. I've told him already, he can choose.'

'Who done it, though?'

'Those concerned *are* being punished, Nicky. I promise you I'm punishing them in the way I'm sure will hurt them most. There will be no need for any revenge in the playground! DO I MAKE MYSELF CLEAR?'

'Yes, Sir,' said Nicky. 'You make yourself as clear as anything.'

Roy sat in his seat, and it was as though there was only him, real and solid, in the whole world. Everything else – the desks, the books, the pictures on the wall, Mrs Blake, the other children – all were shadowy, misty shapes, existing in a different sort of time and space, not joined up with his. He was all alone in his shock and grief. Even Claudette, with her soft brown arm round his neck, whispering words of comfort into his ear – even Claudette was outside in that other space, and not really close to him at all.

Stony-faced, Roy stared blankly ahead, twisting

his fingers, trying to adjust his mind to the enormity of what had happened. He shrugged Claudette's arm away and her eyes, still full of sympathy, showed hurt.

'Come along, Roy,' said Mrs Blake, trying to jolly him out of it. 'Life goes on, you know.'

What did she mean, life goes on? Not Fishy and Goldy's life, that wasn't going on. Their life was ended, down the toilet. Or at any rate *he* would never see them again. And he wished he was dead as well, because now there was nothing left.

'Come on now, Roy! You know you're going to have two of the school's instead,' Mrs Blake blundered on, making it worse. 'And goldfish are all very much the same, aren't they? Pretty soon you won't know the difference.'

But he would, he would! How could two fish without any names, out of the school tank, take the place of his beautiful Goldy and Fishy? Mrs Blake didn't understand. Nobody understood. Even Nicky, who had given them to him, could not possibly understand how special they were to him. He couldn't even cry for them, the sorrow went too deep.

In the dinner hall, Nicky observed Roy's stricken face. He was ashen white and empty-eyed, not even twisting his fingers now. A terrible pain began in Nicky's chest.

'Stay with your class, Nicky,' said Mr Hunt, who was on duty, and hadn't heard about the fish yet. He knew Nicky had been to Mr Nelson, of course, and he knew she was in a mood when she came back, but he didn't know why. So he was not particularly concerned when Nicky ignored him, and pushed her way through the jostling crowds of children, to put her hands each side of Roy's face, turning his head to look at her. 'Who done it?'

He turned his head without answering.

'Come on! I want to know,' said Nicky, giving his shoulder a push.

'Gary,' Roy whispered. 'And Sanjay.'

'Right!' said Nicky.

Her eyes were blue gimlets, marking them down. All of 3B watched with interest, anticipating fun to come. The third year table was dismissed from dinner first. That was a pity – now Gary and Sanjay would bolt into the toilets and there would be no interesting fight to watch, But no, no, Nicky was not waiting to be dismissed! Nicky was getting up from her seat anyway, and pushing past everyone to grab Gary before he could hide. She caught him by the hair, and they both stumbled into the playground. 'What did you do to my brother's fish? Tell me what you done to my brother's fish!'

'Nothing. . . . Ow!' the bulging eyes bulged some more, as Nicky yanked at Gary's hair roots.

'Slob! Creep! Tell me what you done!'

'Nothing. It was Sanjay's idea. Ow-w-w!'

'You drownded my brother's fish, didn't you!'

'You can't drown fish.'

'Don't be clever. There's another one for being clever. And another. And another! You want me to push those ugly sticky-out teeth down your mouth, like you put my brother's goldfish down the toilet? Do you?'

'No-o-o! Leave me! Witch!'

'I'll leave you when I've finished!' She had dragged him to the wall now, and was quite deliberately grinding his face against the bricks. The watching crowd closed in, admiring the way Nicky neatly dodged Gary's flailing arms and legs, uneasy at the sight of Gary's bloody nose.

'Sanjay done it too, it wasn't only me.' He had given up trying to fight back. He was using his hands to protect his face, and one foot to brace himself clear of the wall.

'Yeah? I'll have to do him as well then, won't I! When I finished with you!'

'Sanjay's in the toilets,' someone called. 'Hiding.'

'He's scared!' said someone else.

'Ha, ha, ha!'

'Cool it, Nicky. You're kicking Gary too hard!'

'Yeah – cool it now!'

Mr Hunt arrived at that moment, having received the frantic message from a distraught dinner lady, that Nicky Mitchell was killing someone in the playground. Mr Hunt pushed his way through the crowd, and grabbed at Nicky's arm. Nicky went on lashing out with her feet, and there was yet another painful bruise on Gary's backside. Mr Hunt yanked her backwards so she couldn't reach – and Nicky kicked backwards at him! It was only because she was so deeply hurt and frustrated she didn't properly know what she was doing. She was sorry afterwards, about kicking Mr Hunt, but, of course, afterwards was too late.

'Well that's it, Nicky, isn't it?' said Mr Nelson. 'I mean – what am I expected to do? What do *you* expect me to do?'

'How is your arthritis today, Sir?'

'Never mind my arthritis – you realize I shall have to stop you coming to Easthaven on Wednesday, don't you?'

'It was worth it,' said Nicky. 'Except I'm sorry about kicking Mr Hunt.'

'Mr Hunt will forgive you. Eventually. I'm not so sure about Gary's mother. And speaking of mothers, I shall have to have a word with yours.'

'Oh.'

'There'll be a letter in the post tonight. For obvious reasons, I shan't ask you to take it home with you.'

'Don't you trust me, Sir?'

'I hoped I could trust your good sense this morning!'

'Anyway, I feel better now,' said Nicky. 'I feel so much better I'm not going to do nothing to Sanjay.' She gave a little hopeful, sideways smile at Mr Nelson. 'I *was* going to poke his little piggy eyes in, but I'm not now!'

'Good try,' said Mr Nelson, sadly.


When she had time to think about it, Nicky found she was quite uncomfortably worried about the letter that was coming in the post. The very thing she had been trying to avoid! One of the little juggling balls had come crashing right down now, so Aunty Four-Eyes could do her worst; there was no more worse to do. 'Do you know the seaside of Southbourne?' she asked Joycelyn, in class.

'I heard about it, one time.'

'Do you know how to get there, on the train?'

'Go to the station, and buy a ticket,' said Joycelyn, unhelpfully.

'I know *that*,' said Nicky. 'Who don't know that? I mean what station is it? I meant is it Euston, or Waterloo, or what?'

'Ask Mr Hunt,' said Joycelyn.

'I can't,' said Nicky. 'He's not speaking to me.'

When the bell went, Nicky announced that she was not waiting to be dismissed with the others, she was going straight to Roy's classroom, because he would be needing her this afternoon; and Mr Hunt needn't bother trying to stop her, because she was going anyway. Mr Hunt sighed, and caressed his kicked shins, and shrugged.

'Have you chose your new goldfish yet?' said Nicky to Roy.

'I don't want any new goldfish.' His voice was flat, and without expression, the words barely audible.

'Don't be silly, of course you want them! You do say some silly things, Roy Mitchell! Well *I* want them, anyway. Shall I choose, then? Are you coming to help me? All right, I'll do it on my own. Is that all right, Mrs Blake? Can I go and choose?'

'Come along, Roy,' said Mrs Blake. 'We'll go and choose your goldfish, shall we? You and me and Nicky together.'

'I don't want them,' said Roy. 'I want Goldy and Fishy.'

'Goldy and Fishy have gone to Heaven,' said Nicky. 'As you very well know. You coming to the hall, then? All right, me and Mrs Blake will choose for you. I'll put some water in the bowl, shall I? Come on, Mrs Blake.'

Roy trailed behind them, his face a total blank. 'Look at this beautiful goldfish, Mrs Blake!' said Nicky loudly and ecstatically. 'This big one! Oh *look*, Mrs Blake, isn't he beautiful? Did you ever see such a beautiful goldfish in your life? Can we have him? Can we *really*?'

Roy stood a little way off, twisting his fingers and

87

staring at the wall. 'And *this* one,' Nicky enthused. 'Oh look, he's got a bit of red on him. Look, Roy, you got two beautiful fish again!'

'I don't want them,' said Roy.

'All right,' said Nicky. 'You don't have to keep on saying it. They can be *my* fish. Thank you, Mrs Blake, for these beautiful fish. Good night, Mrs Blake!'

Nicky carried the bowl with great care. 'Gosh, it is heavy! You must be very strong, Roy, to carry this bowl to school this morning! You must be strong like Tarzan!' She chattered at him over her shoulder, trying to rouse him out of his depression, but he didn't answer, didn't even look at her. His feet moved sluggishly, scuffling along the pavement; his eyes wandered from side to side, and over Nicky's head.

'All right,' said Nicky. 'If you won't talk to me, perhaps the fish will talk to me. *My* fish. Good afternoon, fish, how are you today, fish? What do you think of this lovely weather, fish?' She bent her head over the bowl, holding her ear to the opening. 'Oh you don't think it *is* lovely weather! You rather rain!' Without pausing in her stride, Nicky turned her head briefly, to see if Roy was smiling by any chance – and her foot caught in a nasty little hole in the pavement. She stumbled forward, lost her balance, tried to regain it and failed. And the goldfish bowl flew from her hands as she instinctively stretched them to break her fall.

The glass shattered into a dozen pieces, the water poured over the pavement, the fish were floundering and gulping in the gutter. Roy stared blankly at the disaster, almost without interest. Stunned with dismay, Nicky sat one moment more amongst the debris, then scrambled to her feet. She bent to grab at the fish, and they slithered out of her hand. She grabbed again, and managed to hold one. She hesitated, then abandoned the other and ran quickly, quickly, to save the life of this one fish at least, if she could.

Roy trailed after her, still only half aware.

At home, Nicky put the fish in the washing-up bowl in the kitchen – but it was obviously dead. She emptied it into the dustbin, and went to find Roy.

He was in the Back Room, sitting on the shabby sofa, the tears streaming down his face at last. Nicky sat beside him, and put her arm round his shoulders. 'I'm sorry. I'm sorry. I didn't mean to drop them!'

Roy began to cry noisily, his body shaken with sobs. Nicky's arm tightened around his shoulders. 'Oh Roy, don't, don't! Please don't cry any more, I can't stand it, I'm so miserable! I'll buy some more fish for you when I've got some money, I will!'

He pushed her arm away and turned his back to her, still sobbing.

'Roy! Please!'

'Do you think I'm crying about *your* old fish, then?' he said, bitterly, still not looking at her.

'They weren't my fish really,' said Nicky. 'I thought you would understand that. I was just keeping them for you.'

'Well you needn't have bothered, because I didn't want them. I only want Goldy and Fishy, and they're d-dead!'

'Oh Roy!'

'And that's what I'm crying about n-now.'

'Won't you *never* want any more fish?'

'No. I finished wanting fish. Anyway, I don't think

'I'm lucky enough.' He had never sounded more sad, but at least his crying had stopped.

'What you mean, not lucky enough?' she scolded him. 'Now you're talking silly. Now you're saying silly things again.'

'I'm not lucky enough to have fish. I'm a unlucky person.'

'No you're not, you're a very lucky person. You're a very lucky person indeed, and if you don't believe me I'll show you how lucky you are! You're so lucky I'm going to let you choose anything you like for tea. Anything!' she said recklessly. 'You can have whatever you like.'

'Even if it costs a lot of money?'

'I got plenty money,' Nicky lied.

'Can we have Chinese?' Roy had not touched his school dinner and now, with his grief partly out, he was beginning to feel hungry.

'If that's what you choose.' Chinese was expensive, they didn't often have it, but Nicky would have given Roy the food out of her own mouth tonight, if that would comfort him.

'Can we have those crispy balls with the sweet stuff on them?' His eyes gleamed, just a little bit.

'Yes we can, we can. We'll go as soon as they're open.'

In the Lotus Garden, Sonia and Eric were also waiting for their take-aways. 'What are you having?' said Eric.

'If it's any of your business, we're having sweet and sour,' said Nicky. 'And some egg-fried rice.'

'Is that all? That's not much. We're having all this, look, six different things!'

'Everybody isn't as greedy as you.'

'We have to share it,' said Sonia. 'In the whole family.'

'So?' said Nicky. 'We have to share ours.'

'Only two things, between three people?' said Eric, scornfully.

'That's enough for Roy and me,' said Nicky.

'Doesn't your mum want anything to eat tonight, then?' said Sonia.

'She doesn't like Chinese,' said Nicky.

'Yes she does,' said Eric, remembering friendlier days.

'She changed her mind,' said Nicky.

'I haven't seen your mum,' said Sonia. 'Not for ever such a long time.'

'That's funny,' said Nicky. 'She's seen you!'

'When?'

'The other day,' said Nicky. 'She told us, didn't she, Roy? She said, "I saw that Sonia Morris on her way to school, isn't she getting tall?" You must have forgot.'

'I don't think so,' said Sonia, puzzled.

'Our mum's not speaking to your mum,' said Eric.

'And our mum's not speaking to your mum,' said Nicky. 'But she quite likes Sonia, she said.'

'Which day was it?' said Sonia.

'Which day was what?'

'When your mum saw me.'

'Tuesday. Perhaps you didn't see her after all. I think she said she walked up the road behind you.'

'I didn't go to school Tuesday,' said Sonia. 'I had a tummy-ache.'

'Well Wednesday then,' said Nicky. '*I* don't know.'

'My dad took me to school in the car, Wednesday.'

'Some other day then,' said Nicky. 'Don't go on and on about it, it's boring.'

There had been enough money to pay for the meal, but precious little over. 'I've got 46p left now, and that's all,' said Nicky, in the house.

'Is that all you've got really?' said Roy, dismayed. 'Are you joking?'

'That's all. Go on, eat your Chinese now I bought it.'

'What are we going to do though? Without enough money?'

'I don't know,' said Nicky. 'I'll think tomorrow.'

In the night Roy woke, and his sheets were soaking wet. He went to Nicky for comfort, but she was not feeling like comforting anyone, just then. 'What you want to do that for?' she scolded him. 'You supposed to be ten years old! Funny sort of ten years old! Anyway you can change your bed yourself, *I'm* not going to do it for you!'

# 7

# Hungry!

The woman in the hospital was fretting. She wasn't lying in bed any more; the cruel nurses made her sit in a chair for most of the day, which was painful; and even walk about sometimes, which hurt even more. They didn't do it to be cruel, they said, they did it to help her get better. And she *was* getting better, in one way. She was feeling stronger every day. The only thing was, she still couldn't remember her name.

It was very strange, having arms and legs and a body and a face, and no memory of any past life. The woman didn't like not having any memory; it made her feel as though she wasn't quite a real person. Over and over each day, she struggled to force the memories back – but it was as though a thick black curtain had come down over part of her mind, and however hard she tried, she couldn't lift it.

'You're probably trying *too* hard,' the nurse explained. 'Just relax. It'll come when it's ready.'

'It's all very well for you saying that,' said the woman. '*You've* got a name!'

'Well I haven't been in a coma, have I?' said the nurse. 'Which is what we call the long sleep you had. People *do* lose their memories after a coma, sometimes.'

'But I'm fed up with this, I'm fed up with not knowing who I am!' the woman burst out; and she added a few words that were not nice to hear at all.

'Charming!' said the nurse, walking away.

'Oh you lot are so pleased with yourselves!' the woman shouted. 'How would you like to be me, then? How would you like it?' And she let fly with some more not-very-nice language, but since no one took the slightest notice of her tantrum she soon tired of that, and sat glaring dejectedly at the wall.

'It begins with a M,' she said suddenly.

'What does?' said the woman in the next bed.

'Margaret Thatcher!' said the woman in the chair, tartly. 'No! *My* name, of course. One of my names anyway . . . I think.'

'Well that's a start then, dear, isn't it?' said the woman in the bed.

'And I *think* I live in London,' said Mrs Mitchell, sounding quite excited.

Nicky got up in a bad mood. Troubled and confused about what to do, now Mum had been gone a whole week, she took out her ill temper on the house. 'Look at this place!' she complained. 'It's like a rubbish heap. Look at all those cushions on the floor! And the chairs knocked over. And papers and stuff everywhere. Who done all that mess?'

'We both did,' said Roy. 'When we was playing Rough Games.'

'It's "we were", not "we was",' said Nicky sourly. 'Where are your manners? Anyway you can clear it all up after breakfast, that can be your job.'

Roy swore, under his breath.

'Wash your mouth out!' Nicky scolded him.

'Mum says worse than that, sometimes.'

'That's different. Mum has a excuse if she says bad words sometimes. She has a hard life, you know.'

'So do we have a hard life.'

'No we don't, we have a very good life and stop moaning! We have a great life. I do, anyway!'

The milkman rang the doorbell just then, and since it was Saturday he wanted to be paid. 'Mum says she'll pay next week,' said Nicky. 'She hasn't got any change.'

'She didn't have any change last Saturday.' The milkman didn't sound very happy.

'She'll pay next week for absolute certain,' said Nicky.

She went to the bathroom to deal with Roy's sheets. 'It's time they went to the launderette anyway,' she said. 'And some of our things. Our knickers and things. Else what are we going to have to wear if they're all dirty? Hurry up and finish your breakfast, Roy. I could eat four breakfasts while you eat one. You got to take a load of washing to the launderette.'

'You said I got to pick up the cushions.'

'I changed my mind, don't argue.'

'I don't think we've got enough money for the launderette.'

'Yeah. . . . All right then, we won't take the stuff to the launderette after all. I'll do the washing in the kitchen, and hang it on the line. You can pick up the cushions after all, I changed my mind again.'

She pegged out the sheets and the underwear, and Roy's school shirts from last week, and her school dress. There was washing on the next door line as well, Mrs Morris had just finished putting it out; a lady's dresses, and Mr Morris's pyjamas, as well as Sonia's and Eric's things. Nicky went up to Mum's bedroom and fetched a nightie and a petticoat, and Mum's best blouse. She dipped them in water to make it look real, and pegged them on the line with

95

the rest. That would fix Sonia Morris and her nasty suspicious questions!

The bathroom, she observed, was filthy. No use telling Roy to clean that, he wouldn't know how. Nicky scrubbed at tide marks and polished taps. Then she dragged Roy off his bottom to help with the rest of the house. He grumbled a bit; he had slumped himself in front of the television that didn't work, thinking his part was done. But Nicky said there was the hall still, and the stairs, and the kitchen, and their bedrooms; and not to be a lazy slob because for all he knew, for all he knew, Mum might be coming home today, and did he want Mum to think they turned themselves into tramps, just because she wasn't there?

'I don't want to talk about Mum,' said Roy.

'I didn't ask you to talk. Who asked you to talk? I said to clean the house, so do it!'

By the time they had finished, the house had had rather more than the superficial wipe-over it usually got when Mum was in charge. It was also dinner time. 'I'm hungry,' said Roy.

Nicky looked in the cupboard. 'There's one tin of peas. We haven't ate the peas yet.'

'Is that all we're going to have?'

'What's the matter with you, you want to get fat? You want to get as fat as a pig? Peas are very good for you, you know. She looked in the fridge. 'Oh Roy, I forgot, I forgot! There's some of the roast still, from Sunday.'

'It's old.'

Nicky smelled it. 'It's all right, don't grumble. You should be glad to have such a good dinner. There's plenty of children in the world don't get hardly anything to eat at all, you know.'

'Anyway I don't like peas. Can't I have the rest of my birthday cake?'

'We have to save that for our tea.'

'Can't we *buy* something for our tea?'

'That reminds me,' said Nicky. 'I was going to ask you. Roy, do *you* have any money?'

'A little bit. It's mine, though.'

'Don't be selfish.'

'But it's *mine*.'

'Roy, this is special, isn't it. This is a special thing that never happened before. So you have to do a special thing and give me your money, so we can last out a bit longer, and keep the secret a bit longer.'

'I don't want to talk about the secret.'

'Well *don't* talk about it. Just go and get me your money.'

In the secrecy of his bedroom, Roy divided his little horde of money into two piles – one pound thirty-five pence for himself and ninety-one pence for Nicky. 'Is that all you've got?' said Nicky.

'I spent the rest,' said Roy.

'One pound thirty-seven altogether,' said Nicky. 'It's not going to go very far. It's not even enough for Sunday roast.'

Roy's eyes filled with tears. 'Aren't we going to have Sunday roast, then?'

'How can we, if there isn't any money to buy it?'

Roy twisted his fingers, pulling at them until they cracked.

'Don't do that!' said Nicky, sharply.

'I think we're going to starve,' said Roy.

'No we aren't. We aren't going to starve at all. There's still more food in the house, you know; we haven't finished it all yet. There's a half packet of rice

97

I found, I could cook that. And some potatoes still. And some bread. It's a bit mouldy but we can have this jam, look, to cover the taste.'

'The jam's mouldy too.'

'Don't be fussy.'

'And it's Sunday tomorrow, and we supposed to have Sunday roast!'

'But this is special, Roy. We can't have everything the same when it's special.'

'I don't want to talk about it's special. I want us to have our Sunday roast.' He was twisting his fingers frantically. He was being totally unreasonable, and she didn't understand it properly, but she could see that Sunday roast was somehow tremendously important to Roy.

They ate the peas and the hard stale meat in silence, and afterwards Roy slumped again in front of the television that didn't work.

'Haven't you got nothing interesting to do?'

'No.'

'Can't you *find* nothing interesting?'

'No.'

'Don't you *want* to do nothing interesting?'

'No.'

She was irritated for a moment, and then her heart turned over with pity. She picked up Mum's shopping bag, and went to the High Street, and she went with dragging steps, because she was quite a bit afraid about what she was going to do. There was a notice inside Safeway, which said THIEVES WILL BE PROSECUTED. Nicky took one of the wire baskets and put Mum's shopping bag inside it, with the opening facing upwards. It felt as though everyone in the shop was looking at her, but when she peeped out of the corner of her eye, she saw they were all much too busy thinking about their own shopping. There was a notice about detectives in plain clothes, as well as the one about thieves, and that made her uneasy, because it meant you wouldn't know who was a shopper, and who was a detective.

Nicky walked round the aisles, putting things into the wire basket. She had a plan of a sort, though not a very clear one. She was actually not very good at making plans, being more used to acting on the spur of the moment, but she knew she couldn't just trust to inspiration in this case. There had to be lots of packets and tins in her basket, that was the first thing; then no one would notice, perhaps, that her own bag was not quite empty.

She reached the frozen poultry section at last – and this was the first really important bit. Nicky chose a middle-sized chicken, and put it into the wire basket, with the tins and the packets. She carried the basket along, seeking a convenient spot for the next part of the plan. There were not many people in the biscuit tin section. Nicky put the wire basket on the ground, right against the shelves, as though to ease her aching arms. Then she bent over the basket, shielding the sight of it with her body. She hoped that anyone noticing would think she was just rearranging the weight, to make it more comfortable for carrying. What she was really doing was transferring the frozen chicken from the wire basket to her own shopping bag. Then she pushed the shopping bag with the chicken in it right underneath the packets and tins.

She had done it! She was a thief! Well not quite yet, but nearly. It was amazing that nobody challenged her. She expected that at any minute someone would come up from behind, and tap her on the shoulder, and say, 'I saw what you did, little girl. I saw you put that chicken in your bag to steal it. Come with me to the police.' But nobody did say that; it was as though she were invisible. Stealing was really easy, after all.

Heartened by the ease of it, Nicky moved to the frozen dessert section. She was looking for another rich, creamy gateau, one Roy could make himself sick on if he wanted to. Might as well get a good one, while she was about it. There was no freezer at home, but the gateau would keep in the fridge until tomorrow.

Taking the gateau was no more difficult than taking the chicken. Now Nicky had a basketful of things she didn't want, and a bag with two things she was going to steal. There was only one difficulty ahead of her, and that was to get the chicken and the gateau out of the store. And this was the bit she was vague about.

Nicky regarded the long queues at the checkout. She had heard of people passing through the checkouts, and paying for what was in their basket, and there was more in their own bag all the time. It wouldn't work for her, though, because she hadn't got enough money to pay for the stuff in her basket anyway.

There were loads of people waiting to pay, and most of them were taller than she was. Might it be possible to squeeze past them, hidden from the eyes of the checkout lady? Could she pretend she was with her mother really, and just pushing to catch up? She had almost decided to try that one, when she noticed a man standing just beyond the checkouts, and it seemed as though his eye was right on her. Perhaps he was one of the plain clothes detectives! The fear that he might be put her off squeezing past the checkouts, and she went back to her first idea, the one that had occurred to her as she was coming in. With an indrawn breath, signifying to anyone looking that she had just remembered something, Nicky walked briskly round the aisles to the entrance.

The big glass doors opened only one way, but people were coming through from outside all the time. Nicky rested her basket on the ground again, pretending to check the contents with her left hand. The handles of her own bag, protruding through the packets and tins, were held firmly in her right. She was watching her opportunity and she saw it: a whole family apparently – mum, dad, grandma, and a horde of kids and a pushchair, all shoving and pushing their way through the glass doors. It would be the easiest thing in the world, Nicky thought, to yank up the bag, abandon the wire basket, and push through the glass doors herself, under cover of the family which was so obligingly keeping them open for her.

She wasn't even afraid any more.

She could do it easily – and yet she *couldn't* do it! She couldn't do it, she couldn't steal! What was the matter with her? She had gone to all this trouble and now, it seemed, she had just wasted her time.

She grabbed the bag – and hesitated! The family pushing through the doors was nearly through. Another moment, and the chance would be gone. Nicky scolded herself for letting the chance go by, but something very peculiar was happening inside her.

Once she walked through that door, she realized, she would really have made herself into a thief! And she didn't want to be a thief. She wasn't afraid of being caught, she just couldn't make herself be a thief.

Angrily, Nicky glared at the backs of the family now struggling to free a trolley from the stack inside the door; as though it was *their* fault she couldn't make herself into a thief. Then, regretfully, she took the chicken and the gateau back to their respective sections and replaced them.

Back at home, Roy was still sitting, staring blankly at the television that didn't work. His dejection, going on so long, made Nicky uneasy. A nice dinner for tomorrow – now that would cheer him up! Only she had been out to get one, hadn't she, and now if she couldn't steal it she must buy it. She brought in the clothes, and ironed them, and pondered.

There was Mum's post office savings, and Nicky knew where the book was. Mum wouldn't mind; Nicky was sure Mum wouldn't mind, since it was for food, and they really needed food. But somehow Nicky didn't think the post office man would let her have any of the money.

Who had money?

Joycelyn! Joycelyn had had a birthday some weeks ago, and she had got money for her birthday, which she surely wouldn't have spent, because she was saving for some smart red shoes she had seen. Nicky knew where Joycelyn lived, because she went to her birthday party that time. And there was something Joycelyn would like to have, even more than she would like to have the red shoes.

Nicky went to the top drawer of her dressing table, and took out her own most precious possession – a

102

very unusual necklace of multi-coloured stones, that she had seen in the junk shop and longed for. The lady said it cost seven pounds, which was more money than Nicky ever had at one time in her life. She told the lady in the junk shop that she would save up for the necklace, but it would take a long time because she only had fifty pence a week, unless Mum felt generous, and please, please, *please* not to sell it to anybody else. Nicky took the lady the two pounds twenty pence she already had saved, and the whole of her pocket money every week after that, and in the end the lady let her off the last eighty pence because she clearly loved the necklace so much.

And when she took it to school, to show the few people she was associating with at the time, Joycelyn fell in love with the necklace as well. She didn't *say* she wanted it for herself, just gazed at it with unconcealed longing in the warm brown eyes. Well – now she could have it! She could have it instead of the red shoes, which were quite ordinary after all, and would be too small for her anyway, next year.

Joycelyn was surprised to see Nicky standing on her doorstep. Except for the birthday party, Nicky had never been to her house before. 'How much money have you got for your shoes now?' said Nicky.

'Three pounds.'

'Is that all? You had more than that last week!'

Joycelyn looked sheepish. 'There was a nice bracelet—'

'You silly fool, Joycelyn! You should have saved your money for the shoes.'

'I know.'

'All right, you can have it for three pounds.'

'Have what?'

103

'My necklace. You can have it for three pounds. There!' She held it up, and the multi-coloured stones glistened in the sunlight.

'You paid a lot more than that, though. You saved for weeks and weeks, you said.'

'Don't matter.'

'It's your best thing!'

'Oh don't go on and on,' said Nicky. 'Do you want it for three pounds or don't you?'

'I do want it.'

'Good.'

Nicky ran all the way back to Safeway. She put the chicken and a smaller gateau into the wire basket, and paid for them like everyone else, at the checkout. She had exactly fifty pence left, altogether.

And after all, what was the use of what she had done? Food for one more day, or two – and what then? Roy happy with his roast chicken tomorrow, perhaps, and all the money spent again! Perhaps she didn't ought to have spent the money on food. Perhaps she should have saved it, for that other thing they might have to do. Only it was so hard that other thing, she didn't even know where to start. And at least now there would be a nice dinner tomorrow. But if Mum didn't come, if she went on not coming, then what would happen next? What would happen to her and Roy?

She sat beside him, on the sofa with the broken springs. 'Roy, I think we have to do something a little bit hard.'

'What?'

'I think we have to go to Southbourne, to find Mum.'

'I don't want to. . . . Anyway, we can't.'

'If I think out a way, will you come?'

'I don't want to.'

'I know you don't *want* to, but *will* you?'

'No.'

'I think we have to, though.'

'Leave me alone. I don't want to talk about it.'

Confused and uncertain still, Nicky fretted for half the night.

Coming home from Sunday School, next day, Sonia was very tiresome and inquisitive. 'I *haven't* seen your mum for a long time,' she persisted.

'That's because you weren't looking.'

'I was out in the garden this morning, and I was looking in your back, and I never see her at all.'

'Don't be silly, Sonia, you know she always has a lie-in, Sundays.'

'It's like she's gone invisible though.'

'Well she's not invisible to *me*. She's not invisible to us, is she, Roy?'

'I haven't seen her neither,' said Eric.

'Mrs Willams said she never see her for a long time,' said Sonia. 'She told our mum.'

'Why is everybody so interested in *our* mum?' said Nicky. 'Our mum is fine. In fact, she is so fine, she might be going to take us to the seaside this afternoon.'

'We went yesterday,' said Sonia. 'In the car.'

'We haven't got a car,' said Nicky. 'So we're going by the train. My mum says we might go to South-bourne.'

'You should have went in the morning,' said Sonia. 'It takes a long time.'

'It's quicker by the train though. Only my mum says she doesn't know for certain what station we have to go from.'

'Oh.'

'Do *you*? Do you know what station it is, to go to Southbourne?'

'No. We don't go by the train, you see, we go in the car.'

'You don't have to make a big thing about it, Sonia, that you got a car and we haven't.'

Sonia was so unhappy to think she might have been unkind, that she made herself think really hard, to make up for it. 'It might be Victoria.'

'The station?'

'It *might* be Victoria. I know it's Victoria for Easthaven, and I think Southbourne is quite near to there.'

'I'll tell my mum when she gets up.'

'I think she *is* up,' said Sonia. 'There's ever such a nice smell coming out of your house, Nicky!'

'That's because Mum is making roast chicken for our dinner,' said Nicky proudly.

'What's the matter with Roy?' said Eric.

'Nothing,' said Nicky. 'He's just walking more slower than usual.'

Over the meal, Roy did come alive just a little bit. Nicky tried over again. 'We have to talk about Mum, Roy.'

'I don't want to.'

'I know you don't want to, but we have to.'

'I think she's dead.'

'No she's *not* dead, she's *not* dead. But if they find out she left us, she might have to go to prison.'

106

'You said they wouldn't do that to her.'

'It might be different now. Because it's been so long. So we have to find her, and tell her. In case she didn't think of it herself. And anyway, we can't last by ourself for a long time.'

'I don't want to talk about it. I don't want to think about it.'

'All right, *don't* think about it. Don't think about it and see what happens! I bet you won't like what happens, if you go on and not think about it, like now.'

'What then?' He turned away from her, hiding his face and twisting his fingers.

'If they find out Mum left us, and if they put her in prison, they going to do the same to us like they done to her.'

'Put us in prison?'

'No, stupid! Like they done to her when she was a little girl, I mean.'

'Put her in a children's home!'

'Because she didn't have a mum or a dad.'

'And she didn't like it.'

'And *we* won't like it. . . . But that's what they're going to do to us, because we haven't got anywhere else to go.'

'Don't let them! Don't let them do that, Nicky!'

'Come to Southbourne with me, then.'

'No.'

'You know what's going to happen if you don't.'

'I don't want to think about it. I don't want to think about it!'

In fact, thinking about it frightened Nicky too; and she was by no means clear, even now, or sure, that what she had just been saying was right. She went up to Mum's bedroom again, and tried on all the things, and made her face up to look like Mum, if she could. But she didn't look like Mum, she looked like Nicky with the wrong sort of lipstick, and the wrong sort of clothes – and everything was wrong, and a muddle, and she couldn't make up her mind what to do, and Roy was going to be difficult anyway. And there was the letter coming from school as well. And it was all too much. It was too much!

Nicky sat on Mum's bed, and covered her face with her hands. Her thoughts were like a bunch of balloons on long strings, waving about, and floating off in different directions. Her head had begun to ache and throb, with the strain of trying to pull them all together. She had to decide though, she had to decide!

She decided suddenly, and found her heart was as light as air. 'I've decided,' she said to Roy, downstairs.

Roy didn't want to talk to her at all, now. 'Go away,' he said.

'I'm not going away, because you have to listen.'

'I'm not *going* to listen.'

'Yes you are. Don't argue.'

He was silent, not looking at her.

'I've decided we have to go to Southbourne, and I thought of a way to go on the train without a ticket.'

'I don't want to go on the train.'

'I know, but we have to. I've decided.'

He was silent again. Then, after a long pause, he asked, reluctantly, 'How do we get to the train, anyway?'

'We go to Victoria Station. We go on the Number 52 bus, I seen it on the front. And I think we got enough money for that bit. If we haven't got enough to ride all the way, we can walk part of it. Walking is good for you.'

'I'm not going to come.'

'All right then, don't. I'll go by myself if you like. I'll just leave you here all alone, shall I?'

Silence.

'And if they find you're here, all by yourself, they can put you in the children's home without me. I don't mind. I'll be having a nice adventure, looking for Mum.'

'You wouldn't *really* go without me, would you?'

'Watch me!'

"When?'

'When what?'

'When are we going?'

'Tomorrow morning. And you can take that miserable look off your face, Roy, because it is not a miserable thing, it is a happy thing. We are going to find Mum, so it is a very happy thing indeed. *I* think so, anyway.'


The police were talking on the phone to the Sister at the hospital.

'Has she remembered her name yet?'

'Not so far. Her memory's coming back in bits, though. Today she said she thinks she lives in London.'

'Give it another few days,' said the policeman. 'And if she still doesn't remember, we might put out a television appeal. *Somebody* must know who she is.'

# 8

## Looking for Mum

Nicky was in great spirits. She sat with Roy, on the front seat of the bus upstairs, and sang 'Jesus wants me for a sunbeam', loud and raucously. An irritated passenger poked her from behind. 'Do us a favour, love!'

'What's the matter with you?' said Nicky. 'I'm only singing.'

'Is that what you call it? Sounds more like a cat with the stomach ache.'

'Wrong!' said Nicky. 'It sounds like *six* cats with the stomach ache.'

She shrieked with laughter; peal after weird peal bounced around the bus. 'She's a nutter, ain't she?' someone said.

'You all right?' said the passenger behind.

'No, I'm half left,' said Nicky, shrieking some more. The laugh stopped as abruptly as it had begun, and Nicky turned her attention to the splendid view of London unfolding slowly and jerkily, because there was quite a lot of traffic, before them. She was intensely interested in everything she saw. 'Look, Roy! Look at those posh houses. Fancy living in a house like that! Look at the beautiful old things in that shop! Look at the grass, with all the different trees! Look, Roy, like in a picture! Do you think we come to the country?' They were passing Kensington Gardens, where Nicky had never been, although she lived only a few miles away. '*Look*, Roy!'

Roy did not answer her. He sat hunched and stiff in his seat, the china-blue eyes blank, staring at nothing. Home for the last week had been a crumbling fortress; now he was being torn away from the ruins, even. He was leaving the known for the unknown, and he was too lost inside himself, almost, to be frightened.

Everyone was getting off the bus. 'I think this is it,' said Nicky. 'Wasn't it lucky the money was just enough for the tickets!'

They were in a big bus terminal. 'I never see so many buses, did you, Roy?' Nicky marvelled. 'I wonder where it is for the trains.' A taxi hooted them angrily, as they stepped into its path. 'And the same to you!' Nicky called after it. 'Some people got no manners, have they, Roy! Come on, I see where we have to go.'

Victoria Station was intimidating in its hugeness. Nicky had been on a big station once before, but it was a long time ago, and she couldn't remember which one, or where she was travelling that time. Nevertheless it was that memory she relied on, to work out her plan. Reality was disconcertingly different from memory, though; bigger, and harsher, and noisier. Bewildered, Nicky felt a little bit of her confidence ebb away. 'Let's sit down for a bit,' she said to Roy, 'and have a little think.'

There didn't seem to be any seats, so they tucked themselves into a corner and sat on the hard ground, against a wall. Down here they felt even smaller, towered over by trolleys, and moving legs. 'When are we going on the train?' said Roy, speaking at last.

'Don't you listen to what I say?' said Nicky. 'I said we got to think. You can't expect me to know

111

everything all at once. You got to give me a chance to work it out. Where the right train is, and everything.'

'I want to go home,' said Roy.

'Shut up,' said Nicky, losing patience. 'Shut up or I'll belt you one! You're nothing but a drag; you don't help a bit!'

Roy withdrew into stony silence again. For comfort, Nicky fussed through the bags she carried – one of Safeway's plastic carriers, and her own schoolbag stuffed with a woolly each for her and Roy for if it got cold. The Safeway's carrier contained one slice of birthday cake, some very stale biscuits from a tin Nicky had overlooked before, the bread with most of the mould cut off, the packet of cornflakes half empty now, two cold potatoes left over from yesterday's dinner, the remains of the chicken, cut into pieces so they could eat it with their fingers, and a pint of milk left over from breakfast.

There was also the letter from school, duly arrived that morning, now getting greasier and greasier from rubbing against the food. Nicky had not opened the letter, of course, because it was addressed to Mum, and it would not be right to read it, but she had a fair idea what was inside, because Mr Nelson said. When Mum saw the letter, she would realize how important it was to come back quickly.

Nicky scrambled to her feet. 'You stay here with the bags,' she told Roy. 'Stay right here, I'm going to explore a bit. Find out where we have to go for the train. . . . *Roy*, I'm speaking to you!'

His gaze was fixed still, and he didn't move. Nicky prodded him with her foot. 'Snap out of it, Roy, you're getting to be like a robot or something. . . . Oh all right, *be* like that! Make a misery out of it, see if I care! I'm having a great time anyway. A *great* time. You're missing all the fun, being like a robot!'

She walked away from him, deliberately not looking back. Crowds of travellers closed in around her, and when she turned her head at last, she couldn't see Roy anyway, because he was round the corner. She stood near the entrance to Platform eight, but she had no idea where the train waiting there might be going. How were you supposed to find it out? Nicky looked up and down, and she could see now that the station was much bigger than she had thought at first, even. She felt tiny, swallowed up in the vastness of it.

The thing was, she must ask someone. Who? Well not one of the station people, not somebody in uniform. Somebody like that might ask her why she was travelling so far all by herself, which might get complicated. He might even want to see her ticket. So who? An ordinary person, probably . . . a kind person. . . . How about an old person? Someone who couldn't see very well. Who wouldn't notice too much about the one that was asking.

Nicky looked around for such a person, and there was a nice old lady sitting on one of the very few seats, surrounded by baggage. 'Excuse me,' said Nicky. The old lady had silver hair, and a sweet, crumpled face. 'Excuse me, but can you tell me which is the train for Southbourne?'

'I'm afraid I don't know, dear, it's all a great mystery to me,' the old lady confessed. 'I just do what my son tells me – here's my son coming now, we'll ask him.'

The old lady's son was big, and red-faced, and short-tempered looking. 'Look on the Departures

Board,' he said, pointing. 'Doesn't your mother know how to do it?'

'She's busy,' said Nicky. 'Looking after my baby brother.'

'Very likely, but doesn't she know how to *do* it?' His voice sounded really fierce.

'Of course she does,' said Nicky.

'Why does she send you to ask strangers then?' said the old lady's fierce son. 'Where *is* your mother?' he added, in a suspicious tone.

Nicky ran.

The old lady's fierce son lost interest in Nicky almost immediately. He had a train to catch, and a mother of his own to look after, and other people's children were not his responsibility anyway. But Nicky imagined a great burly form, topped by an angry red face, bearing down on her out of the crowd. She dodged, and doubled back, and dived into the ladies' toilet, where she loitered a long time outside the barrier, until a sympathetic customer for the toilet asked her was she short of a ten pence to get in? Nicky said, 'No, it's all right,' and then she said, 'Yes, I am rather short as it happens.' The sympathetic lady gave her ten pence saying she knew from experience how awful it was to want to go when you couldn't. As soon as the nice lady had gone through the barrier, Nicky put the money in the pocket of her jeans, and emerged into the station again. She looked cautiously up and down, but there was no sign of the old lady's son. Trying to look unconcerned, she sauntered back to where she could see the seat on which the old lady had been sitting, but the seat was empty. Cases and all had disappeared. Nicky went back to Roy.

'I'm back,' she announced.

He didn't seem to care much whether she was back or not.

'Didn't you miss me?'

Roy shrugged.

'Anyway, you will be pleased to know that I saw how to go on the train, like I thought, and it's easy. The only thing I don't know yet is, which train we have to go on. So you still stay here.'

Roy shrugged again, as if to imply he wasn't going anywhere anyway.

Nicky stood in front of the Departures Board, and read all the place names very carefully, but she couldn't see Southbourne at all. Every now and again, the whole board rattled and flickered, and the names got changed, and every time that happened Nicky watched anxiously to see if the word South-bourne was going to come, but it never did. A great doubt began to trouble her. Was this the right station after all? Did Sonia make a mistake?

Nicky looked around for someone else to ask. There was a smartly dressed lady sitting over the way, eating an apple and sheafing through some papers she kept taking out of a briefcase. She looked too busy to be nosy about where people's mothers were, and too young to have a big red-faced son. She might have a boyfriend like that, of course, but she seemed to be alone. Nicky approached her. 'Excuse me, is this the right station for Southbourne?'

'Yes,' said the young woman, without looking up.

'Will the name come on the board in a minute?'

'I expect so.'

'When it does, how shall I know which platform to go on?'

The young woman looked at the board. 'It's just come up now. Platform six. Leaving at eleven-fifteen.'

'Do you know what time it is now?' said Nicky.

'For heaven's sake, can't you read a clock? Look! Five minutes to eleven. Anything else you want to know?'

'No, thank you,' said Nicky, quite sweetly.

Twenty minutes to get herself and Roy on to the train. Nicky went back to where she had left him. 'I'm hungry,' he said peevishly.

'You can't be,' said Nicky. 'You only had breakfast a little while ago.'

'I am though,' said Roy. 'And thirsty.'

'You can have a little bit of cornflakes,' said Nicky. 'And some milk. We have to keep the rest for our packed lunch. And for our tea, perhaps, if we don't find Mum before that.'

'I don't think we're going to find her at all,' said Roy.

'That's because you think sad things all the time, not happy ones,' said Nicky.

They sat together in their corner, eating dry cornflakes and swigging milk by turns out of the bottle. 'Come on now,' said Nicky. 'It's time for the train. Come on, Roy, and pick your feet up. You'll wear out your shoes scuffling like that!'

'I'm tired.'

'You only just now got out of bed, nearly.'

'I had all bad dreams, in the night.'

'Forget the bad dreams! *You're* a bad dream! You're like a alien from outer space. It's like you're looking at something else all the time. You're making me feel all funny, Roy, so snap out of it before I give you a kick or something, to help you!'

'I hate you,' said Roy.

'*What* did you say?'

'I said I hate you, and I do!'

'Take that back!'

'No.'

'Take it back, you little creep!'

'I won't. I won't. I hate you!'

In the middle of Victoria Station they faced one another, sparking with animosity. Nicky took a step towards Roy and he backed, nervously. 'If you don't take it back what you just said, I'm going to hit you!' She put the bags on the ground, and took another step towards him. She was angry, and hurt, and she meant what she was saying. Roy backed again, and Nicky lunged at him. She caught him briefly by the shirt, but he twisted out of her grasp and ran. 'I'll get you, you wait!' She pelted after him, then stopped dead, remembering the precious bags. Muttering furiously, she went back to retrieve them. By the time she had them safely in her grasp again, Roy had disappeared from sight.

Uncertain about what to do now, Nicky sat on one of the red bucket seats, nursing her bags and her fury. Serve Roy right if he got lost! Serve him right if she went without him! For a few minutes she toyed with the idea of doing just that, but then she saw him in her mind, helpless and terrified, and knew she could no more abandon him than she could sprout wings and fly. He wanted her to look for him, of course, that was what it was all about; and that was what she was going to have to do. Still fuming, Nicky gathered up her bags and went to find her brother.

She looked in Smith's bookshop, and in the cafeteria, and in all the telephone boxes, and in the booths where you sit to take your own photograph. She walked from one end of the station to the other, and there was no sign of him. She stayed near the Gents' toilet for a long time, in case he was hiding in there, but he didn't come out.

She looked at the clock, and saw that the time was nearly twenty minutes past eleven. The train would be gone! They had missed it, and all because of Roy. There was a boy going into the Gents', and Nicky asked him to see if there was a kid inside who looked about eight; but the boy came back and said there was no kid in there at all.

Again, Nicky walked from one end of the station to the other, and it suddenly occurred to her that Roy might have run out of the station altogether. He might have really got lost! It might take hours and hours to find him, and all the trains to Southbourne would be gone. When she found him she would give him a good thump, for making them miss all the trains.

Someone was looking at her. Nicky felt the gaze coming from somewhere over her right shoulder and she turned sharply, to see who it was. A big spotty girl, wearing a blouse and a skirt that might have been school uniform, grinned and winked.

Why was the spotty girl grinning and winking? Why was she looking, like that? Nicky didn't like being looked at when she didn't know the reason. She turned to walk away, and the spotty girl followed. What was she up to? Nicky ran, and the spotty girl ran. Nicky dodged round a family group, and the mother swore at her for nearly tripping up grandma. Nicky thumbed her nose as she ran, but she was getting to be out of breath; and the spotty girl, she could see when she turned, was still behind her.

Round the corner were the photograph booths. Nicky dived into the first one, and pulled the curtain, and drew her knees up to her chin as she sat on the stool, so no one could see her legs through the gap.

Then the curtain was yanked back, and the spotty girl was bending over her, her hands holding the sides of the booth, pinning Nicky in. 'Go away!' said Nicky, furiously.

'Hold on!' said the spotty girl. 'Weren't you looking for someone?'

'Not at all,' said Nicky. 'I'm having my photograph taken, can't you see?'

'Well not in this one, you aren't,' said the spotty girl. 'This one's out of order.'

'Oh,' said Nicky, feeling a bit silly. 'I didn't notice.'

'You don't have to worry about me, you know,' said the spotty girl, still grinning and winking. 'I'm not going to tell of you.'

'Tell what?' said Nicky. 'I don't know what you mean.'

'Yes you do. You're bunking off school, aren't you?'

'No. What a peculiar idea.'

'It's all right, I am too. Meet another bunker!'

Nicky swallowed, still wary.

'You lost your mate, didn't you?' said the spotty girl. 'I saw you looking. Up and down, you been looking a long time.'

'I don't know what you're talking about,' said Nicky.

'Oh come on, you don't have to keep that up! A little kid – smaller than you. Is he your brother? Anyway, I know where he is.'

'Where? I mean *who*? Who do you know is hiding somewhere?'

'See that hut thing? Where you get the tickets for the Gatwick Express? Well he's underneath it, round the back.'

'I shall go and look,' said Nicky. 'Just to see who it is that's hiding, in such a peculiar place.'

Roy had crawled so far under the ticket office that he was barely visible, and he was all curled up, like a baby before it gets born. 'Get out of there this minute, Roy Mitchell!' said Nicky, prodding his back with her foot.

He didn't seem startled, particularly. He didn't seem aware enough to be startled. He wriggled out slowly, and the eyes that looked up at her were glazed again, only half seeing. He muttered something, under his breath.

'What was that?'

He muttered again, and Nicky shook him. 'I can't understand gobble-gobble. Speak up!'

'I SAID, "I WANT THE WORLD TO GO AWAY."'

'Don't shout!' said Nicky. 'And don't say such wicked rubbish. It's a lovely world. I think so, anyway.'

'I don't like it,' said Roy. 'It's all a lot of troubles.'

Nicky sat beside him on the ground, and put her arm round his shoulders. 'Well that's what you got me for, isn't it, you silly stupid fool!'

'I did want you to find me,' he said, not looking at her.

'Of course you did. I know that. Who don't know that? Only the thing is, you made us miss the train.'

120

'Can't we go, then?'

'Of course we can go. There'll be another train soon.'

'Suppose we don't find Mum when we get there?'

Nicky did a handstand, against the back of the ticket office. 'Can you do this?'

'I said, suppose we don't find her?'

'I'm not going to suppose any bad things that haven't happened yet,' said Nicky. 'Come on, let's see who can make the ugliest face.' She flattened her nose with her fingers, and stretched her mouth into a fiendish grin. 'Come on, Roy, now you do one!'

'I can't.'

'No such word as can't. How about this then?' She bent double and peered at Roy through her legs, rolling her eyes and making idiotic drooling noises. A faint smile appeared on Roy's face. 'That's better!' On all fours, Nicky became a sow, grunting and snorting and scratching herself, against the hut. Roy began to giggle, just a bit.

'Come on,' said Nicky. 'We'll go and see if there's another train yet.'


'The thing is,' she explained, 'you have to wait till someone's talking to the man in the box. Then it's easy to go behind, and he won't notice. I seen lots of people do it. I mean – they probably had tickets all the time, but they didn't bother to show them. It's easy peasy to get on the train, you'll see.'

'How do you know which train is the right one?' said Roy.

'Well I *told* you. You don't listen to anything just lately, do you? Platform eleven this time, it says it on the board. And on top of the board is the time it goes.

121

We got ten minutes. . . . Come on, he's busy now. . . .
Come *on*, Roy!'

But Roy's shoe fell off as they hurried, and he had
to go back for it, and by the time they reached the
entrance to the platform, the enquirers at the box had
moved on again.

'Tickets, please,' said the man in the box.

'Oh, we're not going on the train,' said Nicky.
'We're just having a little look round . . . while our
mum's at the shop. That shop over there! Then we're
going on the train. Not now.'

'Move out the way then,' said the man in the box.
'You're holding up the traffic.'

The children retreated.

'Do your shoes up properly, can't you?' Nicky
scolded. 'You're going to spoil it all. All right, don't
cry, don't cry. I said, DON'T CRY! We shall have to
be a bit careful now, though. Now the man noticed us
already. . . . We shall have to wait till there's lots of
people going past the box, and make out one of them
is our mum.'

There was a surge of late arrivals, and Nicky
pushed through under their cover. 'You see?' said
Nicky, as they ran down the platform, weaving in and
out of the legs and the cases. 'Easy peasy. Come on,
let's get on the train quick.'

Inside the train, they sat side by side. 'Isn't this
fun?' said Nicky. 'Isn't this great? Don't you think
this is great, Roy? Well I do, anyway!'

The train on the opposite platform began to slide
out of the station. 'Isn't it funny!' said Nicky. 'It
seems like we're the ones that's moving, not them!
Don't you think that's funny, Roy?'

They waited a little time more, and Nicky began to

fidget. 'I'm sure it's longer than ten minutes now.' Neither child had a watch, and there was no clock visible from the train. 'Don't you think it's longer than ten minutes, Roy? I thought we supposed to be going.'

The carriage was still filling up. An elderly couple sat opposite Nicky and Roy. 'Just made it!' said the lady, beaming at Nicky. 'You going to the seaside then? All by yourselves?' She didn't seem to think it particularly strange, not like some people, and Nicky smiled back, relaxing a bit.

'We're going to see our aunty,' she said.

'Didn't anyone come to see you off?' said the lady's husband.

'Our mum would have, but she couldn't,' Nicky improvised. 'Because the baby's sick.'

'Oh dear,' clucked the lady, 'I *am* sorry to hear that.'

'Our aunty lives in Southbourne,' said Nicky. 'So it's lucky we can go and stay with her, until the baby gets better.'

'Did you say you're going to Southbourne?' said the lady's husband.

'To stay with our aunty, by the sea.'

'Not on this train!' said the lady.

'This train's going to Brighton,' said the lady's husband.

'The Southbourne train's gone,' said the lady.

'Saw it pulling out as we came on the platform, didn't we, dear?' said her husband. 'Platform eleven – that one just across. This is Platform twelve.'

There was the sound of slamming doors.

'Oh dear,' said the lady. 'I'm afraid you've got on the wrong train.'

From the platform outside, a whistle shrilled.

# 9

## Scatter!

Nicky screamed. 'It's going, it's going, we got to get off!'

She grabbed at her bags and kicked Roy. '*Roy!* Come on. We got to get off the train!'

The elderly lady and her husband were both looking very upset. 'Don't get off if it's moving, you'll hurt yourselves!'

The train gave a little jerk. Nicky grabbed Roy with her free hand, and dragged him to the door. 'I can't open it! I can't open it! Somebody open it for me!' she shrieked.

The train *was* moving. Not very fast, but definitely moving. 'Go on then, hurry up!' A young man was opening the door for Nicky, which was a most unwise thing to do, though he meant well.

Nicky jumped, pulling Roy with her.

They fell on to the platform, and Roy shouted as the shock of the fall brought him painfully into full awareness of what was going on. Nicky did not cry out, but her face twisted up as her knee struck the platform and she rolled over, still clutching her bags.

The platform was empty of passengers – the two trains had taken them all. But from the far end a railman was running towards them and, worse, the guard had seen the children tumbling out. With a screech of brakes, the train shuddered to a halt.

'Get up!' said Nicky, yanking Roy to his feet. Her

knee hurt so much she was surprised to find she could stand, but in fact it was only bruised. 'Run!' she shouted. 'Run!'

The railman was a good distance from them still, and anyway there were lots of convenient obstacles on the platform he needed to swerve around. But the guard, riding at the back, had climbed off the train and was lumbering towards them, consternation over all the folds of his fleshy face. And the guard was between them and the exit from the platform!

Nicky seized Roy by the wrist and hauled him along with her, straight towards the guard, and away from the railman. The railman was young and lithe, he was the one to watch! The guard, poor man, was older and portly, with several rolling stomachs. 'Dodge!' Nicky shrieked, as they were about to run into his arms. She gave Roy a push to the left, while she herself shot off to the right. The guard lunged at air and hesitated, unsure which child to pursue.

The boy was the smaller, – the boy would be the easier to catch. The guard gave chase – Roy was nearly at the exit by now. In blind panic Roy turned, and ploughed along the path which crossed the platforms, inside the barrier. The guard chased him a short way and then, winded, stopped to get his breath. He felt more than a little foolish, and hoped not too many people were looking.

Nicky, meanwhile, was charging straight at the ticket man's box. 'Hey, you!' said the ticket man, who had come out of his box to intercept her. 'I remember you!' He held her by the arms, and Nicky's head whipped swiftly round to bite his hand. The ticket man swore, but let her go, and stood sucking his bitten hand, feeling almost as foolish as the guard.

By now the railman also had arrived at the exit, and he was all for carrying on the chase, but the ticket man and the guard told him not to bother. Clearly no one was really hurt, no one had actually committed the crime of travelling without a ticket, and they all had better things to do than go after a couple of silly kids, playing silly games, who would certainly be too scared to do it again.

Running away from the guard, Roy thought his legs were going to fold up underneath him. They were weak and shaky, but still he kept pushing them to go. There was a pain in his chest as well, and his heart was pumping madly. He ran blindly; round corners, bumping into people, crying quietly deep inside himself.

There was a wall – he had come to the end! No, no, there was another barrier and people coming through, and beyond the barrier the main part of the station again. Head down, following instinct rather than reason, Roy charged at the exit. 'What a rude little boy!' he heard someone say, as he rushed through.

He was out, he was out! Still in this horrible station though; this station that was as bad as any nightmare he ever had in bed. Which way, which way? Ahead of him, and to the right, was the clamour and confusion that had battered him all morning. To his left was a bare alleyway, and through that alleyway, surely, an open street! With the last of his strength, Roy drove his trembling legs through the alleyway and up the road to his left – uphill and round a corner, on and on till each breath was like a knife slicing through his chest, and he could go no further, whoever might be chasing him.

He half knelt, half sat, on a pavement against a wall, and his bottom was sore from where he fell out of the train. But there was no fat guard pounding after him, so that was one good thing. The shuddering gasps that were his breathing slackened and slowed. The sweat that soaked the limp curls, and streaked his face with salty rivulets, cooled in a day turned chill and sunless. Roy wore only jeans and a tee-shirt. He thrust his bare arms under the tee-shirt to warm them, and hugged his thin chest, while his eyes darted wildly this way and that, looking for Nicky.

Less than two hours ago he had run from her, and hidden from her, and from the world, and from himself. But he wanted her to find him really, and she had; and he wanted her to find him now, and he knew she would look till she did. Only hurry up, Nicky! Hurry up! Hurry up!

There was a tear in his jeans, he noticed, and blood soaking through. That was from where he fell, in the station. His thigh smarted from where the blood was coming through, and he felt sorry for himself about that, and he wanted to go to the toilet as well. That was easy, of course, though not very nice, and nobody took much notice of a small boy doing it in a corner. Afterwards he sqatted down again, and waited for Nicky to come.

Suppose she didn't, though? What about the fat guard, and the station man that ran after them, and the ticket man in the box? Did they catch her, and do terrible things to her, and stop her from coming to look for him? What would he do if she didn't come? What would he do?

It was cold. Clouds were piling, grey on grey; three

large drops of rain fell on the pavement in front of Roy, and he shivered. The day had been so warm when they left, they hadn't thought they would need coats. They would *boil* in coats, Nicky said, and coats would be too much nuisance to carry. Woolies would do, she said, and anyway it was going to be a lovely day, she just knew. But the lovely day had not lasted; it was freezing now, and getting more freezing by the minute, and there were goosepimples on Roy's arms, and Nicky had his pullover.

Why didn't she come yet? Roy looked up and down the road, straining his eyes hopefully, his heart beating with sudden gladness when he saw a figure that might be her. But it was another girl after all, someone not a bit like Nicky really. The disappointment was crushing; he felt desolated, more alone than before, even.

Should he go and look for her himself?

No he couldn't, he couldn't! Not back to that terrible station! And anyway he wasn't sure where the station was, except that it was round a corner. And down a road. He remembered that bit because he was running uphill that time, and his legs were all wobbly, like jelly, when he was trying to make them go.

But perhaps Nicky was looking for him in the wrong place. Perhaps she was just going round and round, looking in the wrong places, and he must find her, and show her where he was really. He must hurry, and do it now, before she went farther away from him, perhaps, looking in the wrong place.

Roy heaved himself up. He was stiff from sitting now, as well as cold, and the dried blood on his jeans had gone all hard, and crackly. His right leg had gone to sleep where he had had it doubled under him, and he stamped it weakly a few times, to make the pins and needles come. The sobs came as well as he trotted down the road – sobs of loneliness and fear, gathering volume until people were beginning to look. One kind-looking lady even put her hand on his arm, to stop him and ask what was wrong; but Roy pushed her away and stumbled on, swallowing the sobs now, because people mustn't ask him questions. If they asked questions they might find out the secret.

He ran down the road he had come up. The tears in his eyes made him miss the little alleyway into the station, so that he ran straight past it down the road, down, down, down, – and suddenly he knew where he was! It was the bus terminal, the bus terminal where they came in this morning; this morning that seemed like weeks ago.

And they ran between the buses that time, to get to the train station. So the way in to the train station was just here. Just there, where all those people were going! And Nicky was in there, perhaps, looking for him.

He was frightened to go in, and he was frightened not to go in, because if he didn't go in he might never find Nicky at all. Cautiously, he trotted through the long entrance hall, and he was in the horrid place once more, with trolleys and luggage and people sitting about, and people pushing everywhere, and such a muddle he didn't know where to go first. And he didn't seem to recognize anything for certain, it was all mixed up from before. He didn't know which end of the station he was at, if it was where they sat against the wall, or where they went to go on the train the first time, or where they got on the wrong train;

and at first he forged a blind zig-zag path, too frightened to look properly.

Suddenly he noticed the funny ticket place, where he had hidden underneath, and then he remembered it was Platform twelve they went on, or Platform eleven. Anyway it was the wrong one, wasn't it, but at least there was something he knew now, and perhaps Nicky was looking for him under the ticket place, and he would see her in a minute.

Only she *wasn't* there. There were railway officials in uniform though, all over the place, and Roy didn't know if they were the same ones that chased him before – he was just terrified of all of them. Sick with fear, light-headed almost, he turned and plunged out of the station.

Buses again. And buses didn't just carry people away from home, they took them back again as well. Somewhere amongst all those red buses in the station, there was a Number 52. And the Number 52 would take him home!

But what was the use of going home, when Nicky was here, looking for him round Victoria Station? Unless she got caught by the railway people, which was a thought so terrifying his mind went all foggy, and empty, when he started to imagine it. He crossed over the bus terminal, and was glad when he got to the pavement on the other side. He looked around him, and was bewildered by what he saw. So many streets, so much traffic! Where was Nicky? He was never going to find her!

Roy put his hand into the pocket of his jeans, and felt the secret coins he had hidden there. One pound and five pence. Enough for his fare and more. He ran round the buses, looking at the front of each one, till he found a Number 52. The door at the front was open, and people were getting in. Roy bought his ticket from the driver, and sat downstairs because his legs were too shaky to go on top. He twisted his fingers, and the bus rumbled, and shook, and moved. He wanted to get off then, and look for Nicky some more, but it was too late; the driver had closed all the doors, and they were on their way.

What was happening wasn't real. He was going to a home that wasn't a home! So how could a rubbish like that be real? Anyway, if he liked, he could get off at the next stop. He could still do that, it wasn't too late.

But he sat through the next stop, and the next one, and the one after that, and by now it *was* too late, because he would certainly be lost if he got off; so he went on sitting there, staring blankly out of the window, and not seeing the streets and the shops and the park at all, not even seeing the rain, which sheeted down suddenly and made everything dark, though a clock they passed said it was still only twenty minutes to three.

Roy rubbed his arms to warm them, and thought about going home, and thought this *wasn't* real, any of it. Nothing that was happening was real. When he got home he would find he had dreamt it all; and Mum would be there, and Nicky, and everything would be ordinary, like before. And Nicky would be sometimes horrible to him and sometimes nice, like always, and he wouldn't care if she wasn't always nice, he wouldn't care about that at all. And they would tease him again at school, and he wouldn't care. He wouldn't care about that either.

He thought about school as he got off the bus, and

he wondered briefly if they were out yet, and he
hoped they weren't because he wanted to get home
quickly without anybody seeing him, and asking him
why he didn't go today; because he didn't want to
talk to them today, even if it *was* only a dream.
Confused, and empty, and panicky, Roy ran through
the dark, wet streets. The rain, still tipping down,
soaked his hair and his tee-shirt, chilling him to the
bone. But it was lucky it was raining really, because
everybody was inside, weren't they? Aunty Four-
eyes, and Polly Pry, and everybody. There was
nobody to see him, running home at the wrong time,
and ask him why he wasn't in school.

Gilbert Road! Another minute, and he would be
safe indoors!

The only thing was, the only thing was – he didn't
have a key!

The house was silent, blank. Even on the path you
could feel the coldness coming from it, and the
emptiness. Roy called to Mum and Nicky through
the letter box, but they weren't there. His voice
echoed flatly in the little hall, and his voice was the
only sound in the deadness. He didn't cry; some
things are too bad to cry about. Instead he sat on the
doorstep, and pressed his back against the door.
There was a tiny roof over the step, and that gave
some protection against the rain but not much. And
it was real after all, there was no getting away from it!
The station was real, and the empty house was real,
and he was really here, sitting on the doorstep in the
rain. Cold and despair closed in on him from all sides.
They squashed him; he felt himself shrinking. Soon
he would be just a dot, sitting all alone, outside a
house with nobody inside it.

And it might be quite a good thing to be just a dot — then he could get through the letter box. Or the keyhole perhaps, like Alice in Wonderland when she drank that magic stuff. Or what about that space in the window, where it didn't fit properly? If he was just a dot, he could get through that space. That space was why they had to be specially careful to keep the window locked all the time, because burglars could get in else, Mum said.

And it was a pity the window was locked, because if it wasn't *he* could get in and be a burglar, perhaps. . . . And he *did* unlock it that time, didn't he, when he wasn't supposed to. . . . Did he lock it up, after? Did he even bolt it? He couldn't remember if he locked it up after; perhaps he forgot, and it was open all the time! Perhaps an angel made him not lock the window up, so he could open it from outside, and climb in. Nicky believed in angels, so it might be true!

Roy got off the doorstep, and pushed at the lower sash. It moved. He pushed some more. The rain that lashed down was a curtain of water across the street. No one could have seen him from the windows opposite, even if they had been looking. Roy pushed the window right up, and climbed through.

# 10

# A new hope

Nicky was wet through. The cloudburst had caught her while she combed the streets looking for Roy, and now she was huddled under a shelter in the bus station, waiting for the rain to stop. Her clothes and her hair were soaked. She considered swapping her wet cardigan for Roy's dry pullover, but decided not to because she would miss the pullover too much when she had to take it off to give it to Roy. When she found him. Which she was certainly going to do! Even though she seemed to have looked everywhere already – except in the train station, where she was very much afraid to go.

One place she looked, just before the rain, was up a hill and round into another road. There was a puddle here in one corner, and Nicky had an idea Roy might have made it, but there was no sign of him now. He must be *somewhere*, though. It was silly to be worried that she hadn't found him yet; people don't just disappear, they have to be in some place. She only had to find Roy's place, that was all.

The thing was, though, *Roy* would be so frightened. All alone, and not knowing what to do, he would be just terrified without her. She must find him, even if it meant going back into that horrible station, where the railman with the fast legs was, and the ticket man she bit.

The day was really dark now, like a little night,

almost. Sitting on the pavement, on the bus terminal, Nicky was miserable with cold; and the longer she sat the colder she got, and the more she wanted to go to the toilet as well.

Would the rain never stop? Nicky watched the buses coming in, and the people who got off them struggling into macs and putting up umbrellas. She watched the people getting on the buses, going home to their nice dry houses and their tea. When she found Roy, they would go home too, she decided.

She thought about the problem of bus fares. There was the ten pence the lady had given her for the toilet, but that wasn't enough for one fare, let alone two, and anyway she was going to need it pretty soon. Nicky watched the buses coming in, queuing up one behind the other, waiting to go out again. People got off the back one, and then the bus was empty. After that, sometimes the driver got out of his cabin and searched the bus a bit to see if anything had been left behind; and sometimes he sat in his seat, eating sandwiches. She never saw him go upstairs. The back bus became the middle bus, and then the front bus, and the driver would open the front door to let the new passengers in. But she and Roy couldn't go in that way, clearly, because the driver would want them to buy a ticket, and they hadn't enough money. The driver was always very careful, she noticed, to make sure that everybody had a ticket.

The middle door was the thing, the one the people came out of. She and Roy must push in, while everyone was getting out. They must keep their heads down, and run upstairs – lucky the stairs were just opposite the middle doors – and they must hide right at the front, where the driver wouldn't see them even if he *did* come up. They would get home like that, then, after the rain stopped and she found Roy. She felt warmed, and comforted, thinking about it.

But the rain went on and on, less heavy now but persistent. Nicky began to think she was so wet she couldn't get any wetter, after all, so she might as well go on with her looking. Besides, she really must go to the toilet in the station, she couldn't put it off any longer. And while she was there, while she was there, she might as well do that other thing she was scared of, and search the station to see if Roy was inside it, all the time.

People were beginning to give her funny looks anyway, sitting on the pavement all by herself so long. Nicky made a hideous face at one woman who was staring at her; the woman flushed and turned her head, and Nicky felt quite powerful because she could make the woman do that. She contorted her features again, embarrassing the others who were looking, so she could feel even more powerful, and braver for going into the station, where she didn't want to go.

She felt braver anyway, after she had spent the ten pence, though it was a pity having to waste her last bit of money on something so uninteresting! She could have shared it with Roy otherwise, but never mind! She began her round of the station and the first place she looked, of course, was under the ticket office where she had found him before. But he wasn't there, and he wasn't in any of the other places this side of the barrier.

Dared she?

He might be stuck! All the time she was looking for him outside, perhaps he had got stuck behind the barrier, and didn't know how to get out. Oh poor Roy, stuck behind the barrier! And look at her, a cowardy custard, too scared to go in and look for him! And she wouldn't *be* a cowardy custard, she wouldn't!

She inched closer to the barrier, and peeped at the ticket man in the box at Platform eleven. But the ticket man had changed into a ticket lady, which was an encouraging start. She pushed her way on to the platform, just like before, and ran the way Roy had run, and it was easy to get out, easy! She looked in a few cubby-holes, just to make sure, but of course he wasn't there. Why should he be, when it was so easy to get out of the station?

Out into the rain once more, then, to search the streets. Up and down, round and round, poking into corners and alleys, trying farther and farther from the station, calling Roy's name, until her legs dragged, and there was a blister on her heel, and her spirits were right down there in her heels somewhere, with the blister. She was cold from fear, as well as from the rain – exhausted, and finally despairing. She had lost him. She had lost him, and she couldn't look any more because her legs wouldn't go any more, and it had to be admitted, she didn't know what to do!

A clock on a high building told her the time was nearly half past six. She had been searching for hours, and soon it would be night. She couldn't stay here all night! The rain had stopped, but there was no sun to dry her clothes, and now she was no longer moving, the chill of the damp evening sank into her bones. She couldn't think any more, she couldn't think! She just wanted to be home, and curled up in bed, and going to sleep warm and snug, and forgetting. She would think of something tomorrow. Tomorrow she would think of a way to find Roy. It was terrible to be going home without him, but what else could she do?

Wearily, Nicky dragged her unwilling legs back to the bus station, and found the queue for the Number 52. Nicky pushed into the bus which was just disgorging its passengers. She kept her head down, so the driver didn't see her, and the dismounting passengers couldn't have cared less. With the last of her strength, Nicky scrambled up the stairs and crouched on the floor between the front of the bus and the front seat, until the new passengers started to come in. Then she sat up, and gazed desperately out of the window, hoping against hope that by some miracle he might, even now, come into view.

The bus was moving. She was leaving him, she was leaving him! He was all alone out there somewhere, cold and hungry and terrified – and she was leaving him! She would have got out then, but her legs would not obey her brain's command to them to move. Numb with exhaustion, Nicky went on sitting there, while the bus pulled out of the station and began its ponderous journey back to north-west London.

From her high seat, Nicky saw again all the things which had given her such delight that morning, but this time she saw them without joy. Really and truly, this had been a very bad day indeed. She didn't think she remembered having a day as bad as this, ever. It would be only right if something nice could happen, to end this day. Like, for instance, if Mum had come home all by herself after all. Like, for instance, if Mum was home now, making tea in the kitchen, her bag and her coat and her other things scattered all over the Back Room. It would be only right, if something like that could happen.

'Tickets please!' said a voice behind her.

It was the bus Inspector, and instead of something nice, here was something else bad! All the virtuous people who had bought tickets were finding them, and holding them out for the Inspector to inspect. 'Can I see your ticket please, love?' said the Inspector to Nicky.

'I think it's in my pocket,' said Nicky, pretending to look.

'Hurry up,' said the Inspector, 'I haven't got all day.'

'It must have went on the floor,' said Nicky, pretending to look there.

'You haven't *got* a ticket, have you?' said the Inspector.

'I lost it,' said Nicky.

'Do you realize you can be prosecuted for travelling on a bus without a ticket?' said the Inspector. 'Had up in Court!'

'Will I go to prison?' said poor Nicky.

'More than likely,' said the Inspector, to give her a good fright. 'So buy a ticket or get off the bus. Now. Before I change my mind and take your name and address.'

Nicky got off the bus, and shivered as a little wind cut through the wet wool of her cardigan. Her legs were rested a bit, but stiff, as she forced them to follow the bus route another mile and a half. A long, weary, limping mile and a half.

And she might have known it, she might have known it! The bad things of this day were still not finished because, home at last, there was that awful old Polly Pry, standing outside the house, looking very self-righteous and rather pleased. 'I've been knocking and knocking at your door,' said Mrs Williams. 'And ringing. And I can't get nobody to answer. Isn't your mother in?'

Nicky tried to look unconcerned and ordinary, but her knees were strangely wobbly now, and her brain seemed as stiff as her legs. It was quite a hard struggle to think of a lie. In fact, she suddenly thought, she was sick of telling lies. She would like never to have to tell another. 'Mum's ill in bed,' she said. 'She can't be bothered answering the door.'

'What about your brother then? Isn't he in?'

'He's ill too. They both got the 'flu.'

'In *July*?'

'Can't you get the 'flu in July?'

'I never heard of it,' said Mrs Williams, with a sniff.

'You haven't heard of everything.'

'Maybe not, but I've heard of burglars!'

'What d'you mean?'

'What I say. Burglars. Getting in through open windows. And don't tell me I'm a nosy old bag for having my eyes open!'

Nicky saw it then; the Front Room window wide open, and the curtains blowing about. Nicky stared at the open window in bewilderment. 'Mum must have opened it to get some fresh air,' she said faintly.

'I never see that window open before since your mum come here to live!'

'She opens it sometimes.'

'Well she must have forgot to shut it then. Gone upstairs and forgot it. I know there's nobody in the Front because ... well anyway, I know. And she should thank this nosy old bag for noticing. You can't leave the downstairs windows open these days. Not unless you want to have the burglars in.'

'She must have forgot to shut it,' said Nicky. 'Like you said.' Her head spun. Who had opened the window? *Who?*

'I was in two minds to call the police,' said Mrs Williams. 'In case a burglar got in already.'

'Oh we don't want the *police*!' said Nicky.

'He might have got in while your mum was upstairs in bed. And she never heard him. Us nosy old bags do have their uses, you know.'

'We don't want the police, though.'

'He might have forced that window anyway, and your mum never opened it at all. Aren't you scared to go in there? By yourself? In case he's still there? Where have you been, anyway? You're soaking wet!'

'Getting the medicine of course. For Mum and Roy. It's a special medicine for 'flu you get in July. I have to hurry up and give it to them. Excuse me.'

She was terribly frightened, in fact. She left the front door a little bit open in case she needed to run out; then she stood in the hall listening, her ears strained to catch the slightest sound.

Silence.

She peeped into the Front Room. Nothing had been disturbed; no ornaments were missing, no drawers spilled out. Which Mrs Williams must have seen herself, when she came poking and prying and sticking her long nose in. The nasty old thing just wanted to give me a fright, Nicky thought.

But someone had opened the window.

The sofa was a bit wet – which was not surprising with all that rain coming in. And there *was* a cushion

141

on the floor, but the wind might have blown that, she thought. Were those wet footmarks on the carpet?

Nicky went into the Back Room and the kitchen, and everything was just as they had left it. She went to the front door again and looked out. Mrs Williams had set her heart on getting *some* excitement out of this occasion, and she stood there still, her eyes gleaming hopefully. 'Go home!' Nicky shouted, furiously. 'Go home, and do your washing up!'

No burglars, because burglars stole things, and messed things up, and they hadn't. But *someone* had opened the window. Of course the window had been closed when they left that morning, of course it had! She would have seen it otherwise, she couldn't possibly have missed a thing like that!

So who had opened the window?

She had better close it, of course, before someone *did* break in. What happened to the special lock? It had been undone! With the special key! From *inside*!

So who had opened the window?

Mum?

Nicky's heart did a little dance. 'Mum!' she called. 'Mum!' She forced her aching legs up the stairs, treading hard on the blister and not even noticing. She stood in the doorway of Mum's room, and gazed with shining eyes. 'Mum!'

There was no doubt about it. There was someone in Mum's bed!

She was only deceived for a moment; the body in the bed was much too small to be Mum's. She pulled back the cover and there he was! 'Roy!'

He had been asleep but he woke up now, and the china-blue eyes filled with tears immediately. 'Why didn't you come to find me, at the station?'

She hugged him until the sobs subsided, rocking him in her arms. 'I did, I did, I looked for you everywhere!'

'I thought you would f-find me if I stayed still, but you didn't c-come!'

'I must have not looked in the right place. . . . How did you get home, Roy?'

'I went back in the station, but you weren't there,' said Roy, not answering her question.

'Were you frightened?'

'Course I was. . . . I thought you got caught, I thought you got c-caught!'

'Oh, poor Roy!'

'I hurt myself when we come off the train. Look!'

'Oh, poor Roy! I think I know where there's some plasters.'

'It stings.'

'Never mind. You're home. You're *home*! And I thought I lost you.'

'And I thought I lost *you*.'

'We thought we lost each other, but we didn't. . . . How did you get home though, Roy?'

He turned his head, not answering.

'Well come on, how?'

'I just came.'

'You're hiding something.'

'No I'm not.'

'How did you get home, then?'

'How did you?'

'I came on the bus. Some of the way. The Inspector made me walk the rest, because I didn't have a ticket.'

'That's the same thing happened to me,' said Roy.

'The same thing? Really? . . . You're telling a lie!'

'No I'm not.'

'Yes you are. You couldn't do the same thing as me, you couldn't think of it.'

He turned right round then and lay, twisting his fingers miserably.

'So what happened really?' said Nicky.

'I got some money,' he admitted in a small voice.

'What money?'

'Just some money . . . this!'

'Where did that come from? You didn't *steal* it, did you?'

'No! It's mine. It's my own.'

Light dawned. 'You mean it's your *pocket* money?' said Nicky.

'Yes.'

'You were supposed to share that.'

'It's mine, though,' said Roy. 'It's mine!'

Nicky was hurt beyond words. 'You had all this money in your pocket, all the time, and you let me think we were skint?'

'It's my money.'

'I shared *everything* with you, Roy. I nearly *stole* for you, did you know that? I give my best beads to Joycelyn to get some money for you. You didn't know that, did you? And I only spent the ten pence the lady gave me because I was bursting to go to the toilet.'

Roy squirmed. His fingers twisted frantically, and he kept swallowing.

'I looked for you everywhere,' Nicky went on. 'I nearly *killed* myself looking for you, do you know that? All round the streets, and I got wore out. And a big blister on my foot, look, so I can't walk properly!'

He was ashamed. More ashamed than when he wet the bed. More ashamed than when he couldn't fight. He buried his face in Mum's pillow, and held out the money to Nicky, not looking at her.

'Keep it!' said Nicky, bitterly. 'I don't want it.'

'Go on!'

'I don't want it. It's yours, you said.'

'I don't want it neither though. I want it to be for you. I want it to be for you. . . . I want it to be for *you*!'

She stood by the bed, looking down at the money in his hand. 'We could have some chips, I suppose,' she conceded, at last.

'*You* have them. You have them all.'

'Don't be silly. We'll have them with the chicken. Presently. When I had a little rest.' She lay beside him on Mum's bed, and closed her eyes.

'Nicky. . . .'

'What?'

'I'm sorry I kept the money.'

'It's all right.'

'I'm not going to do anything like that, ever again.'

'All right, all right, you don't have to go on about it.'

'Nicky.'

'I'm having a rest!'

'Can I just say one thing?'

'All right then, just one thing.'

'. . . What will it be like in the children's home?'

'Quite good, I expect.'

'You said it would be horrible.'

'No I didn't. I never said it would be horrible. I said *Mum* thought it was horrible. . . . That was a long time ago, it's different in children's homes now. I expect.'

'You said I wouldn't like it.'

'Well I changed my mind. I expect you will like it very much, and so will I.'

'Nicky. . . . ?'

'What *now*?'

'Will we be in the same children's home, you and me?'

'Of course.'

'Suppose they put us in a different one to each other?'

'I won't let them.'

'Do you promise?'

'Yes. . . . Can I go to sleep now?' She was still for a while, then fidgetty. 'Roy. . . .?'

'What?'

'I can't go to sleep. It's funny, isn't it, I'm so tired and I can't go to sleep! It's like I'm still running, and I keep on seeing buses and things, in my head. Don't you think that's funny?' She climbed off the bed and went to the window. Bedraggled and grubby from the day's adventures, together the children looked out at a threatening world.

Nicky did fall asleep later though, right in the middle of the meal. They were eating it out of their laps, because Nicky was too tired to sit up to the table properly, and Nicky fell asleep on the sofa, with one chip halfway to her mouth. Her head lolled awkwardly, and the food slid from her lap, to make yet another greasy stain on the shabby carpet.

Nicky's head dropped to Roy's shoulder. She was heavy against him, and he wriggled sideways, easing her head right down on to the sofa. He stood up, his chips in his hands, and looked at Nicky lying there; fast asleep, worn out with looking for *him*. Her head was still at an awkward angle. Unaccustomed to bothering about someone else's comfort, Roy

146

pondered a moment, unsure what to do. Then he went upstairs and fetched a pillow from Nicky's bed. He lifted her head quite gently, and put the pillow underneath, and stood back to see if she looked more comfortable now. She shivered suddenly, in her sleep, and Roy went upstairs again to fetch a blanket. He lifted Nicky's feet on to the sofa, and covered her with the blanket. The clothes she wore were the same ones she had worn in the rain, and still damp, and Roy wasn't sure if he ought to try to get any of them off. But he didn't want to wake her, and anyway she wasn't shivering any more, so perhaps she was warm enough now.

He tucked the blanket round her, and it felt good doing that.

He finished his supper at the table, and went back to tuck the blanket round Nicky again, and it felt good.

He went upstairs, and changed into his pyjamas and got into bed. Then he got out again and went downstairs to see if Nicky was still covered up. He pulled the blanket a tiny bit higher round her shoulders, and tucked it under her a bit more.

And he felt good!

She came into his room, early in the morning. 'Wake up! I want to talk to you.'

But Roy didn't want to wake up. It was nice being asleep, and he was having nice dreams for once. 'Leave me!' he grumbled.

'I'm all stiff,' said Nicky, cheerfully. 'And I've got all bruises. Look at my bruises, Roy!'

'I think I've got bruises too. All down my leg.'

'Let's look at each other's bruises, and see who's got the biggest.'

'Later,' said Roy.

'Now!' said Nicky.

'It was a bad idea to go to that station,' said Roy into his pillow. 'I don't ever want to go to that station again. I don't ever want to go to *any* station again.'

'I know, I know. . . . This idea is not about a station!'

Roy turned over, and opened his eyes. 'What idea?' he said, suspiciously.

'Oh good! You've properly woke up!'

'What idea?'

'My new one. That I thought of in the night.'

'What did you think of in the night?' said Roy, not at all sure he wanted to hear the answer.

'We-e-ll, you know Sonia—'

'What about Sonia?'

'You know what she said. The other day.'

'No,' said Roy. 'What?'

'About Southbourne. Where Mum is. Sonia said it is quite near to Easthaven!'

'So?'

'So we're *going* to Easthaven! All of us. Tomorrow!'

He began to see what she was getting at, and there was a nasty sinking feeling, in his stomach. 'I know what you're going to say.'

'What? What am I going to say?'

'You're going to say we have to run away from the outing, and go to Southbourne to find Mum.'

'Don't you think it's a good idea?'

'I don't want to do it,' said Roy.

'I thought you'd say that.'

'I don't want to do any more of your good ideas. I don't like your good ideas!'

'Do you want to go in the children's home then?'

148

'I thought we decided it yesterday. I thought it was going to be all right. You said it would be all right.'

'I changed my mind again. I think it's going to be horrible after all, and you won't like it one little bit.'

He had thought it was settled. He even didn't mind too much, yesterday, about the children's home. Now Nicky was frightening him, and muddling him, and turning everything upside down again. 'I don't want to do your ideas! I don't want to get in trouble! I don't want to get lost!'

'I won't let you get lost. I'll look after you, I promise.'

'I don't want to get in trouble, then.'

'Well you won't get in trouble! Tell me how you can get in trouble. We won't go on any trains again. We won't go on any stations.'

'Mr Nelson will be angry with us. And Mrs Blake.'

'Mum will make that all right when we find her. Everything will come right, when we find Mum. *Everything* . . . I *think* so, anyway.'

'I don't like your ideas, though. They don't work properly. . . . All right, what will we do then, when we get to Southbourne?'

'Well, look for Mum, of course, to stop *her* getting in trouble. Though I'm not sure she still deserves it, for staying away so long.'

'We can't do it anyway,' said Roy, suddenly.

'Why not?'

'Because you aren't going on the outing. Don't you remember? You beat up Gary, don't you remember, Nicky? So Mr Nelson said you couldn't go.'

'That's nothing,' said Nicky. 'You don't think I would let a little thing like that stop me, do you? I'll ask Mr Nelson to change his mind. Mr Nelson is a kind headmaster, I think he will give me another chance.'

'All right, I know something else! What about the letter Mr Nelson wrote? He'll expect Mum to answer the letter. He'll expect Mum to come to school. Today.'

'I'll think of a story.'

'*And* Mr Nelson won't like it because we bunked off school yesterday.'

'I'll tell him I was ill. No – I'll tell him Mum was ill. And you.'

'You're always telling people Mum is ill. They won't believe it, if you keep on saying it so many times.'

'Can you think of a better story then? See? You can't! Anyway, I already said it to Mrs Williams. I said you and Mum both got the 'flu. It's a very good excuse indeed. I think so, anyway. I'm going to say you and Mum are ill, and I stayed home to look after you, so there!'

Roy was silent, twisting his fingers.

'So what about tomorrow? Are you coming with me, like I said?'

'I suppose I shall have to.'

'Don't strain yourself to sound enthusiastic!'

He turned away from her, struggling with his apprehension.

'You will be pleased this time, Roy. Everything will go right this time, I just know. . . . You don't believe me, do you?'

Roy shrugged.

'And there's one more good thing for you,' said Nicky, 'you will have to stay home from school today.'

'What!'

'You will have to stay home from school. To make it real about the 'flu.'

'I don't want to!' he wailed.

'What's the matter, I thought you'd be pleased! You don't like school, you know you don't!'

'It's lonely by myself.' He had felt so good when he awoke, and now he felt miserable again.

'Well, get busy at something,' said Nicky. 'To make the time go by.'

'I don't want to get busy. I don't want to stay home from school. You always make me do things I don't like.'

'Oh, bad luck!' Her harshness brought the tears to his eyes, and his shoulders began to quiver. 'Cheer up, Roy,' she said in a softer tone. 'I will look after you, you know. I won't let anything bad happen to you this time. It will be good this time, you'll see. I just know!'

'How are we going to get there though, Nicky? The bit from Easthaven to Southbourne. How are we going to get there?' Surely she would see now that her plan was hard, and mad, and impossible!

'I think it might be near enough to walk,' said Nicky.

# 11

## Will he or won't he?

Nicky went straight into school and up to Mr Nelson's office. 'Good morning, Mr Nelson, how is your arthritis today?'

'Good morning, Nicky. Bad, thank you very much.'

'And your other things, that I forget what they're called?'

'How about coming to the point?'

'Yes, Sir.'

'Well?'

'Will you let me off, Sir? *Please!*'

'Isn't your mother coming to see me today?'

'She can't, actually, she's ill.'

'I'm sorry to hear that.'

'She's got the 'flu. It's a special 'flu you have in July. Roy's got it as well. That's why I was away yesterday, Sir – I had to look after them both. It was very hard work, and I had to walk about a lot, and I had to go and get their medicine, and it was a very long way because the first chemist didn't have it. And the second chemist didn't have it neither. And I got a blister on my foot, so now you and me are the same as each other!'

'And I'm supposed to let you off because we've both got gammy legs?'

'No, Sir, not that.'

'Go on, I'm listening.'

'Well, Sir, it was me done the wrong things on Friday, wasn't it?'

'Indeed it was.'

'So it's not fair if Roy has to be punished.'

'How is Roy going to be punished?'

'Mum says Roy can't go on the outing if I don't.'

'Oh, Nicky, really!'

'I know what you're thinking, Sir. You're thinking about I make a baby of him, but it's not that. It's about he's not well, and I got to keep an eye on him.'

'Are you sure he's well enough to go anyway?'

'Oh yes, Sir, he's at home today, but he will be well enough to go tomorrow, the doctor said. And the doctor said it will do him so much good to go to the seaside. But he can't go unless I do.'

'H'm!'

Mr Nelson did not know what to make of this tarradiddle about the 'flu you get in July. The stories children offered were not always strictly true, but who had the right to judge that? And Mr Nelson was glad of any excuse, really, to give Nicky another chance.

'I'll tell you what.'

'Yes, Sir?'

'Suppose you were to be perfect for a whole day? I'm only supposing, mind, I don't imagine for a moment you can really do it!'

'Want to bet?'

'I don't mean ordinary good, I mean extra specially good.'

'I shall be like a angel!' said Nicky, with a joyous face.

'Gary and Sanjay will have to have the same chance, of course.'

'That's all right, Mr Nelson, I don't mind,' said Nicky, generously. 'I don't mind how many creeps go on the outing, as long as me and Roy can go.'

In Assembly, Mr Nelson talked to the school about going to Easthaven. They had been looking forward to it, he knew, and so had all the teachers, and now the great day had nearly come! The weather forecast was hopeful, he was glad to tell them, in spite of yesterday's rain, but they must all remember their warm clothes, just in case, and their packed lunches, of course.

Just one serious thing he had to say, and they must all listen to it very carefully. Some of them didn't go to the seaside very often, he knew – perhaps some of them had never been before. So they might not know that you have to treat the sea with respect. There could be dangers; they must all be quite sure to stay with their teachers and their groups, and not wander. Then everyone could have a happy day, and come back safely.

In the classroom, Nicky turned the pages of the big atlas. 'Come on, Nicky,' said Mr Hunt. 'Maths time!'

'In a minute.'

'*Now!*' said Mr Hunt.

'Oh yes, Sir, yes, Sir!' Nicky scuttled back to her seat. She had nearly found what she was looking for, and she had to leave it in order to be perfect! She began to work ostentatiously, hunching over her book, and screwing up her face to show how hard she was concentrating. 'Have you noticed how good I'm being, Sir?'

'Was I supposed to?'

'Yes. Will you tell Mr Nelson I'm being good?'

154

'Oh I don't know about that,' said Mr Hunt. 'Mr Nelson wouldn't be specially interested, would he? Do you really think Mr Nelson would be interested?'

'Oh, Sir!' said Nicky. 'You're teasing me.'

'We should have outings more often,' said Mr Hunt, marking Nicky's work.

'Can I look at the atlas now, Sir?' said Nicky.

'Why the sudden passion for maps?'

'I want to see where we're going, tomorrow.'

'Where the rest of us are going, you mean. Where you *may* be going, I understand, if you can manage to achieve the impossible.'

'Oh, Sir!'

She opened the heavy book, and found the map of England. There it was, there it was – Easthaven! . . . And there *it* was! Almost touching! Only a titchy-witchy centimetre away. You could walk that easy, just like she said to Roy. A brilliant idea began to form, in her mind.

'You look happy,' said Mr Hunt.

'I'm *extremely* happy,' said Nicky.

'Is the sea really dangerous, Sir, like Mr Nelson said?' said Joycelyn.

'No, no,' said Mr Hunt. 'Mr Nelson just said that for fun. Just to fill up the Assembly time.'

'Oh, *Sir!*'

'Anyway, what does it matter? A few lost, a few drowned, what's the difference?' That was Miss Powell's joke, not his, but Mr Hunt was often too lazy to make up his own jokes.

'You don't *mean* it, Sir!'

'Every word of it. . . . Come on – playtime! Books away, chop, chop!'

'You didn't tell us yet. Why the sea is dangerous.'

155

'*Playtime!*' said Mr Hunt, who didn't want to miss a second of his break.

By now the whole class knew about the second chance Nicky had been given, and the terms of it, and some of the boys thought it might be fun to tease her a bit. And safe, today, since she couldn't do anything back.

'Pity if we got to have *you* in the coach, after all!'

'Get lost!' said Nicky.

'Pity if we got to listen to you singing!'

'Yeah, give us all a pain!'

'Make the driver crash!'

'I can sing if I want to, so bad luck!'

Marcus came close, and pushed his heavy face near to hers, and blew down her neck.

'Push off!'

Marcus danced about, taunting her. 'Come on then, make me, make me!' He got behind her and blew again.

'Leave me!'

Good – she was getting angry. They all began blowing then, as many as could get close enough; until Mrs Blake, on duty that morning, came striding on her spindly legs and shooed them off.

'I didn't hit them,' Nicky pointed out.

'Well done!' said Mrs Blake, who had also heard about the second chance.

'Did you notice, Mrs Blake, I didn't hit *any* of them!'

'Yes, I did notice. Well done!'

'Will you tell Mr Nelson?'

'I shouldn't be a bit surprised.'

Nicky sat on the steps, feeling very pleased with herself. Two good reports, anyway. But ordinary good wasn't enough, Mr Nelson said, it had to be extra specially good to count. What could she find to do, that was extra specially good? Helping the teachers would count like that, wouldn't it?

After eating the school dinner for which she had not paid, Nicky lurked outside the staff room. Miss Powell emerged soon, carrying a pile of books. 'Shall I carry them for you, Miss?' said Nicky.

'What are you doing in school?' snapped Miss Powell. 'You're supposed to be in the playground.'

'I want to help,' said Nicky.

'OUT!' said Miss Powell, who had heard about the second chance but wasn't interested.

'Can't I ask in the staff room,' said Nicky, 'if anyone wants me to help?'

'There's only Mr Hunt in the staff room.'

'Where are the other teachers?'

'For heaven's sake, how should *I* know? In their classrooms, I suppose.'

'Can I go round the classrooms and ask?'

'Give me strength!' said Miss Powell.

'*Please!*'

'Oh go on then,' said Miss Powell, to put an end to the pestering. 'But straight out if nobody wants you, understand?'

'Cross my heart and hope to die!' said Nicky.

She found Miss Greenwood, putting out painting things all by herself. 'Hello, Miss Greenwood, would you like some help?'

Miss Greenwood regarded Nicky nervously. Her class were first years, and she had very little contact with the fourth year children. And Nicky Mitchell, in particular, had a reputation for difficult behaviour, Miss Greenwood knew – violent behaviour, even!

She did not want this dangerous child in her classroom, but she didn't want to offend her either. 'No thank you, dear,' she said. 'I can manage.' Miss Greenwood was one of the teachers who had *not* heard about Nicky's second chance.

'But Miss Greenwood, it's too much for you all by yourself,' Nicky persisted. 'Please let me help.'

The blue gaze was unnerving. 'All right then,' said Miss Greenwood, weakly.

'I'm good at putting out paints,' said Nicky. 'I can do it all for you, if you like. And you can go to the staff room and have a cup of tea. . . . And then you can tell Mr Nelson I'm doing the paints for you.'

'I don't think I'm allowed to leave you on your own,' said Miss Greenwood.

'Well never mind,' said Nicky. 'You can tell him after. You won't forget, will you?'

'No, no, I won't forget.' In fifteen minutes the bell would go; and this eccentric person, whose motives Miss Greenwood could not begin to guess, would have to go to her own class. Roll on fifteen minutes! And in the meantime, it had to be admitted, it was useful to have another pair of hands. . . . Now what was the other thing she meant to do? Oh yes, the room was stuffy: the day had turned out really fine and warm, she must get the bottom windows open as well as the ventilators. She struggled with a sticky sash.

'I'll do that for you,' said Nicky.

'It's all right,' said Miss Greenwood, struggling some more.

'I'm strong,' said Nicky. 'Let me!' The window was very stiff indeed. Nicky climbed on to the radiator.

158

'What are you doing?' said Miss Greenwood, alarmed.

'If I stand high, I can pull instead of push,' said Nicky. 'That'll be better.'

'Get down before you fall!' said Miss Greenwood. 'I'm responsible for you, you know.'

'Oh I won't fall,' said Nicky. 'I'm a good climber.'

She was right on the high windowsill now, her feet firmly planted among some roughly fashioned clay pots, left to dry before they could be painted. She bent to wrench at the window, and it was awkward because she had to crouch sideways, and her own knees were in the way. She shifted to find a better position.

'Mind the pots!' said Miss Greenwood.

The window gave suddenly, and Nicky's foot shot backwards – and five clay pots lay on the floor, shattered into little pieces!

Miss Greenwood was very upset. 'Their pots!' she wailed. 'They were so proud of their pots! They're going to be heartbroken!'

Nicky, also, was very upset. 'We can mend them, can't we,' she tried. 'Look, I can mend them with some glue.'

'They're past mending,' said Miss Greenwood, bitterly. 'Why didn't you get down when I told you?'

'I only wanted to help.'

'Well now you've helped enough. Now please, please, go away! Before you do any more damage!'

'You won't tell Mr Nelson, will you? Mr Nelson won't be interested in the broken pots, will he?'

'At the moment, I'm only concerned about what I'm going to tell my children.'

'Haven't you got any more clay?' said Nicky. 'Shall I make some more pots for them?'

'It wouldn't be the same.'

'I'm sorry I broke them. I'm as sorry as anything I broke them. I wish I could do a magic spell and make them come together again. But you don't have to tell Mr Nelson, do you? There's no sense worrying him about it, is there? He's got enough to worry about, hasn't he? With his arthritis, and his other things that I can't remember their names. . . .'

The incomprehensible chatter went on and on. 'Go away!' begged Miss Greenwood, almost hysterically. 'Go away before I *do* tell him!'

Nicky went. She looked for somewhere to hide, so she could watch if Miss Greenwood went to tell Mr Nelson. She flattened herself against the wall, just round the corner from Miss Greenwood's room, and kept peeping. Miss Powell, on her way back to the staff room, found her there. 'Why are you lurking?'

'No reason.'

'Are you going peculiar?'

'No.'

'Get out to the playground then, I shan't tell you again.'

Nicky stood alone in the playground, with a face like thunder, and when Joycelyn came up, she turned her back on her. 'What's the matter?' said Joycelyn. But Nicky wouldn't tell her, and afterwards in class she sat brooding, not looking at anyone.

'What's wrong, Nicky?' said Mr Hunt, but Nicky wouldn't tell him either.

After a while she put up her hand. 'Can I go and see Mr Nelson?'

'Is it important?' said Mr Hunt.

'Yes, Sir.'

'Will you cheer up if I let you go?'

'It all depends what Mr Nelson says?'

'Go on, then.'

Mr Nelson was not in his office. The secretary didn't know where he was, but thought he would be back soon. Nicky hung around for a few minutes, then found she couldn't bear to be still. She began to wander round the school, looking for him.

Miss Greenwood's class were having painting. Nicky thought Miss Greenwood might have got over being angry by now; she could try some more pleading, perhaps. Nicky pressed her face against the glass panel in the door, and tried to catch Miss Greenwood's eye. Miss Greenwood, looking up from helping one of her little ones, saw Nicky's face peering through the door, and flinched. Nicky put on a wistful smile, but her nose and lips were partly flattened against the glass, so the smile looked unfortunately like a leer. 'Go away!' Miss Greenwood mouthed at her.

Nicky was about to try again, when she saw Mr Nelson coming along the corridor, and went to meet him, falling into step beside him. 'You're limping ever such a lot, Sir.'

'So I am.'

'Did anybody say anything about me, Mr Nelson? Any of the teachers?'

'Actually, yes.'

'Was it good? What they said?'

'Very good.'

'I think you should go home early today, Sir, and rest your arthritis for tomorrow.'

'What an attractive thought!'

'Well, why don't you?'

'Because I have a hundred things to do here.'

'Why don't you put a notice outside your room, "PLEASE DON'T DISTURB"? Then nobody can interrupt you from doing your hundred things.'

'Good idea, but, alas, not fitting!'

It wasn't too late, though, it wasn't too late! As soon as Mr Nelson had limped away, Nicky went back to Miss Greenwood's class to try once more. The sight of Nicky's face leering against the glass panel yet again was terribly disconcerting. Miss Greenwood waved her away. The face disappeared, and a few moments later came back, its earnest contortions even more grotesque. Miss Greenwood felt the hysteria rising.

She went to the door and opened it herself. 'If you've got something to say, why don't you come in and say it, instead of pulling those ghastly faces outside?'

'I didn't want to disturb you.'

'Well you *are* disturbing me. I'm trying to teach and you're bothering me.' She was dreadfully upset still about the pots. One or two of her little ones had been in tears. It was too much to have to suffer even *more* of Nicky Mitchell's attentions. 'You're bothering me! You're being very rude! Now what is it?'

It was bad luck that Miss Powell, on her way back to class after a free period, came along at that moment, and heard the agitated complaint. 'Not you again!' said Miss Powell to Nicky. 'What are you doing this time, prowling round the school? What is she doing to annoy you, Miss Greenwood?'

'Oh – looking through the door. Making faces.'

Miss Powell gave Nicky a little push. 'Get up to my room!'

'But Miss Powell, I didn't mean—'

'MY ROOM! Go on, in front of me, where I can see you!'

Nicky muttered something under her breath. 'Did I hear you calling me an interfering ugly cow, by any chance? Oh, I thought I did! I must get my ears attended to! Go on, stand there by my table. All right, you lot, find yourself something to do for two minutes. . . . Did you hear me, Jason Charles? Something to *do*, I said, other than concerning yourself with someone else's business. Right, Nicky, I shouldn't think you need bother looking for your swimming costume tonight!'

'It was a accident though,' said poor Nicky.

'What was? Making faces through Miss Greenwood's door?'

'No. When I knocked the pots over and they all got broke. It was a accident.'

'Oh, you broke the pots! When was this?'

'Dinner time. It was a accident. I didn't want Miss Greenwood to tell Mr Nelson.'

'Why should she, if it was an accident?'

'I thought she might.'

'How did the pots get knocked over?'

'I was only trying to open the window.'

'How?'

Silence.

'How, Nicky? How were you trying to open the window?'

'I only climbed a *bit*.'

'Did Miss Greenwood tell you to climb?'

'. . . Not really.'

'Did she tell you *not* to climb?'

'. . . She might have.'

163

'It wasn't an accident, then, was it? It was a very serious piece of naughtiness.'

'I thought she would be pleased if I got the window open. *Please*, Miss Powell, don't tell Mr Nelson!'

'I'm not going to tell him. You're going to tell him yourself. Now. About your disobedience, and the damage to Miss Greenwood's pots, and your rudeness to Miss Greenwood, and your rudeness to me on the stairs coming up, and don't tell him you didn't say it, because I know you did!'

Nicky trailed sorrowfully to Mr Nelson's office. 'Oh dear,' the headmaster sighed. 'Trouble?'

'Yes, Sir.'

'Bad?'

'Yes, Sir.'

'What have you done?'

'Lots of things.'

'Cheeked someone?'

'Yes, Sir.'

'Damaged something?'

'Yes, Sir.'

'Oh dear!'

'Yes, Sir.'

'Punched someone's head in?'

'No,' said Nicky, brightening. 'I didn't do that. Not today. Not all day!'

'You haven't been perfect, though.'

'No.'

'And we agreed you must.'

'I know. . . . All right, Mr Nelson, you needn't say it, I'll say it for you! I can't come on the outing tomorrow, can I? There, I said it myself. . . . I did *try* to be good, but it went wrong.' Perhaps the children's home wouldn't be *too* bad. 'Never mind, Sir, eh?'

'Nicky,' said Mr Nelson, thoughtfully, 'tell me something. . . . Have you been to the seaside at all this year?'

'No, Sir.'

'Did you go last year?'

'No, Sir.'

'Have you *ever* been?'

'I think so. I can't quite remember. Eric's dad *nearly* took us in his car, once.'

'So you don't really know what the sea's like.'

'Yes I do. I seen it on telly.'

Mr Nelson looked down at some papers on his desk, because he was having a lot of feelings he didn't want Nicky to see.

'All right. Remember to bring a warm coat for tomorrow. And make sure Roy has warm clothes as well. You often get cold winds by the sea, even on a nice day.'

Nicky stared at the strands of hair across the dome of Mr Nelson's head. 'Sir. . . .'

'What?'

'I *love* you.'

# 12

## A leaking secret

Roy, too, had been having a troubled day. That morning time had seemed endless. Roy mooched about the house, lost without the television, his mind empty of motivation. There were a few books and comics in his room, and he thumbed through them listlessly, but he wasn't much of a reader and soon gave that up. The pieces of last year's Christmas presents, cheap and flashy toys now falling to bits, were piled in a depressing heap in the corner. He went into Nicky's room, to see if she had anything better.

Nicky was rarely idle, but since she was often better at starting things than she was at finishing them, her room was rather full of such items as half-completed jig-saws, bits of abandoned embroidery, a poem she was writing but had tired of, and so on. Nothing of interest to Roy.

He went downstairs; slowly, one step at a time, so as not to get there too soon. He thought of making another WELCOME HOME banner for Mum, because that was a good idea he had had once, and he didn't have many! But there didn't seem much point in making a WELCOME HOME banner for some-one who never came, and anyway Nicky broke up the first one they made, and anyway he didn't want to think about Mum.

He took a ball into the back garden, and began

kicking it. Mrs Williams called to him, over the wall. 'Why aren't you in school?'

'I got the 'flu.'

'Why aren't you in bed then?'

'I'm a little bit better today. I'm going to school tomorrow.'

'How's your mum?'

He was confused suddenly, being asked about Mum. What was he supposed to say?

'Well, cat got your tongue?'

'She's in bed. Her 'flu is worser than mine.'

'Did you have the doctor, then?'

'No.'

'Oh? I thought your sister went for the prescription.'

'I mean, yes. We did have the doctor. I forgot.'

Mrs Williams gave Roy a sharp look. '*You* didn't have the 'flu though, yesterday!'

'Yes I did. I did.'

'No you didn't. You was out last night. I saw you.'

'I wasn't out! I wasn't!'

'I *saw* you. Quite late. Going up the chippie with your sister.'

'Oh yes. I forgot.' His fingers twisted frantically. He wished he had never come in the garden – whatever made him do it?

'You seem to be forgetting a lot, today.'

He shrugged, not looking at her.

'*I* think you're telling me a story!'

Roy ran indoors. He sat on the sofa with the broken springs, shaking. Polly Pry thought he was telling a story! Polly Pry didn't believe him! What would happen now?

He went up to Nicky's room, which had the best

167

view over the back gardens. Mrs Williams had gone in her house, which was something. Roy came down again, and fiddled with the television that didn't work, and tried to forget how he nearly gave away the secret.

Mrs Williams had taken up her post at the front. The day promised to be warm and dry, not like yesterday. That rain yesterday was really something! Funny, Mrs Mitchell choosing yesterday, of all days, to open that window wide. Which was a thing she never did in her life before, Mrs Williams would swear! And she must have done it *after* the girl went to get the medicine, because the girl didn't know it was open till she came back. And what a time to be getting medicine anyway! She must have had to find an all-night chemist ... and she was wet through. . . . But stop a minute, stop a minute, the rain finished a long time before. So the girl must have been out for hours anyway. How funny! And that meant, that meant, the *window* must have been open for hours!

Mrs Williams thought it was funny, yesterday – and now she thought about it again it seemed even funnier. Whoever heard of getting out of a sick bed, and coming downstairs and opening a window wide, to let all the rain in? And then going back to bed, and leaving the window wide open for the burglars!

That girl was hiding something, yesterday.

The boy was hiding something this morning, as well. He looked quite scared when he ran in, just now.

The two of them were hiding something? What?

Something to do with the mother?

Mrs Williams looked at the Mitchells' house. She

looked at the Front Room window, firmly locked now. She looked up at the window of the front bedroom, where Mrs Mitchell was supposed to be lying, ill in bed. *That* window was closed, when surely it ought to be open a bit. A warm day like this, and she had been in the room all night. Surely the room would be stale, and stuffy, now. Surely she would need some fresh air.

If she *had* been in it all night!

Suddenly Mrs Williams felt quite excited. She tried to remember when she had last seen Mrs Mitchell, and she couldn't. More than a week ago – it must be more than a week! And that Mrs Morris said she hadn't seen her, either. Just casual, just in passing, like it was only a coincidence – but perhaps it wasn't just coincidence after all.

Where *was* Mrs Mitchell, really?

At last, and after a lot more thought, Mrs Williams left her post by the gate, and went to knock at the Morrises' front door.

Mrs Morris was giving the kitchen a good clean, which she always did on Tuesday mornings. She was very particular about her house, and she always did the same jobs on the same days, and she didn't like having her routine interrupted. She didn't mind a gossip when it was the right time for a gossip, but the right time was not now, when it was her morning for cleaning the kitchen. She prepared to get rid of Mrs Williams as soon as she could, because that woman was a terrible time-waster, and if *she* had nothing to do but stand by her front gate all day, then other people did!

'I want to ask you something,' said Mrs Williams.

'I was just doing the oven,' said Mrs Morris.

'It won't take a minute,' said Mrs Williams. 'It might be important!' She implied, more important than the oven.

'Well what is it?' said Mrs Morris, implying it had better be.

'About that Mrs Mitchell.'

'Oh *her*!'

'You know you said you never see her for a long time—'

'Well that's how it goes, innit? Sometimes you don't.'

'Do you think she's really living there though, in the house?'

'*What?*'

'Do you think she's really there?'

'That's going a bit far, isn't it? She must be there! The kids are there, and don't I know it! And they can't be living on their own.'

'I suppose not.' Mrs Williams was beginning to wonder if she was making herself look like a silly old fool. She had made herself look a silly old fool quite a few times, lately, jumping to conclusions, and spreading rumours that turned out not to be true. But you had to do *something* to liven up the dull days. 'There's something funny going on, though. There's something funny going on! You mark my words, there's something funny going on in that house!'

'Well whatever it is, that woman's had all the help she's getting from me,' said Mrs Morris.

'What about them kids though? Nasty little things they are, especially the girl, but somebody got to look out for them.'

'The mother was there on Sunday, I do know,' said Mrs Morris after thinking a bit. 'She was cooking roast dinner, you could smell it. And there were some of her things on the line, Saturday. That tarty blouse, for one! No no, she's there all right. Worse luck.'

Mrs Williams was quite disappointed, as well as sorry she had made herself look like a silly old fool. She went into her house to get some lunch, and thought about her disappointment, and started to think she had let her suspicions be quietened a bit too easily.

Roy also was feeling hungry. He went to the kitchen to see if there was anything to eat, but the cornflakes packet was empty, and all he could find were two cold potatoes and the cut-off bread which had gone mouldy again. He drank the milk which the milkman had left that morning, looked at the mouldy bread ·and the cold potatoes once more, and his stomach heaved.

Dinnerless, he went to sit on the sofa again, wishing the time away till Nicky should come home.

The doorbell, ringing suddenly, made him jump. At first he thought he would just ignore it, but then there was a lot of knocking as well, and finally the letter box rattled, and someone was shouting through. 'Come on, Roy, I know you're there!'

It was Mrs Williams, and of course she *did* know he was there, so he couldn't pretend he wasn't. Trembling again, he went to the door to answer it.

'I've come to ask you a question, Roy.'

'What?'

'You may think it's a funny question.'

'What is it?' His heart was hammering madly.

'Us nosy old bags got our uses.'

'What uses? What do you mean?'

'I got to make sure nothing bad is happening to you, Roy.'

'Nothing bad *is* happening to me.'

'I got to make sure you're being properly looked after.'

'I *am* being properly looked after. Nicky looks after me.'

It was the wrong thing to say, of course. His terrified face showed he had realized his mistake.

'I should have thought you'd say your mum looks after you.'

'Well she does. As well.'

'Is your mum really in the house? Tell the truth now!'

That was the question, then. He thought it was going to be that, and it was.

'Yes,' said Roy, nearly shouting.

'Now, this minute, is she in the house?'

'YES!'

'Are you sure?'

'Of course I'm sure. Go away! Go away!'

He banged the door shut, and ran to sit on the sofa, sick with fear. She knew the secret, she knew the secret! Polly Pry knew the secret, and now she would tell it to everyone! And it was his fault she knew the secret! He got muddled, and said the wrong answers, so she guessed it. He dared not tell Nicky what he did. Nicky would *kill* him!

He tried to block the whole thing out of his mind, and pretend it hadn't happened; but it lay like a stone, like a dark heaviness, within the wall he tried to build around it.

Nicky came home, jubilant. 'We're going, we're going, we're both going! Go and find your swimming things, and your coat for tomorrow, because Mr Nelson says it might be cold.'

172

'I'm hungry,' said Roy.

'You're always thinking about yourself.'

'It's all very well for you; I suppose you had your school dinner.'

'Isn't there anything to eat at all?' said Nicky.

'Only mouldy bread. Can't we get some chips again, with the leftover money?'

Nicky shook her head. 'We have to have a packed lunch for tomorrow. Everybody has a packed lunch for the outing. I shall have to buy some bread, and we can have some of that for our tea.'

'Only bread, for our tea?'

'Oh don't make such a fuss! It's only for one day.'

'But I'm *hungry*.'

'Well, bread will fill you up. . . . I know, I know, I'll fry the bread! In the frying pan! And these old potatoes, I'll fry them as well! M-m-m! Tasty! Plenty starving children in the world would be glad to have such tasty things to eat, so stop moaning!'

In the end, Roy found he was not as hungry as he thought he was, after all. There was this nasty lump of guilt that was making him feel quite full. And he dared not tell Nicky, he dared not – but he kept having this horrid thought about Polly Pry, running up and down Gilbert Road, telling everybody the secret. He kept trying to push the thought away, and it kept coming back.

In fact, Mrs Williams was *not* running up and down Gilbert Road telling everyone the secret. Up to now, she hadn't told one person the secret – unless you could count Mrs Morris. She hadn't told, because she wasn't sure. There was something funny going on, Mrs Williams was sure of that, but what she was

thinking was more than funny, it was downright
scandalous. So scandalous it could hardly be true.
She thought it was true this morning, and now she
thought it couldn't be – could it? Well the boy hadn't
admitted anything. He was scared, but he hadn't
admitted anything. Perhaps she'd got the wrong end
of the stick after all. Perhaps she really was a silly old
fool, and she would just make herself look sillier,
telling people about it.

On the other hand . . . Mrs Williams went over the
evidence for 'on the other hand'. First, Mrs Mitchell
had not been seen by the neighbours for over a week.
Second, there had been a lot of racket going on in that
house. Screaming and crying from that boy, much
more than usual though he seemed to have gone quiet
lately; as well as noisy play no adult could have put
up with after a hard day's work. True – Mrs Mitchell
often took herself out in the evenings, but she hadn't
been seen doing that either, as far as Mrs Williams
knew. Third, there was the funny business of the
window, and Mrs Williams couldn't see how that
fitted in anyway, but it was very, very *funny*. Fourth,
there was that boy so scared of questioning, you'd
think someone was trying to kill him!

It seemed to add up, whatever Mrs Morris said. So
did she ought to tell *them*? The Authorities? Did she
ought to go to the Authorities, and tell them what she
suspected, and just let them get on with it?

Who *were* the Authorities, exactly? Mrs Williams
tried to think who it was she ought to go to, and found
she didn't really know. If the dustbins hadn't been
emptied, you rang up the council. If a dog was
barking all night, you told the RSPCA. But what if
two children were living alone in a house? The police,

she supposed. But Mrs Williams was a bit uncomfortable about going to the police. She had been
to the police quite a few times lately, about things
that turned out to be mistakes. She had the idea the
police were getting to be rather impatient with her.

She must be a bit more certain, before she said
anything to *them*.

Should she waylay that girl, coming home from
school, and see what *she* had to say for herself? No –
only get a load of cheek!

What she would do, she would go all up the road,
and down the road, and ask everybody in their front
gardens if they saw that Mrs Mitchell lately. She
wouldn't say why she wanted to know, she would just
ask. After she had done that, she would make up her
mind about going to *them*.

The twins had come indoors for bedtime. 'What have
you got on your face, Pamela?' said Mummy,
suspiciously.

'Nothing,' said Pamela, rubbing hard at her mouth.

'Strawberry jam,' said Pandora, rubbing at hers.

'You've got it as well!' said Mummy. 'You little
monsters! You've been at my lipstick!'

'Not *your* lipstick,' said Pamela. 'We found this.'

'You *found* it?' said Mummy, horrified. 'And you
put it on your mouths? Somebody's lipstick you
found in the road?'

'Not in the *road*,' said Pandora. 'We wouldn't do a
disgusting thing like that, would we, Pamela! In the
road? Ugh! . . . It was in an old handbag.'

'What handbag? What are you talking about?'

'It was only an old one. They didn't want it – they
threw it away.'

'Where *was* this handbag?'

'In the garden. Behind the playhouse.'

'Show me,' said Mummy.

'Now look what you've done!' said Pandora to Pamela. 'You silly stupid pea-head!'

'Pea-head yourself! Turnip-head! Cauliflower-head!'

'Brussels sprouts-head!' said Pandora, following Mummy and Pamela out to the garden.

'Mangle-wurzle-head!' said Pamela to Pandora, over her shoulder.

'Where's this handbag?' said Mummy.

'Here it is. It's a very old one, you see. They just didn't want it any more, so they threw it over our wall.'

'What else was in it, besides the lipstick? Was there any money?' said Mummy. 'You had better tell me the truth,' she added, grimly.

'Of course there wasn't any money. People don't throw away money!'

'Keys?' said Mummy. 'Letters?'

'There were some keys.'

'Do you think people throw away keys, then?' said Mummy.

'They were old keys, I expect,' said Pandora. 'That didn't fit any more.'

'This is not a handbag somebody just threw away,' said Mummy. 'This handbag was stolen!'

The twins' faces radiated delight. 'It was *stolen*,' Pamela told Pandora.

'Tell me something I don't know,' said Pandora.

'I think the police may be interested in this,' said Mummy. 'How long have you had it?'

'Oh the police, the police!' squealed Pandora. Her rapture knew no bounds.

'How long?' said Mummy.

'Oh a long time,' said Pamela. 'Weeks and weeks!'

'She's barmy,' said Pandora. 'Weeks and weeks indeed, when it's only days and days!'

'Hours and hours,' said Pamela.

'Minutes and minutes.'

'Seconds and seconds.'

'Split-seconds and split-seconds!'

'*How long?*' said Mummy.

'It was before last Saturday,' said Pamela.

'But after the Saturday before that.'

'And letters?' said Mummy. 'Were there any letters in the bag? Anything at all, besides the keys?'

'No,' said Pamela, uncomfortably.

'Are you sure?' said Mummy, looking at her hard.

'Of course she's sure,' said Pandora. 'There was only the keys and the lipstick and the eye stuff and some tissues, and some old bits of paper.'

'What did you do with the bits of paper?'

'Put them in the bin, of course. We didn't want *them*.'

'That's a pity,' said Mummy. 'They might have been clues.'

'What are clues?' said Pamela.

'Dunce!' said Pandora, scornfully. 'Everybody knows that clues are what the police have. Everybody except you!'

'What do they have them *for*, though?' said Pamela.

'You never know,' said Mummy. 'You never know what might be useful. . . . Now are you sure there was nothing else inside the bag? Besides the things you've told me?'

'Absolutely certain sure, cross my heart a thous-

and million times!' said Pandora, firmly suppressing any pricks of conscience she might have about the mutilated 'cheque book', at present buried under the heap of dressing-up clothes, soon to join the handful of Safeway's receipts, and advertising leaflets, already consigned to the garden dustbin.

Mrs Williams turned her old bones over, and lay on her back with her eyes open, thinking out her suspicions once again. She had asked at least ten people and no one, not one person, remembered seeing Mrs Mitchell since more than a week ago. Some of them didn't even know her, of course, at least not by name. People didn't know their neighbours these days, the way they used to. Mrs Williams couldn't be certain, even now, but it was surely time to do something about it.

The police, then, in the morning.

No, not the police! Mrs Williams had a better idea. She wouldn't go to the police, who were getting fed up with her; she would go to the school. She would go and see the headmaster, and tell it all to him. *He* would know what to do. She would go to the school in the morning.

Mrs Williams had no way of knowing, of course, that she would arrive at the school to find it almost empty. That she would tell her story to Miss Powell, the deputy head, who would be quite uninterested; who would dismiss Mrs Williams's story, in her mind, as probably the ramblings of a poor old thing gone a bit ga-ga. Who would promise to tell Mr Nelson as soon as the outing returned – and promptly forget all about it!

# 13

# The outing

The coaches rolled through open country. In the front one, Nicky was singing 'Jesus wants me for a sunbeam', while everyone else was singing 'Ten green bottles'.

The morning had started cloudy, but the sun was doing its best, and little patches of blue sky were beginning to appear. Suddenly, in a burst of glory, the sunshine streamed through, lighting up fields and woods and hedges with the promise of a lovely day. Nicky's caterwauling stopped abruptly, and she turned sideways in her seat to give enraptured attention to the panorama of green and gold outside.

The children tumbled off the coaches for a break. 'No, this is not the sea; this is not the sea! It's just for everyone to stretch their legs and go to the toilet,' said Mr Hunt.

'All right, Nicky?' said Mr Nelson, limping up behind her.

'Sir,' said Nicky, 'what do you think Heaven is like?'

'I can't say I've ever given it much thought.'

'I used to think it was like the park. Where the swings are. But now I think it's like this place.'

Mr Nelson thought Nicky Mitchell was going to get more out of this outing than all the rest of them put together. Pity about Roy, though. The ''flu you get in July', of course! Certainly the boy did not look well. There were dark shadows under his eyes, and round his mouth – and hadn't he lost some weight? 'All right, Roy?' said Mr Nelson, to encourage him.

'What?' said Roy.

'Don't say "what" to Mr Nelson,' Nicky scolded him. 'Say "pardon, Sir". Where are your manners?'

Everyone piled back on the coaches. Some of the children were getting restless now. 'It's a long way,' they complained.

'Not far now,' the grown-ups lied.

Nicky started up 'Jesus wants me for a sunbeam' again, and the coach protested. Obligingly, Nicky changed to 'All things bright and beautiful', which she considered far more appropriate to the occasion than 'Ten green bottles'.

'Shut up!' said Marcus.

'Yeah, shut up!' said Eric Morris.

'Your voice make us all feel ill,' said someone else.

Nicky turned, and grinned; turned back, and carolled on.

'Tell her, Sir,' Marcus complained.

'I can sing if I want to, can't I, Mr Nelson!'

'I think that's enough now, Nicky,' said Mr Nelson.

'See?' Marcus taunted her.

'See, Nicky?' said Eric. 'Mr Nelson says you got to stop.'

'Shut your mouth, creep!' said Nicky.

'It's *your* mouth is supposed to be shut,' said Eric.

'Yeah,' said Marcus, 'it's your mouth that's supposed to be shut!'

'You can shut yours as well,' said Nicky. 'Or I'll shut it for you.'

'Witch!' said Marcus.

'Take that back,' said Nicky, getting out of her seat.

'Sit down, Nicky,' said Mr Nelson.

'When that thickhead takes back calling me names!'

'Sit down!' said Mr Nelson.

She sat, but with a bad grace.

'Witch!' hissed Marcus, going on with it.

'That will do, Marcus!' said Mr Nelson, sharply, at the same time as Nicky's head whipped round in her seat.

'Thickhead!'

'Witch!'

Nicky lunged out of her seat and hit Marcus, hard on the nose so the blood came; and Mr Hunt had to get out of *his* seat, at the back of the coach, to stop the punch-up which followed. Mr Hunt did not like having to leave his seat just to stop a fight. He had been sitting next to Miss Greenwood, who had arrived for the outing dressed in a green and purple sundress, with her hair done a different way; and Mr Hunt had suddenly noticed that she was really rather attractive. He had been chatting her up at the back of the coach all morning, and was not best pleased at having to stop.

'Take Nicky back with you, will you, Mr Hunt?' said Mr Nelson. He felt tired, all of a sudden, and very old.

'He started it!' said Nicky, still furious. 'That thickhead started it! That sack of potatoes with the turnip on top!'

'That will do,' said Mr Nelson.

Now Miss Greenwood had to change places with Nicky, which did not suit her at all. She sat next to

Roy, but couldn't be bothered to talk to him. Mr Nelson dragged himself on to his arthritic legs and limped forward, swaying as the coach turned a corner. 'Miss Greenwood, that little one of yours by me is feeling sick, I think,' Mr Nelson invented. 'Needs your motherly touch!'

It's like Musical Chairs, thought Miss Greenwood, sulkily, and wondered how she could manoeuvre herself nearer to Mr Hunt again.

Mr Nelson sat next to Roy. 'Nearly there now! I'm getting really excited, aren't you?'

'Yes,' said Roy, turning his head and twisting his fingers.

He didn't look excited, he looked withdrawn. 'Brought your swimming things, then?' Mr Nelson tried again.

'Yes,' said Roy.

'Can you swim yet?'

'No,' said Roy.

'Better not go in the water anyway, perhaps, if you've had the 'flu.'

Roy did not answer, and Mr Nelson gave up. Mr Nelson was sorry for Roy, but there was no denying he was a dreary little thing. The two of them sat together, in uncomfortable silence, until the coaches sailed into the town.

They were moving sluggishly now, in jerks, behind the line of traffic making for the seafront. 'We want the sea! We want the sea! We want the sea!' Nicky grabbed at Mr Hunt's arm and held it. Her eyes were wide open, brilliant with expectation. 'Oh, Sir, oh, *Sir*!'

'When you've quite finished with my arm . . .' said Mr Hunt, good-humouredly.

'Sorry, Sir.'

'It's only the *sea*!'

'*Only!*'

They turned a corner, and they were on the front. And there it was, and it was different from the telly, and different from her blurred and distant memories. It wasn't just blue, or green, like she thought it would be, it was twenty different colours all at once, all moving and changing and throwing the sunbeams back at the sky. And it was *enormous*. As far as you could see, and further, and you could sail over it, like the little boats, and your troubles would go smaller and smaller. You could sail over the huge sparkly sea, and your troubles would go to nothing. And the brightness would fill you up, so there was no room for anything else.

'You approve then, Nicky?' said Mr Hunt, teasing her. 'You feel you're getting your money's worth?'

Nicky did not think that silly remark was worth answering, so she didn't answer it.

The coaches made for the far end of the promenade, where there was a great green space. They would sit here, Mr Nelson said, and eat their packed lunches before they did anything else. Then they would pick up the litter, every tiny scrap. And then, only then, would they go to the beach.

Nicky and Roy sat together to share their bread sandwiches. Sitting on the grass you couldn't see the sea, because there was a wall in front of it. They could have been in the park, or anywhere. Nicky stood up again, and stretched on tiptoe, craning to catch a glimpse of the lovely, shining water. 'Sit down, Nicky, and eat,' said Mr Hunt.

Nicky took a bite of the dry bread. 'M-m-m!' she

exclaimed. 'Chicken! I got chicken in mine, Joycelyn, what have you got in yours?'

'Chicken,' said Joycelyn.

'What have you got in yours, Eric?'

'Chicken.'

'Isn't that a coincidence?' said Nicky. 'We all got chicken in our sandwiches! . . . Oh look, look, Roy! Tinned salmon! I bet nobody else got salmon sandwiches, only us, Roy!'

'Haven't you got no crisps?' said Eric.

'*Crisps?*' said Nicky, scornfully. 'Who wants *crisps?* Me and Roy got chicken sandwiches and salmon sandwiches and egg sandwiches. Our mum made them for us last night. We don't want crisps, do we, Roy?'

'You've got all bruises down your leg, Nicky,' said Eric, just noticing.

'No I haven't.' Nicky pulled her skirt down quickly, to cover them. She would have preferred to wear her jeans for the outing, but she only had the one pair, and they were too grubby, from Monday.

'Yes you have,' said Eric. 'All round your knee.'

'Don't be personal!' said Nicky.

'What have you got to drink?' said Eric. 'What have you got, Roy?'

'He's not thirsty,' said Nicky, quickly. 'I'm not thirsty neither. We don't get thirsty, me and Roy, so we didn't bother to bring any drinks.'

'I've got two Cokes,' said Joycelyn. 'You can have one of mine if you like.'

'Thank you,' said Roy, his eyes brightening just a little bit.

'You don't need it, Roy!' Nicky scolded him. 'You got chicken sandwiches and salmon sandwiches and egg sandwiches. You don't need Coke as well, that's just being greedy.'

'I didn't see any chicken in your sandwiches,' said Eric, 'I think it was just bread.'

'He must be a *little* bit thirsty,' said Joycelyn.

'If you didn't see the chicken in my sandwiches, you must be blind,' said Nicky.

'I think he *is* thirsty,' said Joycelyn. 'Can't he have the Coke, Nicky? I don't want to carry it around with me the rest of the day, it's heavy!'

'All right then. Just this once. Just so you don't have to carry it.'

'How much money have you got to spend, Joycelyn?' said Eric.

'50p. How much have you?'

'The same. How much have you got, Nicky?'

'Mind your own business,' said Nicky. 'And you can give me some of that Coke, Roy. You don't have to drink it all.'

The children had been divided into groups, eight or so to a group. There were plenty of grown-ups to look after the groups, because a number of mums had been recruited to help. Nicky Mitchell, naturally, could not be given to someone's mum to mind, so Mr Hunt was stuck with her. He was also stuck with her misery of a brother, since Roy had apparently been ill, and had to stay with Nicky. Mr Hunt assembled his group, and threatened them. 'Keep together, all of you! I don't want to be counting you every five minutes, to see if anyone's missing.'

'I thought you said it doesn't matter if we drown,' said Nicky.

'Well yes, you can drown if you like,' said Mr

Hunt. 'It's all right to drown, but apart from that, keep together.'

They trooped on to the beach of sand and shingle. There was a little wind, and the air was sharp – tingling, and heady. Nicky stood with upturned face, and smelled the wonderful air. 'I wish this day would go on for ever and ever!' she said.

'Can we swim now?' someone asked.

'Not yet, you've just eaten,' said Mr Hunt.

'Can we paddle, then? Can we paddle, Sir, *please*!'

'All right,' said Mr Hunt. He sat on the beach, lazily juggling pebbles in his hand. 'Stay where I can see you all.'

Nicky took off her shoes. The beach was wide, and gritty, and hurt her feet; the sharpness underlined her joy. The wind cut through the hot rays of the sun. Incredulously, Nicky felt the first cold wave breaking over her ankles, and seeping smoothly back. She watched it go, over the shingle, leaving her feet all clean and new.

Roy did not go to the water's edge with the others. He sat on the beach by himself, a little way from Mr Hunt, playing half-heartedly with the knobbly sand. 'Why don't you go with your sister?' Mr Hunt suggested. He had just seen Miss Greenwood coming towards him with her group. She would sit down with him, probably, and her group would go paddling, and he and she could continue the flirtation they had started on the coach. This would be very agreeable, but better without Roy Mitchell spilling depression all over them.

Roy did not answer.

'Don't you feel well?'

Roy shrugged.

'You shouldn't have come if you're not well enough, you know. Oh hello, Miss Greenwood, having fun?'

Miss Greenwood's group were clinging all round her. Those who could not reach hands or arms were clinging to her skirt and her bag. 'A prize for the first one to find fifty shells!' said Mr Hunt.

'Should we encourage them to scatter?' said Miss Greenwood, with her best tinkly laugh. 'Won't they get lost?'

'Nah, they won't get lost,' said Mr Hunt. 'They'll mind each other! Wouldn't you like to go looking for shells, Roy? I suppose not. . . . Oh well!'

Miss Greenwood gave Mr Hunt a silly smile, and Mr Hunt forgot about Roy anyway.

A policewoman had brought the bag, to show to Mrs Mitchell. 'It's mine!' said Mrs Mitchell, at once.

'Are you sure?'

'I only lost my memory! I still know my own bag!' She rummaged through the contents, eagerly. 'There was more in it than this! There was more things in it!'

'Money?'

'There must have been!'

'Papers? Letters?'

'I suppose so . . . I dunno.'

'How did you lose it, do you think? Did you leave it somewhere? Throw it away?'

'Throw it away? Throw my bag away? With keys in it? Do you think I'm mad?'

'What happened then? You can't remember at all?'

'. . . I was running,' said Mrs Mitchell, suddenly.

'Running. Yes? Running where?'

'I don't know, do I? I lost my memory, haven't I?'

'All right. How about *why* you were running?'

'It was important, it *was* important!' Mrs Mitchell began to look really distressed. 'It was important, but I can't remember. . . .And I'm sick of this not knowing what's going on! It was important that time, and I can't do nothing about it because I don't know what it was!'

'All right,' said the policewoman. 'I'm pushing you and I probably shouldn't. When you try too hard, it stops the memories from coming. I tell you what I'll do. . . . You're quite sure the bag is yours?'

'Positive.'

'I'll leave it with you for a while, and see if that helps to bring things back. Don't force it, just try to relax and let it come.'

'Relax?' said Mrs Mitchell, fretfully. 'Some chance!'

The children were dressing themselves after swimming – modestly, under coats and towels. Mr Nelson, who had no group of his own, came limping along on his gammy leg, tactfully averting his eyes.

'Boo!'

'Are you trying to give me a heart attack, Nicky, on top of my other tribulations?'

She linked her arm in his, affectionately. 'How is your arthritis now, Mr Nelson?'

'Bad, thank you very much. I don't think this sea air agrees with me. Too damp. It seems to be suiting you though.'

'I'm having a *great* time!' said Nicky. Her face glowing, the blue eyes looked gladly into his. 'Mr Nelson, will you tell me something?'

'If I know the answer.'

'Does this beach go on and on?'

'What do you mean?'

'Does it go on and on, all round the country, like this?'

'Well – I suppose there's some sort of foreshore, all round the country. . . . That is—' He concentrated, trying to get it right.

'Oh look, Mr Nelson! Look at your hair!' said Nicky. 'It's gone all funny!' The wind had lifted the long strands that were supposed to go over the bald bit, and was blowing them straight up in the air. 'Does it go on and on, then?'

'My hair?'

'*No!* Not your hair! The beach! Could you walk all round the country, on the beach?'

'Actually, no. There are things like headlands . . . and docks.'

'What a pity!'

'Is it?'

'Not really . . . I was just wondering, though.'

'Wondering what?'

'How far *this* beach goes on.'

Mr Nelson laughed. '*I* don't know. Miles and miles, anyway.'

'Miles and miles which way?'

'Well – that way!'

To the right, at the other end of the promenade, there was a small harbour. To the left, the beach curved gently into the far distance.

'That's what I thought.'

'Happy now?'

'Yes, I am. Did you see me swimming, Sir?'

'No, I'm afraid I missed that great treat.'

189

'I can swim ten strokes now, without touching the bottom.'

'Well done!'

'Is that enough for a width, at the baths?'

'Nearly, I should think.'

'We're going for a walk soon,' said Nicky. 'When we're all dressed.'

'Well, make the most of it. Coaches leave at three-thirty, remember.'

'Oh *Sir*! It's too short, Sir! What time is it now?'

'Just past two o'clock.'

'The beach is getting bigger, look!'

'Of course, the tide is going out.'

'How much further will it go?'

'A bit more, I think. Then it starts to come back in. Some seaside places it goes out for miles and miles, but not here.'

'How funny.'

'Didn't you know?'

'I think so. . . . I forgot. Anyway, you told me now, didn't you, Sir!'


The police lady said not to think too hard – but how was she supposed to stop? The thoughts in Mrs Mitchell's head whirled like spinning tops. She was running, running, running! She did it again in her mind. The bag was in her hand as she ran. The bag swung from her hand – and then? What happened then?

It was no use, she was trying too hard. It was like the police lady said; the memories would never come while she struggled to find them. If she could have a little sleep, now! Would that cow of a nurse let her get on the bed? Probably not. How would *she* like it, having to sit on this chair with broken ribs?

All right then, if she couldn't sleep, she'd have a read. She stretched for a magazine, and yelled a bit, because the broken ribs hurt when she did that. She began to read a love story. It was a silly story, Mrs Mitchell thought; the characters in it did not seem real at all. Then a twist in the plot caught her interest, and she began to read with more attention. Then, because she still tired easily after the accident, Mrs Mitchell's eyelids began to droop. She forced them open, because she wanted to know the end of the story, she really did.

Her head began to nod. The magazine slid off her lap and on to the floor, and Mrs Mitchell slept, after all.

Roy thought it was funny that Nicky didn't seem to be doing anything about running away from the outing. He didn't mind that they weren't running away from the outing yet, he just thought it was funny. He also, in some dark and distant corner of his mind, thought it was funny that no one had yet come to tell them the secret was found out – after Polly Pry went round telling everyone in Gilbert Street. But he didn't think *much* about that, because it was all such a long way away.

He didn't even think much about the things that were near, like how funny it was they weren't running away yet. He didn't think much about anything, because everything that was happening, was happening in a sort of dream.

Joycelyn was quite concerned about him, looking so dazed and unhappy. She kept putting her arm round him, as they trailed along the promenade, and Roy didn't mind when Joycelyn did that, because she was a big girl after all, and allowed to be motherly. It was Nicky who didn't seem to like it. 'Leave Roy alone, Joycelyn, he's my brother, not yours!'

'He's not well though,' said Joycelyn.

'You mind your own business!' said Nicky, unkindly.

With a hurt and puzzled face, Joycelyn withdrew her comforting arm, and stumbled ahead, to join up with some of the others.

'Can we get ice creams, Sir?'

'Go on, then,' said Mr Hunt. 'Miss Greenwood and I will sit on the wall and watch you.' He meant, they would sit on the wall and look at each other. 'Aren't you and Roy going for the ice creams, Nicky?'

'Me and Roy don't like ice cream.'

Roy gazed with ill-concealed longing at the cones and lollies being licked by others. 'Have you spent all your money, Roy?' said Mr Hunt, tactfully. He knew very well they had had no chance to spend money, up to now.

'Yeah,' said Roy.

Mr Hunt thought Mrs Mitchell was a very poor sort of mother, not finding any money at all for her children to spend on the outing. 'Oh come on, let me treat you,' he said, putting his hand in his pocket.

'Roy doesn't like ice cream,' said Nicky, firmly.

They were all walking along the promenade again, straggling with their ice creams behind Mr Hunt and Miss Greenwood. Nicky linked arms with Roy, and slowed his steps till the two of them were last. 'In a minute!' she whispered. 'When I say! Follow me, and hide!'

Suddenly, it wasn't like a dream any more, it was uncomfortably real! Nicky still held Roy's arm, and their steps were getting slower, and slower. They were almost still. Nicky was watching Miss Greenwood and Mr Hunt ahead, making sure they didn't turn round. No need to bother much about the other children – they were much too interested in their ice creams, licking them slowly, making them last.

'Now!' said Nicky, yanking at Roy's arm.

'Gotcha!' said another voice, behind them.

Someone had clamped a heavy hand on Nicky's shoulder, and she turned round furiously. 'What d'you want?'

'Only playing,' said Jason Charles.

Playing was the right word. He and his group were having a wonderful time, playing up Karen's mum, who had kindly come to help with the outing. Someone had slipped up badly, putting Jason Charles in Karen's mum's group. 'You're supposed to be with Karen's mum!' said Nicky.

'I *am* with her,' said Jason, not realizing yet that he wasn't getting a welcome. 'There she is, look!' Grinning, he pointed way down the promenade, where Karen and her mum were floundering along, desperately trying to count heads as they went.

'Well go back to her!' said Nicky. 'Go on, Jason! Mr Nelson said we got to stay with our groups.'

'What about you, then?'

'I can't help it if you're holding me and Roy back, can I?'

'Come on, Nicky,' said Jason, disappointed. 'Let's you and me have some fun!'

'Get away, creep!' Nicky shouted at him.

'What's the matter with *you*?' said Jason.

193

'Creep!' Nicky yelled again, frustrated and frantic.

'All right!' he yelled back. 'Witch!'

'Come on, Nicky, keep up!' called Mr Hunt, turning round to see what all the shouting was about.

# 14

# Escape

Mrs Mitchell awoke. She had slept only half an hour, but she felt wonderfully refreshed. Moving in the chair, her hand touched the bag beside her, fingered it, closed around the strap – and remembered!

The bag was swinging from her hand that time – swinging, swinging, and then not swinging! Something happened to stop the swinging. . . . What. . . ? And then she was screaming. . . . There was a tug, and her hand was hurting, and she was screaming! 'He took it!' she shouted, suddenly. 'He took my bag! He stole it!'

'He took her bag!' shouted the woman in the next bed. 'She remembered! Nurse, nurse, she remembered!'

Mrs Mitchell was sobbing. 'He took my bag, and it had all my money in it! He took all my money so I couldn't. . . .'

'Yes?' said the nurse, trying not to show how excited she was feeling. 'What couldn't you do?'

'I couldn't go . . . I couldn't go . . . the train . . . the train was going . . . I . . . .' Mrs Mitchell's voice trailed off, uncertainly.

'You wanted to go on the train?' said the nurse, trying to help her.

'I think so . . . I don't know, now . . . I thought I would remember it all, but I didn't.' She was dreadfully disappointed. 'I *thought* it was something about a train. . . . I don't know now, it's gone away again.'

'You're doing *very well indeed*!' said the nurse, firmly.


Nicky was getting anxious. Three o'clock by Sir's watch, and they hadn't managed to run away yet! With Mr Hunt being so interested in Miss Greenwood today, it ought to be easy, but the trouble was they kept bumping into other groups. People from the school were everywhere; it was really very annoying.

They were in an amusement arcade now. Most of the teachers wouldn't let their groups play the machines, but Mr Hunt was not being at all strict today, and anyway he was playing the machines himself, with Miss Greenwood. Those of the two groups who had run out of money were clustered round watching, cheering Sir and Miss on. Nicky held Roy's wrist, tight. 'Let's go this way. Over here, look! Stand where nobody can't see you. Here!'

She looked around, carefully. The machines hid Mr Hunt and Miss Greenwood from sight. If she couldn't see them, they couldn't see her! The way was clear to run now – but where? On the pavement outside would be Mrs Blake, or Mr Nelson, or Karen's mum, or somebody else from the school.

Three o'clock! More than three o'clock now! It was a little walk to the coaches, so they would be going soon. Could she work it so Mr Hunt would go without her and Roy? Was there somewhere in this place so she and Roy could hide, so Mr Hunt would think they went out when he wasn't looking? He would be cross they'd left the group, but he would think they'd gone back to the coach by themselves, most likely. He would come after them to tell them off, but he wouldn't find them because they would be left behind in the machine place, really. And all the other groups would be gone to the coach by that time, so outside would be safe, and they could run across to the beach, and run along the beach, and run and run till they came to Southbourne, where Mum was!

It was only a little way. It was only a teeny, weeny way. She saw it on the map.

Nicky peered about her, looking for a good hiding place among the machines. There were spaces between them in some places. If she and Roy squeezed into one of those spaces – against the wall would be good – and if there were people in front of the space, then Mr Hunt and Miss Greenwood and the other kids wouldn't see them. Nicky found a popular machine, one with lots of people around it. 'Excuse me,' she said, elbowing her way through the little crowd to push Roy into the little space.

'I don't like it here,' said Roy.

'You grumble too much,' said Nicky.

She bent her knees, to be as low as possible, and made Roy bend his. 'It's making my legs ache,' Roy complained.

'Shut up,' said Nicky.

'How long must we stay like this?'

'Till I say it's time to come out.'

'There they are, Sir,' said Eric Morris's voice. 'They're hiding, Sir!'

'What's the big idea?' said Mr Hunt, quite crossly. 'You nearly made us late for the coach.'

'Only joking,' said Nicky, coming out of the hiding place with Roy. She felt foolish, and worse.

'All keep together now,' said Mr Hunt, leading the way.

'Nicky doesn't *look* as though she was joking,' said Miss Greenwood, glancing back. 'She looks as though she's casting evil spells.'

'She probably is. Take no notice,' said Mr Hunt.

'Is she quite right in the head?'

'As mad as a hatter,' said Mr Hunt. 'Come on, Nicky, cheer up! We've had a great day out, but all good things come to an end, you know.'

Not this one, Nicky thought, fiercely. Not this one yet!

She began to pretend a tremendous interest in the souvenir shops they were passing. Holding Roy by the wrist, she lingered and dragged, and shrieked with ecstasy over displays of shell ornaments, and seaside pottery. 'Come on, Nicky,' called Mr Hunt, over his shoulder. 'We haven't time for that now. It's three-thirty already, you know.'

'Sorry, Sir. Coming, Sir.'

But she had manoeuvred herself to the back of the group, and the gap between the two of them and the others was getting wider and wider.

Mr Hunt didn't seem to be bothered about them any more, he was chatting up Miss Greenwood like anything again. And no sign of the other groups; they were all back at the coaches, of course! It was now. It must be now.

At the right moment, and with no one looking, Nicky and Roy bolted up a side street and melted into the town.

In the coach, Mr Nelson counted heads. Two missing; he counted them again. 'It's Nicky and Roy,' someone said. 'Nicky and Roy's not here.'

'Mr Hunt?'

'Not those two again!' said Mr Hunt. 'That girl's a real pain in the neck!'

'I thought she was up to *something*,' said Miss Greenwood.

The other coaches were searched, and there was a quick scan of the promenade and the beach. 'What's she playing at?' said Mr Hunt, beginning to be worried.

'I thought she was up to *something*,' said Miss Greenwood.

'Who saw where they went?' Mr Hunt bellowed at the coachload of children. 'Come on, someone must have seen them disappear!'

'Perhaps they drowned, Sir,' said Marcus.

'Perhaps they went back in the sea, and got drowned!'

'Ha, ha, ha!'

'That's not funny!' said Mr Hunt, sharply.

'I thought she was up to *something*,' said Miss Greenwood.

'So you said,' Mr Hunt snapped at her.

'Joycelyn?' said Mr Nelson.

'Nicky didn't want me today,' said Joycelyn. 'She wouldn't even let me cuddle Roy.'

'This is beyond a joke!' said Mr Nelson. The pains in his gammy leg were like twisting corkscrews, and now his ulcer was beginning to gnaw as well, reminding him how much he longed for home, and rest, and a good hot meal. 'The other coaches will have to go on,' he said wearily. 'They can warn the parents this one will be late. Mr Hunt, will you go and look round the streets? They can't have gone far.'

'Shall I come as well?' Miss Greenwood offered.

She put her head on one side, and gave Mr Hunt a smile full of wistfulness and sympathy.

'No, it's all right, I'll go on my own,' he replied. This job required a manly stride, and he did not want Miss Greenwood trailing at his heels.

When he came back, after ten minutes or so of manly striding, some of the children in the coach were singing 'Why are we waiting?', some were falling asleep in their seats, and the rest were showing ominous signs of attacking one another through sheer boredom.

'No sign?' said Mr Nelson, unnecessarily.

'They seem to have vanished off the face of the earth,' said Mr Hunt.

'I thought she was up to *something*,' said Miss Greenwood, before she could stop herself.

Mr Hunt found he had gone off Miss Greenwood quite a bit. All of a sudden he thought she was a silly little thing, and rather wondered what he'd been seeing in her all day.

'Can't wait here for ever, you know,' said the driver, who was getting grumpy.

'And we can't leave two children to find their way home alone,' said Mr Nelson.

'Not *my* problem,' muttered the driver.

The problem was Mr Nelson's, of course, and he was feeling very old, and troubled, and uncertain about what to do. 'It would be a kindness,' he said to the grumpy driver, 'if you would take the coach very slowly round the streets, while we all look out for the missing kids. Someone can stay here in case they turn up on their own.'

The driver muttered something which sounded like 'Not my job', – but he did as Mr Nelson asked.

'Eyes peeled, everyone!' Mr Nelson told the children. 'And a gold star for the first one to spot them!'

Everyone cheered up at having something important to do. 'There they are!' said Marcus, suddenly.

'Stop!' said Mr Nelson, to the driver. 'Where, boy, where? I don't see them!'

'They went round that corner! I just saw their backs!'

Everyone crowded to the windows to watch. Mr Hunt jumped from the coach while it was still moving, and pelted round the corner. Everyone cheered, and jumped up and down. 'Can I have my star, Sir?' said Marcus. 'Can I have my star?'

'Let's just see if it's true,' said Mr Nelson.


Roy and Nicky had gone a long way into the back streets of the town. They had run and run, and in the end they had gone into a church because they had done enough running, and Nicky wanted somewhere safe and dark to hide. Mr Hunt's manly striding had not taken him as far as the church, and he would hardly have thought of looking inside, anyway.

Nicky and Roy sat close together, and Nicky tilted her head. She had never been in this kind of church before. There were beautiful pictures, made of coloured glass, in the high-up windows. 'Look, Roy!' said Nicky, in amazement. 'Look at that!'

Roy was not interested. He wanted this adventure over, and he wanted it over soon. 'We supposed to be looking for Mum, not looking at pictures,' he said.

'You don't have to stop doing one thing, just because you're doing something else as well,' said Nicky.

'I do,' said Roy.

Nicky sat right back in her seat and gazed, and gazed, and it was as though she wasn't sitting any longer; but floating up, to where the beautiful windows were. 'There's lots of things I didn't know about before,' she marvelled. '*Lots* of things!'

'When are we going?' said Roy.

'Presently,' said Nicky.

It was when they came out that they saw the coach. Outside the dark church, they blinked in the sudden brightness. There was a clock in the tower of the church. 'Twenty minutes past four,' said Nicky, with satisfaction. 'They'll be gone now. They'll all be gone back to London.'

'I don't think they'll go without us,' said Roy.

'I bet they didn't even notice!'

'I bet they did, then! They count!'

'Well anyway,' said Nicky, trying to persuade herself, 'I don't think they care really. Mr Hunt doesn't care, he said! He said, "A few lost, a few drowned, what's the difference?".'

'I bet he was joking.'

'No – he said he meant every word of it.'

'What's that then?' said Roy, pointing.

'Run!' said Nicky, dragging him round the corner. They dodged through a maze of streets, then ran straight down. Down, down, down to the sea. Across the promenade, and down the steps, and along the beach under cover of the wall: and Nicky's foot was hurting again from the blister, but it was the pains in their chests and the stitches in their sides that forced them to stop. And anyway the sand and shingle had come to an end; the beach was all loose pebbles now, that their feet sank into, so they couldn't run properly, only plod. They collapsed on to the pebbles, and their breathing came in great shuddering gasps, so it was several minutes before they could say even one word to each other.

And meanwhile a very subdued Mr Hunt was once more climbing into the coach empty-handed.

'It *was* them!' said Marcus.

'Are you sure, now?' said Mr Nelson.

'I just saw their backs,' said Marcus.

'It wasn't them!'

'It was. They had their bags!'

'It wasn't, it wasn't, Sir!'

'*I* never saw them!'

'Nor I didn't, neither.'

'Marcus is making out! He just wants his gold star!'

'He never had a gold star, Sir, before!'

'Ha, ha, ha!'

'Shut up, all of you!' said Mr Hunt.

'I think Marcus must have been mistaken,' said Mr Nelson. 'Good try, lad! Thank you for trying.'

'Do you think they got lost, Mr Nelson? Nicky and Roy, do you think they got lost?'

'I don't see how I can assume anything else. But we can't hold the coach up any longer for them. Drop me at the police station, please, driver.'

'Miss Greenwood's crying,' said Eric.

'Would you like *me* to stay, Mr Nelson?' said Mr Hunt. What a miserable end to a carefree day!

'No, no, you can go back to London and help Miss Powell cope with the mother. A nice little job for you!'

'Miss Greenwood's crying,' said Eric.

'Perhaps they'll turn up before the coach gets back,' said Mr Hunt, hopefully.

'In that case I'll phone through to Miss Powell.'

'Sir,' said Eric, 'Miss Greenwood's crying!'

'Mind your own business!' snapped Mr Hunt.

'It *was* them I saw,' said Marcus. He sulked about it, all the way back to London.


A police car, with Mr Nelson in it, was scouring the streets of Easthaven. A policewoman had been left at the coach place, in case the children came back there; but Mr Nelson was in the car, because he was the one who knew them. As the minutes crawled with the crawling car, Mr Nelson became more and more anxious.

The police officers in the car addressed each other as John and Mike. They had introduced themselves as P.C. Something, and P.C. Something else, but Mr Nelson was so worried about the missing children, he forgot the policemen's names as soon as they said them.

'I can't imagine what's happened! I can't *imagine* what's happened!' Mr Nelson kept repeating.

'We'll find 'em, don't worry,' said the police officer called John. 'Not such a big town, this.'

'I wouldn't be so concerned if I thought they were just lost,' said Mr Nelson. 'But how can you get lost in a seaside place? For all this time? They know the coaches are at the seafront. And there are signposts everywhere, even if they don't twig you have to keep going downhill. Something must have happened to them. *Something* must have happened.'

'We've done the toilets,' said John. 'They aren't trapped in there.'

'Bright kids, are they?' said the policeman called Mike. 'Got their heads screwed on?'

204

'The girl's all there and twice the way back,' Mr Nelson told him, 'if a little unpredictable. The boy's got a poor opinion of himself, but he's no fool really. They *can't* be just lost. . . . Anyway, they only had to ask. . . . Ask! Oh dear God, suppose they asked the wrong person!'

'Don't jump to conclusions, Sir,' said John. 'It's far too early days for that!'

He was only a youngster, younger than both of Mr Nelson's sons, but the uniform gave him authority, somehow. 'You would say so?' said Mr Nelson, humbly seeking reassurance from this whipper-snapper.

'Lord, yes!' said John.

'We shall find they're just playing around and forgot the time,' said Mike. Mike had thought that from the beginning.

'For two hours!' said Mr Nelson.

'You did say the girl was unpredictable,' said John.

'But not that irresponsible!' said Mr Nelson. 'I don't believe it. I don't believe she could be!'

'Kids can be pretty vague about time, can't they?' said Mike.

'True,' said Mr Nelson.

'Well there you are,' said Mike.

'Got watches have they?' said John.

'No,' said Mr Nelson. 'There is that. Only . . . if they're just playing . . . where is there else to look?' They had searched the arcades thoroughly. Several times. They had searched the shops. They had searched the beach, and all around the harbour.

'They'll turn up!' said Mike. 'And you can have a great time bawling 'em out for playing up.'

'The trouble is,' said Mr Nelson, 'I can't stop thinking about all these horror stories we keep hearing. About missing kids.'

'It's *not* that,' said John, firmly.

'They nearly always turn up safe and well,' said Mike. 'Almost always.'

'Life was much safer when I was a boy,' said Mr Nelson. 'Our parents didn't have to worry so much about us. If a kid got lost – well, someone brought him back, that's all. Took him to the police station or something.'

'Most people would still do that,' said John.

'No one has brought Roy and Nicky to the police station,' said Mr Nelson.

'Shall we try further along the beach?' said Mike. 'It gets a bit desolate, nothing to attract a kid, I wouldn't think. . . . Still, you never know!'

They passed the harbour again, and drove along the coast road beyond it for about a mile. 'You're right,' said Mr Nelson. 'It *is* desolate.'

They turned round, and went to the end of the promenade the other way. Mr Nelson was remembering something. 'I was just wondering . . . how far this beach goes on,' Nicky had said. 'Could you walk all round the country?' 'They might have gone this way,' he suggested. 'To see how far they could walk.'

'It's hard going over the pebbles,' said John. 'I wouldn't think they'd get far.'

They drove on for another mile. 'I can't see them going any further than this, can you?' said Mike. 'There'd be no fun in it.'

'I'd like to go on the beach for a minute,' said Mr Nelson, to John and Mike.

The beach was as the policemen had said. Every

step over those pebbles was a labour. 'You're right,' said Mr Nelson. 'They wouldn't have come as far as this. Not along the beach.'

'And we didn't see them on the road,' said Mike.

'We'll crawl back and keep looking,' said John. 'If they *are* on the beach somewhere, we can't miss them.'

There were not many people on the pebbly beach at all. There didn't start to be a lot of people again until they came to the promenade at Easthaven.

The crowd of parents waiting outside the school was noisy and excitable. A cheer arose as the late coach turned the corner. 'Have you found them?' said Mrs Morris, getting it muddled, although she knew really that Mr Nelson had stayed behind to look.

'Where's Miss Powell?' said Mr Hunt, embarrassed about having to look *any* of the parents in the face.

'Inside by the phone,' said someone.

'I hope *you* behaved yourself,' said Mrs Morris to Eric.

'Of course!' said Eric, as though he never did anything else.

'If I'd knowed that Mr Hunt wasn't properly responsible, I'd have made time to come myself,' said Mrs Morris, who was actually feeling quite guilty about not giving up her time to do that anyway. The letters sent home two Fridays ago, asking parents' permission for their children to be taken on the outing, had also asked which parents would be willing to help. Mrs Morris had thought about it, but Wednesday was her day for turning out the bedrooms, which made it inconvenient to help with the outing.

'Well done!' said Miss Powell, inside. 'Got shot of that little monster at last!'

'It's no joke,' said poor Mr Hunt.

'How did you manage it? We've all been trying for years!'

'A special talent obviously,' said Mr Hunt. 'A gift!'

'Don't you wish you'd stayed behind, like me?' said Miss Powell.

'Fervently,' said Mr Hunt. 'Come on . . . the million dollar question . . . has the mother been told?'

Miss Powell looked a bit uncomfortable 'Actually—'

'Actually, what?'

'Well, it's probably nothing.'

'*What's* probably nothing?'

'Well – Nellie rang through to say he was at the police station, and why, and it was before half past five so I tried Mrs Mitchell's work number. No home phone, as you probably know. And they say she hasn't been to work all week! Or last week, I *think* they said.'

'She's got the 'flu,' said Mr Hunt.

'Well, that might explain it, but—'

'What?'

'Well, I didn't take it seriously at the time. I mean, I didn't think it exactly warranted urgent action. But now I'm beginning to wonder—'

'Wonder what?'

'Oh – some old busybody came up here this morning, babbling something. Senile, I thought, poor old thing. . . . But it is a bit surprising that Mrs Mitchell hasn't heard it on the grapevine anyway, about her kids – and come haring up the school. To tear us limb from limb.'

'I shall tear *you* limb from limb in a minute,' said Mr Hunt, 'if you don't come to the point.'

'Yes . . . well . . . you may have gathered I'm a bit embarrassed about it. That I didn't take more notice. When the batty old crow said she thought Mrs Mitchell isn't in the house. At all.'

'What!'

'Roy and Nicky have been living on their tods for a week, she seems to think.'

'*What!*'

'So you see, you may not be the only person who made a mistake today, mate!'

Mr Hunt pressed the Mitchells' doorbell.

'Are you ringing for Nicky's mum?' said Eric, who had come out to see the fun.

'No, I'm ringing for the Queen of Sheba,' said Mr Hunt.

'Nicky's mum's got the 'flu,' said Eric.

'So we've all been told,' said Mr Hunt.

'Isn't it true then?' said Eric.

'That's what I'm trying to find out,' said Mr Hunt.

'Perhaps she's asleep.'

'Perhaps.'

'Shall we break a window, and climb in?'

'No.'

'Shall we call the police?'

'Which house does the batty old crow live in?' said Mr Hunt.

'*Who?*' said Eric.

'All right. The one round here that knows it all.'

'There!' said Eric. 'Can I listen?'

'No. Go back to your house. It must be your bedtime or something.'

Mr Hunt rang Mrs Williams's doorbell. 'I'm Nicky Mitchell's teacher. How do you do?'

'Not too bad considering. What is it then?'

'You haven't heard what happened? On the outing?'

The one afternoon she *didn't* spend at her front gate! What had she missed? What had she missed?

'No. What?'

Mr Hunt could see she was a bit put out. 'From what I hear, you're the only one round here with half a grain of sense,' he flattered her. 'So I'm sure you'll be the one to help find out what's been going on.'

'Some people think I'm a silly old fool,' said Mrs Williams. 'But I'm not. . . . What happened to them two little perishers then?'

'Disappeared,' said Mr Hunt.

'I'm not a bit surprised,' said Mrs Williams.

'Would you like to tell me why you said that?' said Mr Hunt.

Mrs Williams told. All she knew, and a few additions she couldn't help making up, just to make the story more interesting.

'Right! Now will you come with me in my car and tell the police?'

Mrs Williams could hardly believe her luck.

'Can I come, Sir?' said Eric, still lurking on the pavement.

'You can mind your own business,' said Mr Hunt.

# 15

# A walk into trouble

'I'm tired,' said Roy, for the hundredth time.

'All right,' said Nicky. 'We can have another little rest now.' She looked up at the cliffs behind her. 'There's no cars going along the top. I don't think there's any road there now . . . and nobody on this beach only us! I never was anywhere else before, where there was only us, were you, Roy?'

'I wonder if they did all forget us,' said Roy. 'Mr Nelson, and the coach, and everybody. I wonder if they all forgot by now.' He felt very forgotten, out here on this deserted beach. Out here it was easy to believe that nobody in the world cared about him and Nicky. That they had all gone back to their safe and cosy homes, and not cared a bit. 'I don't like it here,' he said.

'You're not supposed to like it, you're supposed to do it.'

'We should have gone by the road. Why didn't we go by the road?'

'If we went by the road we could get lost. This is more better.'

'I want to go *home*.'

'We have to find Mum, you know we do.'

'We aren't going to find her,' said Roy.

'Yes we are,' said Nicky. 'Don't argue. When we had a rest, we're going to walk along this beach until we come to Southbourne. It's not far, I saw it on the map.'

'We come a long way already.'

'Well that proves it!' said Nicky. 'It can't be much further. We must be nearly there.'

'I feel as if someone knocked me over the head,' said Mr Nelson, 'with the proverbial sledge-hammer!'

The London police had phoned the Easthaven police, and now Mr Nelson was struggling to come to terms with this astounding new development. 'How the devil did they get away with it? How the devil did they pull the wool over everybody's eyes? Well anyway, there's got to be a connection, hasn't there? Two kids alone in a house, and now the same two go missing! Wouldn't you say there's got to be a connection?'

'We aren't a hundred per cent sure,' said Detective Inspector Kendall. 'About the mother not being there all that time, I mean. But it looks like it. And there's certainly no sign of her now.'

The two uniformed police constables had disappeared, and in their place were these plain clothes officers – a detective inspector, no less, and a young woman introduced as Detective Constable Shaw. This was no longer a search for two naughty children, lost or larking about. The matter now was deadly serious.

'Could they have gone to relatives?' said Detective Constable Shaw, suddenly.

'Is that a possibility?' said Inspector Kendall. 'Have they got relatives in Easthaven, perhaps?'

'As far as I know they have no relatives at all,' said Mr Nelson. 'Anywhere. Or none they would know of. The mother was brought up in a children's home, and the father's disappeared. Which was no loss to anyone, from all accounts.'

212

'The father?' said Detective Shaw. 'Could the father have taken them?'

'The least likely thing in the world, I should say,' said Mr Nelson.

'I'm wondering about the mother,' said Inspector Kendall. 'Suppose they met the mother here by arrangement and. . . . No? A nonstarter?'

'Who can say?' said Mr Nelson, wearily. He told them what he knew – all he could think of the Mitchells' family background.

'You look tired,' said Detective Shaw to Mr Nelson.

'It's been a long day,' Mr Nelson admitted.

'And getting late now,' said Inspector Kendall. 'There really isn't much more you can do here. You've given us a good description of the kids, and of the mother, in case anything turns up at that end. Why don't you get the train back to London and keep in touch from there?'

'Not yet. I can't go yet!'

'But you look all in?'

'We have to forget about them just being lost now, or playing about, don't we?' said Mr Nelson.

'Oh yes,' said Inspector Kendall. 'There's certainly more to it than that.'

'Couldn't we just go round the town again?' said Mr Nelson. 'Just once more? Suppose they went into hiding for a bit and came out later?'

'There are half a dozen police officers searching the town at this minute,' said Inspector Kendall. 'On that very theory amongst others.'

'But I'm the one who knows the children! And I think, with respect, they'd be more reassured if I was there when they're found than if it was only your lot. They must be scared enough already.'

'I wish I'd had a headmaster like you,' said Detective Shaw, gently.

'I second that,' said Inspector Kendall.

'Come *on*,' said Nicky.

'I'm tired,' said Roy, again. 'I want another rest.'

'You had a lot of rests. You had enough rests,' said Nicky. 'And you're a nuisance being tired. *I'm* not tired. Look at me – I'm not tired a bit!' She strode out, limping because of the blister, through the dragging pebbles. 'See? I'm not the least little bit tired!'

'Well I am, and I can't go on any more.'

'Yes you can, you can. You have to *think* you can.'

'We should have got the bus. Why didn't we get the bus?'

'Without a ticket? And get caught by the Inspector? Where is your sense? Where is your intelligence?'

Roy sat down suddenly, on the stones.

'What's the matter now?'

'I told you, I'm tired.'

'But we're nearly there.'

'How do you know?'

'We come such a long way already, we *must* be nearly there.' She was secretly quite puzzled, actually, that they hadn't reached Southbourne by now. It looked such a tiny distance on the map.

'Perhaps we're going the wrong way,' said Roy.

'It's not the wrong way,' said Nicky. 'You have to look at the sea, and go left – I practised it in my head.'

'Perhaps you made a mistake. Like about the train.'

'I didn't. I practised it a hundred times. I didn't practise the train.'

'Anyway,' said Roy, 'I don't like this horrible beach, and I'm not going to walk on it any more.' Why should he, when it was clearly becoming a long walk to nowhere?

'Yes you are,' said Nicky. 'You *are* going to walk on it.'

'No I'm not.'

'You are, don't argue!'

'You can't make me.'

'All right, I'll go on by myself.'

'Go on then.'

'I mean it, you know,' said Nicky.

'I don't care.'

'Yes you do.'

'I don't,' said Roy. 'I'm tired, and I don't care what you do.' At that point, it was almost true.

'All right, then.' Ignoring the stabbing pain in her heel, Nicky pushed her aching legs another ten paces, then turned her head to look.

'I'm not joking!'

Roy didn't answer. He was lying on the pebbles now, curled up with his back to her. Nicky did another ten paces, then turned to look again. Roy had not moved. He was all by himself, a sad little speck in a great stony desert. Nicky frowned, hesitated, and plodded slowly back.

'Roy?'

No answer.

'Come on, Roy, I know you can hear me!'

Still no answer.

Nicky prodded him with her foot. 'Leave me!'

'Get up.'

'No.'

'I said, "Get up".'

'I'm not going to, I'm staying here.'

'It's going to be night soon.'

'I don't care.'

'*Please*, Roy.'

Silence.

Nicky sat down beside him, and leaned over him, rubbing her cheek against his. 'Come on, Roy! Just a little bit more, eh?'

Silence.

'Don't spoil it, Roy! Now we come all this way, don't spoil it now, *please*!'

He had gone so far into himself that he almost didn't hear her. The stones were hard and knobbly against his side, but he hardly felt them. He just wanted to go to sleep. He wanted to sleep, and sleep, and sleep, and forget everything.

Nicky's patience snapped. 'You're a creep, Roy Mitchell, do you know that? You're a useless creepy worm!' It was safe to shout – there was no one to hear. Frustrated, and exasperated, Nicky grabbed Roy's shoulder and pumped it backwards and forwards. 'Say something, can't you, you creep! Something. Just anything.'

Silence.

'I wish I didn't have you for a brother,' said Nicky, bitterly. 'I wish I had a different brother. I wish I had a brother that wasn't a baby. I wish I had a brother that wasn't a coward. . . . I wish I had a brother that didn't wet the bed!'

He heard that. Bending over him again, Nicky saw

the tears rolling down his cheeks. Not frantic tears, not hysterical tears, just the silent crying of despair. 'I didn't ought to have said that, did I?' said Nicky. She watched his tears with anguished eyes, then burst into noisy sobs.

Roy shifted, and turned slowly. He watched, almost with detachment, the unaccustomed sight of Nicky crying. 'I can't help all those things what you said.' His own words seemed to him to be coming from a long way away.

'I know. I'm sorry.' Her crying stopped.

'Actually,' said Roy, 'I wish I was like you.'

'Do you?'

'Yes I do. I always did.'

'Oh you don't want to be like me!' said Nicky. 'You don't want to be like me, I'm *horrid*.'

'I rather horrid than . . . those things you said.'

'I won't say them again, though. I won't, I won't, won't ever say them again, I promise!'

They were silent then, for a long time. Distressed, confused, in turmoil.

'Nicky,' said Roy, at last.

'Yes?'

'Suppose we go along the beach like you said, and get to Southbourne?'

'Yes?'

'Suppose we do. . . . ?'

'Yes?'

'Well – what will we do, exactly, when we get there?'

'You *know* what we're going to do. We're going to look for Mum.'

'I know, but – how?'

'Just look. You know what looking is, don't you?'

'But it will be like Easthaven. There will be lots of streets, and shops, and houses. How can we look in all of them?'

'We'll find the caravan park. Somebody will tell us where it is.'

'She might not be there.'

'We'll wait till she comes back.'

'But suppose she isn't living there any more?'

'We'll think of something.'

'But *what*?'

'I don't know, do I? You can't expect me to know everything before it happens. . . . All right, I *do* know as a matter of fact. I *do* know. . . . We'll ask at the caravan park if anybody knows where she's gone, that's what we'll do! There – that's what we'll do. Satisfied?'

Roy turned on his side again, away from her. 'Supposing nobody remembers?'

'Somebody will. You'll see. . . . Are you coming, then?'

'How far is it?' said Roy, speaking into the pebbles.

'Well I don't know, do I? I don't know everything. Anyway perhaps it isn't stones like this all the way. Perhaps it gets more easier to walk on, like it was at Easthaven. Let's try, Roy, eh?'

Silence.

'Eh? You coming then? . . . Roy?'

'All right,' he said, but he didn't move.

'Come on, then!' she hauled him to his feet, and he stood with downcast eyes. 'Come on, Roy, it's getting to be late.'

'You come first, and I'll come after.'

He didn't want to be looked at. He didn't want anybody looking at him, especially Nicky. He was all those things Nicky said he was, and he was never going to be anything else, and he didn't want anybody looking at him. He trudged behind Nicky, his eyes still on the ground, keeping several paces between them.

Right foot . . . left foot . . . right foot . . . left foot, and the pebbles sucking at his legs all the time. The bag with his coat, and the swimming things he hadn't used, felt heavy as stones. The evening was chilly now, and Roy could have done with wearing his coat, only he was too sad to put it on. And there was only this beach in the whole world now, with the sea on one side, and the cliff on the other, and the sky with no sun in it any more. Every now and again Nicky turned, anxiously, to make sure he was following. And every time she did that he stood still, to make her turn round again.

Gradually the beach became firmer, the covering of pebbles not so thick. Then there was shingle again – even small patches of sand. It should have been easier to walk, but it wasn't, because Roy's legs had turned into lead weights, and he had to concentrate really hard on lifting them, even over the firmer ground. He slowed, and stopped, and next time Nicky turned to look, there was a great yawning gap between them. 'Come on!' she urged.

'I can't.'

'What do you mean, you can't?'

'I can't. My legs won't go.'

'Well *make* them go.'

'I can't.'

She came back to him. 'There isn't any can't, we got to.'

'I can't,' said Roy.

'Yes you can.' Nicky went behind him and gave him a push. He stumbled a few steps forward and stopped again. 'See? Your legs *do* go. Now come on. We're nearly there.'

'You said that before. A long time ago.'

'So we must be nearly there now.'

'I don't think we're ever going to get there.'

'That's because you think bad things all the time.'

'If I think good things,' said Roy, 'they don't happen.'

'So? You got to *make* them happen.'

Roy sat down abruptly, on the beach.

'Get up.'

'No.'

'You miserable, moany, weak, draggy, *creep*!'

'You promised you wouldn't say those things any more.'

'I changed my mind.'

He was too weary to care, anyway. What did it matter if she called him names? What did anything matter? When she grabbed him by the armpits and yanked him to his feet he made no resistance, just hung on her arms like a dead weight.

'Stand up!'

He stood, numb and hopeless.

'Now come on! We're going a bit further whether you like it or not. We're going because I say so. We're going round that corner. We're going to see what's round that corner, because I think it's going to be Southbourne!' She seized him by the wrist and dragged, and he stumbled after her because her grip was like a vice, so he had no choice. The beach was curving to a point, and in spite of pain and misery, the point *was* getting nearer.

Nearer, nearer. Even Roy felt his hopes rising, just a little bit. There must be *something* different round this corner, there must be *something*. 'What's that notice over there?' said Roy.

'Never mind the notice. We haven't got time to look at notices,' said Nicky.

They were round! And there was nothing very different, only a much narrower beach, and farther on again another corner. Nicky swallowed her disappointment, not to show it to Roy. 'It must be round the next corner!' she said. 'Southbourne must be round the next corner. . . . All right, we'll rest just a little bit . . . just a little bit, till we get our breath back.'

'The sea's come nearer,' said Roy.

It was after supper on the ward, and mercifully everyone was allowed back to bed. Mrs Mitchell hauled herself up on her pillows, wincing at the pain from her broken ribs. She wriggled sideways, so she was sitting right on the edge of the bed. Then she held the bag so it swung from her hand. Backwards and forwards swung the bag, and it was like that other time, when she was running and the bag was swinging. She was running, and it was dark, and the bag was swinging, and the sea was on the other side, black and shiny, and the sand below looked black as well because it was night time, and she was running and frightened because it was night time, because it was late and – because it was late and – *there might not be a train*!

Suddenly it was there, all of it, all the memories coming back with a rush! Mrs Mitchell opened her mouth and screamed. The nurse came hurrying, and

Mrs Mitchell clutched at her. 'My children! My children! Who's looking after my children?'

'It's all right,' the nurse soothed her. 'Someone will be.'

'But I have to know, I have to know!'

'As soon as you tell us your address, we can go and find out for you.'

'It's 24 Gilbert Road, London NW10,' said Mrs Mitchell. 'Roy and Nicky Mitchell. I was running to get back to them. I didn't ought to have left them, and I'll never do it again! I won't, I won't!'

'I'm sure they're all right,' said the nurse.

'But all this time, all those days . . . Who's been looking after Roy and Nicky all this time? Oh I must go to them, I must go to them!' And Mrs Mitchell, weak and hurt as she still was, threw back the covers to get out of bed.

'When you're better,' said the nurse.

'But I have to know now!'

'Of course, of course – we'll tell the police right away. They'll see to it, don't worry.'

'I got sunburned today,' said Nicky, touching her cheeks. 'My face is all hot. Did you get sunburnt, Roy?'

'The sea's getting *really* near,' said Roy. 'There's not much beach left to sit on.'

'We stayed here too long anyway,' said Nicky. 'I only meant it to be a *little* rest. Do you want some more bread before we go? All right, please yourself. It's probably a bigger beach round the corner, like before. And it will be Southbourne, I just know. Don't worry, Roy, we're nearly there!'

'Suppose we aren't, though?'

222

'We will be – you'll see!'

Roy dragged himself upright, and began the weary trekking once again. Over and above the other feelings, a strong uneasiness was forming in his mind. The tide was coming in fast. In some places they had to keep right against the cliff, not to get their shoes wet. And the cliff was very high, and steep. Near the bottom there were places you could climb, otherwise it went straight up. Stiff as he was, and aching all over, Roy began to hurry. 'You *have* cheered up,' said Nicky, pleased.

'I don't think we can get round that corner,' said Roy.

'What d'you mean?'

'Look – there's all water!'

Nicky focused her eyes ahead, and frowned.

'We'll have to paddle, that's all.'

'Suppose it's too deep?'

'You *would* suppose that! You *would* suppose a bad thing like that!'

Roy began to run. 'Wait for me!' said Nicky.

The tide swirled around the point. Nicky put her bag on the ground, took off her shoes, and began to wade. The water was up to her knees. She lifted her skirt and took a few more steps. Suddenly she was floundering, waist deep in water. She turned, and struggled back to what was left of the beach.

'We're going to be drowned,' said Roy, and his face was white with fear.

'Don't be silly,' said Nicky. 'Of course we're not going to be drowned!'

'We are, the water's too deep!'

'Well we don't have to go in it, do we?' said Nicky. 'We can go back the other way. Round the other corner.'

'There was that notice,' said Roy. 'And you wouldn't let me read it.'

'Well – they should make the letters so you can read it from far away! Anyway, it was probably only about you mustn't drop rubbish.'

Going back, there were places where they actually had to paddle. Places which had been dry beach, before. The children hurried, because a great dread had seized both of them; and they were hurrying, and hurrying, only not nearly fast enough because it was like a nightmare, when you try to run and you can't. Suddenly your legs are all paralysed, and you can only go slow, when it's terribly, terribly important to go quick.

The point, which they had rounded dry-footed the first time, was quite impassable now. 'I'll swim,' said Nicky wildly, though she knew she was capable of no such thing. 'I'll swim, and carry you on my back.'

'We're going to drown,' said Roy, in terror.

'No we're not then,' said Nicky. 'I'm not, anyway, and if you think I'm going to let *you* drown, you can think again!'

'You can't swim round the corner, you know you can't! We can't get round this corner, and we can't get round the other corner. And the water's coming deeper all the time!'

'So? It's only the tide coming in. It'll go out again, Mr Nelson said. It does that all the time. It comes in, and it goes out. We'll just stay here, that's all, and wait.'

'Where?'

'On the beach, of course, dummy! Where do you think?'

'Suppose there isn't any beach any more?'

'Of course there will be a beach! There's always a beach. Did you ever hear of a seaside without a beach? Well, then!'

(Had Sir said otherwise? She must have misunderstood!)

'I can see places now where there isn't any beach,' said Roy. 'I can see lots of places where there isn't any beach, and the water's come right up to the cliff.'

'Well . . . we just find a place where there's plenty of beach left,' said Nicky. 'And we sit down and wait for the tide to go out. And I'm going to take off my wet dress and put my coat over me. And you can look the other way, Roy Mitchell, because I don't want any boys peeking at me while I do it!'

Mr Nelson paced on his gammy leg, dot-and-carry-one, up and down the station platform at Easthaven, waiting for the train which was already overdue. He was dreading the thought of the long rail journey, and the long tube journey the other end, and not knowing all that time if there was any news of the missing children. He could use the public phones at Victoria Station, of course, but his hearing was not as good as it used to be, and there was always so much background noise there.

The train came in, and Mr Nelson hoisted himself on board, better leg first, worse leg dragged painfully after. He found a seat by the window, so he could go on looking right to the last minute, as the train pulled out of Easthaven. The sunny day had become a cheerless evening, with a covering of cloud across a dull sky.

There was a noise outside – a message coming over the station tannoy. Mr Nelson tried to hear what the

225

tannoy was saying, but the sound was all muffled and distorted, and being inside the train didn't help, even though the carriage doors were still open.

'What's it saying, Dad?' said the little boy opposite, who surely should have been in bed.

'The usual, I expect,' said his father. 'Excuses about the train being late. Or the next one being cancelled. That sort of thing.'

'Who's Mr Nelson from London, then?' said the boy.

Mr Nelson heaved himself and his arthritis out of his seat.

Doors were slamming farther down the platform. 'Where do I go?' said Mr Nelson, to the railman who was slamming them.

'Depends where you *want* to go, mate. Where was it you was thinking of going?'

'The message! Over the tannoy just now. The one in Ancient Mesopotamian.' The railman gaped, unsmiling. 'Oh never mind,' said Mr Nelson. 'Where's the station master's office?'

Mr Nelson performed the painful dance which was the nearest he could get to a run, first to the station master's office, and then to the police car waiting for him outside. Inspector Kendall smiled, and opened the door for Mr Nelson to get in. Detective Constable Shaw was there as well.

'You've found them!' said Mr Nelson, eagerly. 'You've got me off the train to say you've found them!'

'Sorry,' said Inspector Kendall. 'Sorry to raise your hopes – I'm afraid it's not as good as that.'

'Not – not bad news I hope!'

'No, no . . . we think we know where they may be.

There's a good chance you can help us find them, so we're asking for your help again after all.'

'Good!' said Mr Nelson. 'Because I didn't want to go back to London anyway. What is it then? What's happened?'

'Well, for a start we've found the mother.'

'She was at home all the time?' said Mr Nelson.

'Indeed she was not!' said Inspector Kendall. 'Your old sharp-eyes up in London was quite right, she *has* been missing for a week and a half. She's been missing because she's been in hospital, unconscious!'

'In hospital!'

'And unconscious,' said Detective Shaw. 'Unconscious at first, that is. Then she couldn't remember who she was. Then this evening she finally *did* remember who she was, and started going frantic about her kids.'

'Which is how we came to know about it,' said Inspector Kendall. 'Hospital phoned their local police station. Their local station phoned the woman's local station in London. The very people we were already in touch with, of course. From when your chap and the old biddy went to see them about the mother being missing. Do you follow?'

'I'm trying to,' said poor bewildered Mr Nelson.

'Anyway, London got straight back to us,' said Detective Constable Shaw. 'And we came racing to snatch you out of the train.'

'And all this has happened in the last – what . . . couple of hours?' Mr Nelson marvelled.

'That's the way it goes sometimes,' said Inspector Kendall. 'The breaks all come at once.'

Mr Nelson's head felt big, and tight. In a moment it would go off pop. 'I still don't understand,' he said.

'The mother in hospital! But how did she get? . . . I mean . . . are you saying the kids didn't know what happened to their mother?'

'Couldn't have,' said Inspector Kendall.

'She couldn't be identified,' said Detective Shaw.

'Her bag was lifted just before the accident,' said Inspector Kendall.

'Accident?'

'She was knocked down by a car. No blame to the driver, she just ran across without looking. Right under his wheels.'

'And she only got her memory back this evening!' said Mr Nelson.

'That's right.'

'So as far as the kids were concerned, she just went unaccountably missing!'

'That's right.'

'But why in God's name didn't they tell someone?'

'I'm still trying to puzzle that one out,' said Inspector Kendall.

'I think *I* understand it,' said Detective Shaw. 'The kids were covering for the mother. She's quite open about what she did – now! She was supposed to be away one night at a caravan park, and she told the kids to keep it quiet because she'd get in trouble for leaving them. When she didn't come back, they went on keeping it quiet.'

'Does that make sense to you?' said Inspector Kendall.

'Oh yes,' said Mr Nelson. 'That makes very good sense to me. That is exactly what I should expect Nicky Mitchell to do. I wish someone would explain the rest of it though. Like, for instance, where we're going now.'

The car was making speed along a coast road. 'We're going over to Southbourne,' said Inspector Kendall.

'About ten miles if I remember,' said Mr Nelson. 'But why Southbourne?'

'Ah now, this is where it all comes together,' said Inspector Kendall. 'The hospital your kids' mother is in is at Southbourne. Which is where she had the road accident that put her there.'

'I *see*!' said Mr Nelson.

'You do?' said Inspector Kendall.

'I think so,' said Mr Nelson. 'You mean – the kids will have gone to Southbourne to find their mother!'

'Ever thought of joining the Force?' Inspector Kendall joked.

'But – ten miles!' Mr Nelson smiled only briefly; he was not in the mood for humour.

'Kids find ways,' said Inspector Kendall.

'Bus?'

'Quite possibly, there's a good service.'

'If they have the money for the fare,' said Mr Nelson.

'Since when did having no money stop kids from riding on buses?'

'They could have tried to hitch a lift, which God forbid,' said Mr Nelson.

'Amen to that!'

'Looking on the bright side,' said Mr Nelson, 'and presuming they get to Southbourne safely, they'll go to the caravan park first.'

'Probably.'

'And find their mum not there, so what then? Wander the streets looking for her, I suppose.'

'More than likely.'

'And it's getting dark.'

'Rapidly.'

'What about the mother?' said Mr Nelson, suddenly. 'Poor silly woman, she must be going out of her head with worry!'

'I think they're stalling her for the moment – but of course she's clamouring for news. They can't hide it from her much longer that her kids are actually missing.'

'Can't this car go a bit faster?' said Mr Nelson.

# 16

# Touch and go

Even Nicky had gone silent. They were standing now, leaning on the rough wall of cliff, and their feet were ankle deep in water. A new wave broke against the rock behind them, pulled out, and settled. Now the water level was five centimetres above the bottom of Roy's jeans. Nicky turned her head, and her eyes swept upwards. 'Do you think there might be somebody on top?' she said.

'We're going to drown,' said Roy. There was not enough light to show the whiteness of his face, but his voice came out hoarse and tight, and the hands with the twisting fingers were trembling.

'If there was somebody up there, they could help us,' said Nicky.

'We're going to drown,' said Roy.

'Not if somebody would fetch a boat round for us,' said Nicky. 'I think we got to shout, Roy. I think we got to forget the secret now. I think this is a emergency.'

'There's nobody there,' said Roy.

'Come on,' said Nicky. 'Shout!' She shrieked her best, but there was no response. 'You're not helping!' she reproached Roy. 'Come on, both of us!'

Roy added his feeble cries to Nicky's piercing ones, but the answer was only a chill, uncaring silence.

'What's the matter with you?' said Nicky. 'You can shout louder than that!'

231

'It's cold,' Roy whimpered.

'You got your coat,' said Nicky. 'What more do you want?'

'The water's cold.'

'Of course it's cold,' said Nicky, impatiently. 'It's meant to be cold. What do you expect – bath water?'

'I'm s-scared!' said Roy.

'No use being scared,' said Nicky. 'That's not going to help.' She strained her eyes in the almost-dark. 'I think we could climb a bit over there,' she said. 'To make us higher.'

There was a jutting-out piece of rock, rather less than a metre high, and quite easy to climb on to. They sat not uncomfortably, their legs dangling over the side. 'It's nearly to my feet now, Nicky,' Roy whispered.

'Perhaps there's a better ledge farther on,' said Nicky. 'A higher one. . . . Did you notice before, if there's a better ledge? Shall we go and look? We can still paddle, the water's not really deep.'

'It might be *very* deep further along, though. And it's all dark. We might drown while we're looking!'

Nicky stood, and peered upwards. He might be right, and anyway it might be easier to persuade him to climb from where they were. Better, too! Get them higher – farther above this nuisance sea!

She felt around with her hands, then began to climb.

'Don't!' said Roy, in alarm.

'Don't what?'

'Don't climb, you'll fall!'

'It's all right, I'm a good climber. There's another good ledge up here, I can feel it. You could climb it as well.'

'I can't, I can't!'

'Yes you can. Watch me!'

Her fingers gripped the perch, while her toes scrabbled at the rocky cliff face, seeking a foothold. She dug in her toes, and pulled on her arms. It was painful, but not all that hard. She straightened her elbows and leaned over the perch. 'Easy peasy!' she shouted to Roy, as she manoeuvred one knee on to the new ledge. The jagged rock scraped the inside of her leg, as she wriggled it further in. 'I made it!' she called. 'Come on, now you!'

Roy stood on the ledge below, his face against the rock. 'I can't!'

'Yes you can! Try!'

'I can't, I can't!' He was panicking. Nicky lay full length on her higher perch, and stretched her hand downwards. 'Catch hold my hand. I'll pull you!'

He looked up. He was terrified by the gap between them, and he couldn't reach her hand, however hard they both stretched. 'I can't,' he whimpered.

Nicky sat on her safe perch and considered. There was no getting away from it, this was a very tricky situation. It was Mr Hunt's fault. Everyone asked him to explain why the sea was dangerous, and he couldn't be bothered. Just because it was playtime, and he wanted his cup of tea! He never said about the tide could come in high, and cover all the beach. And it was coming up now all the time – look at it! And how was anyone supposed to know how much farther it would come?

It wasn't up to Roy's ledge yet, but it soon might be! For all she knew it could come higher, and higher, and higher. It could cover Roy all over, and he was

233

too panicky to climb, and if he tried he could fall, and hurt himself.

'All right, Roy,' she called, to calm him. 'Don't you worry. Don't you worry, Roy! I know another way.'

'What?'

'I'll climb to the top. Get someone to help.'

'You can't!'

'I *can*, Roy, it's not too hard for me!' Well, she had to say that, since there didn't seem to be any choice.

'There's nobody up there.'

'I can run till I find someone.'

'Don't climb! You'll fall!'

'I won't! When did you ever see me fall? Well, then!'

'You can't climb the top bit, anyway. It's straight up at the top, I can see!'

'You're a liar. It's too dark to see as far as that.'

'I saw before. . . . Nicky, don't *leave* me!'

She had started already, though. She stood on the ledge, her hands moving upward. This was more difficult. Instead of rising straight, the cliff face now bulged outwards. Nicky felt, gripped, pulled herself, clung, and was frightened. Out, farther out, and now her head overhung the ledge altogether. Slowly, painfully, centimetre by centimetre Nicky hauled herself round the bulge. Her hands found one crack after another, her feet and knees took as much of her weight as she could manage. She hoped there would not be many more bulges like this one, because really this climb was the most frightening thing she had ever done in her life.

She had made it! She was round the bulge, now what next? Her hands moved farther up, to grip a piece of rock. One toe found a new foothold, the other would be next to move. She hauled on her hands, while the free leg swung, jabbing at the rock. And the piece of rock she was holding broke clean away!

She fell. She fell feet first, overshooting the safe ledge, grabbing at it with hands that slipped over rough rock and were torn. Her knees struck one jagged spur of rock, throwing her sideways, so that her head crashed against another. She half slithered, half fell, all the way to the bottom, just missing the ledge where Roy sat. And Roy screamed, and screamed, and screamed.

He screamed for help, and there was nobody to hear. He screamed for Nicky to get up, because she was slumped against the cliff, he could see that much, and he didn't think her face was in the water, but it might be! Fearfully, he climbed off his shelf, and found her head; and it wasn't in the water yet, because the rock was propping it up. He lifted it, and saw in the bit of light reflected off the water, how her eyes were closed, and her mouth drooped open.

The little waves coming in broke against the cliff, receded, then rolled in again. At the highest point of the last wave, the water was nearly up to Roy's waist. He dragged Nicky by the head, and heaved her body partly on to the shelf. The moving water took her weight, and he left her lying there, legs still trailing in the sea, while he climbed, sobbing, back on to the shelf himself. He lifted Nicky's head again, and it was quite, quite limp.

She was dead! Roy was quite, quite sure that Nicky was dead. And he wanted to run, and run, from this horrifying thing that had happened, but there was nowhere to run to, so he just retreated as far along the downward-sloping shelf as he could. He turned his back on Nicky, and he turned his back on the oncoming sea, and buried his face against the rock. While the water came higher, and higher, and higher.

He didn't care about the water. If Nicky was going to be dead, then he might as well be dead too, because he couldn't manage without her. Who would look after him, if she wasn't there? Who would punch people's heads in for him, if she wasn't there? No, if Nicky wasn't there, he might as well be dead!

And then he felt the water, cold over his feet, and he didn't want to die after all. He didn't want to drown, he wanted to be alive, even if he was going to be by himself for ever. He pounded at the cliff with his fist, and cried, because he wanted to stay alive really, and anyway he was terrified of the dark cold water, that was going to come up, and come over his head, and come in his eyes and his nose and his mouth, so he couldn't breathe.

And the water was over Nicky's face now, probably, but it didn't matter if she couldn't breathe, because she couldn't breathe anyway, because she was dead. And then there was another thought, pushing through the numb terror that held him. Perhaps Nicky wasn't dead after all! Perhaps she was just unconscious! People could be unconscious as well as dead, he forgot that! And she was drowning, she was drowning because he had left her face lying in the water! Sick with horror, Roy wanted to run again, and run and run and run, because he had let Nicky drown, and she was drowning now, perhaps, and he was too terrified to go back and see.

Only he *must* go back, he *must*, because it might not be too late. Sobbing, and gulping, and clinging to the cliff face, Roy stumbled up the slopy ledge, back to the place where Nicky lay. The first wave of the rising tide washed over Nicky's face as Roy grabbed her head to lift it up.

She moaned, and muttered, and Roy's heart came right up into his throat. 'Nicky! Nicky!' She didn't answer him, because she had lapsed into unconsciousness again – but she was alive! She was alive!

She was heavy though, he couldn't hold her like this much longer. Whimpering with loneliness and fear, Roy struggled into a sitting position, with the sharp rock sticking into him; his back against the cliff, and Nicky lolling against his chest. He held her head very carefully, from behind, and begged the water not to come any higher. Well anyway, not *much* higher. Because like this he could keep Nicky from drowning, but if he had to stand up he didn't see how he would be able to lift her – she was too heavy.

It was very dark now. Only a few pale stars glimmered in the cloudy sky.

Inspector Kendall, Detective Constable Shaw and Mr Nelson were combing the streets of Southbourne; and the uniformed police were looking too. No one had seen the children at the caravan park though, and that was bad news. Had they come here after all? Had the police worked it out wrong? Or had the children come to some harm on the way?

'We warn them and warn them about taking lifts from strangers,' said Inspector Kendall to Mr Nelson. 'We warn them, and you people warn them as well, I know. And they don't take it in! They just don't take it in!'

'Actually, I don't think Nicky *would* hitch a lift,' said Mr Nelson. 'I'd say it's not in her character. She's a daredevil, but she's wary of people in some ways. Both the kids are; the mother encourages it.'

'Good!' said Inspector Kendall. 'We still have to cover the possibility, of course, but I'm inclined to think you're right. . . . Look, Sir, you obviously know this girl pretty well. Can't you get into her thinking? Come up with something we've missed?'

'Nicky's thinking isn't like anyone else's,' said Mr Nelson.

'Then concentrate on what's special about it. Try!'

Mr Nelson closed his eyes. 'She asked about the beach!' he said, suddenly. 'Dotty questions about walking round the country on the beach.'

'*Did* she!' said Inspector Kendall.

'You think they might have attempted it?' said Mr Nelson. 'To walk from Easthaven to Southbourne, along the beach?'

'Do *you* think so?'

Mr Nelson pounded his forehead with his fist. 'Yes, yes, yes! I'm an idiot! It should have been obvious!'

'I don't think you can,' said Detective Shaw, trying to remember all the details of the coastline. 'Walk all the way along the beach, I mean. Anyway, it's ten miles!'

'The kids might not realize how far it is,' said the Inspector.

'They *wouldn't* realize how far it is!' said Mr Nelson. 'Unless someone told them. If they were going by a map they'd have no idea of the real distance. . . .We did look for them on the beach, though. This afternoon. We went a fair way.'

'Perhaps not far enough,' said Inspector Kendall.

'They surely wouldn't have got far over those pebbles,' put in Detective Shaw.

'That's what I thought this afternoon,' said Mr Nelson. 'But that was before I knew there was a purpose. They would have got just as far as Nicky set her mind to going, I promise you!'

'Not *too* far, I hope.' Detective Shaw's voice was troubled.

'Let's go!' said Inspector Kendall.

'Good God, yes!' said Mr Nelson. 'Poor little devils, it must be pitch dark out there!'

'That's not what's worrying me,' said Detective Shaw.

'Something I haven't thought of?' said Inspector Kendall.

'Something dangerous?' said Mr Nelson, anxiously.

'What about Gull Point?'

'Good God, yes!' There was a new urgency in the Inspector's voice. 'What time's high tide?'

'Just about now, I think,' said Detective Shaw, glancing at the clock on the dashboard.

'Something dangerous?' said Mr Nelson, again.

'There is a notice,' said Detective Shaw. 'Of sorts.'

'*Something dangerous?*' said Mr Nelson.

'Not *too* dangerous,' said Detective Shaw, soothingly. 'Not *really* dangerous. Unless you were crippled or something. I mean, you can get caught by the tide, but you wouldn't drown. Even in a very high tide there are places you can climb, and stand.'

'If you can see what you're doing,' said Inspector Kendall. 'It's a long shot they're there, of course, but we won't take any chances!'

And he reached for the car radio.

Roy was terribly cold. He thought he had never been so cold in his life. Where he sat, the water lapped at his tummy, but when a high wave came it was up to his chest. The waves pulled at him, but not very much. He hoisted Nicky's body higher, and for the third or fourth time she came to, and struggled. 'Keep still! Keep still – the water!' She gabbled something that made no sense, then went limp once more. He was frightened that she really had died this time, and then he was more frightened because he felt the water against his chin. He stretched his back as high as it would go. He crooked his arm round Nicky's neck, pushing up from the shoulder, so he could keep her head clear if the water came any higher. His arm ached, and ached, and ached.

If he was standing on the beach now, he reckoned, the water would be over both their heads.

He would have to stand on the ledge, he would surely have to stand! Nicky's weight was across his legs. He struggled to move her, and she wasn't as heavy as she had been because the water was helping to lift her. He heaved, and pushed her to the side, and the arm that was still round her neck nearly broke off, or so it felt. He hunched up his knees, and pushed with his feet against the rock. But as he heaved her up by the neck, her weight dragged intolerably on his arm and his back and his knees; and he sank back, dropping them both lower into the water.

He was going to drown! They were both going to drown! If he pushed Nicky right away he could stand himself, and then he'd be all right. But *Nicky* would drown. And it would be a horrible thing if Nicky drowned, because he needed her. And anyway, anyway, it would be a horrible thing if she drowned because she liked being alive so much! He shouted at her to wake up properly, so she could help herself, and she moaned again, and coughed, and said, 'What is it?'

'Come on!' shouted Roy. 'You got to stand up! The water!'

'What water?' said Nicky, indistinctly – and drifted off again.

Frantically, Roy tried to think of another way. If he let her go for a minute, and stood up without her weight against him, and then bent down for her – he might be able to lift her, like that!

Now! Just for a minute while he stood! . . . But he dared not let her go, even for a minute, because if she was unconscious she wouldn't know how to hold her breath. If he let her go, even for a minute, she might die after all. He began to twist until he was kneeling, facing the rock now, still holding Nicky under the chin. It was hard, and it hurt, and he cried. He had to change arms in the middle of it, and he kept slipping, and it took him ten minutes to do it, but he was kneeling upright at last, and holding Nicky quite a bit higher out of the water.

At that point, Nicky came back to full consciousness. And strength. And panic.

She felt the water, and she felt Roy's grip round her neck, and she thought she was choking. She fought him, threshing at him with arms and legs. 'No!' Roy screamed. 'No! I'm helping you! I'm helping you!'

But Nicky was too confused to understand. She struggled, and threw her arms about, and kicked. And dragged them both off the ledge.

241

'Can't this car go faster?' said Mr Nelson, again.

'Don't worry too much, Sir,' said Detective Shaw. 'They'll be all right, even if they're there. You'll see!'

'They're able-bodied kids,' said Inspector Kendall. 'They aren't just going to sit down on the beach and let the water come over their heads, are they?'

'They'll be scared to death!' said Mr Nelson. 'I'm not too concerned about Nicky – she's a survivor. But Roy's a weak sort of boy. Not physically, but, you know, nervous. He'll have nightmares for the rest of his life, I shouldn't wonder.'

'Well – he's got a tough sister to look after him, hasn't he?'

'Where's the sea?' said Mr Nelson. 'We seem to have lost the sea.' He hadn't noticed, the first time, how the road turned inland.

'There's no coast road for three or four miles just here,' said Inspector Kendall. 'There are cliffs over there, and a beach, but a bit lonely. Not many places to get down. People mostly go to Southbourne or Easthaven. Much better beaches there.'

'Tide's turned!' said Detective Shaw, cheerfully. 'Several minutes ago, by my calculations.'

'And here's the turning for the cliff,' said Inspector Kendall. 'This is where we foot it – the danger stretch is that-a-way.'

They all piled out of the car, and Mr Nelson lurched dot-and-carry-one over the dark turf. If the children were there, he wanted to be there too. He wanted to shout down to them not to be frightened. To hold on, and not be frightened, because the water wasn't going to come any higher, and they weren't

242

going to drown, and they were going to see their mum soon, and everything was going to be all right.

'Take it easy now,' said Inspector Kendall.

'Don't fall and break something, whatever you do,' said Detective Shaw. 'Otherwise we'll have to get the ambulance for *you* . . .'

'There it is!' said Inspector Kendall, looking up.

There was a droning, and a whirring, and a light in the sky.

Roy dragged himself up, coughing and spluttering. What happened? His feet were on shingle, and his head was above the waves. Where was Nicky? Where was Nicky? He felt her against him, floundering about under the water. Frantically, he groped for her armpits, and heaved. She came up in terror, but she knew where she was, and she wasn't fighting him any more.

They coughed, and clung to the rock, and to each other. And they were shocked, and bewildered, but they hadn't drowned yet, they hadn't drowned! The water wasn't as deep as Roy thought it would be – funny, that! But anyway they hadn't drowned. Nicky was sobbing and retching, though, and Roy was terrified they might drown still if Nicky went unconscious like before, because he didn't have much strength left now, for holding her up.

They sobbed together, in the dark and cold, and Roy thought, why doesn't an angel come? One of Nicky's angels that she believes in! If angels are real they ought to come now, Roy thought – because if they don't do it soon it might be too late.

There was a whirring noise somewhere, a droning sound getting louder. It was a sound Roy had heard before, but the noise of the sea confused him, so he couldn't think for a moment what that other noise was. Then the whirring was right overhead, and there were flashing lights as well, and an angel *was* coming. He was coming out of the sky, on a winch, lowered from the police helicopter that had come to save them!

'Which one first?' said the angel.

'This one,' said Roy. 'She hurt herself.'

'I'll have to leave you alone for a minute, son,' said the angel. 'Not long. I'll be right back. All right? All right, then?'

'Yes,' said Roy.

'You'll do,' said the angel.

He took longer than he said he would, or it seemed like that. And it wasn't very nice standing all alone, chest deep in wavy water, waiting for the angel to come back. But the angel, who was a policeman really, was pleased with him. *Him!* And Nicky was safe now. And he had held her in the sea, didn't he, and that felt good.

It felt good!

The children were taken to the same hospital Mum was in, so they did find her in a way, after all. She came to see them for a minute in the night, and they were going to see her again tomorrow, and the nurse said she didn't think Mum was going to be punished for leaving them that time, because she was sorry now, and she was never going to do it again, and anyway she'd been punished enough already. So that was all right.

Nicky was supposed to rest next morning, because of the knock on the head, but it was impossible to keep her in bed. She kept getting up, and hobbling the length of the ward, so she could boast to everyone about her marvellous brother who saved her life in the sea. She was a bit disappointed she didn't lose her memory, like Mum, but you can't have everything!

It worried Roy, at first, that people said it was him saved Nicky, when really it was the helicopter. He mentioned it to a number of people that it was the helicopter that saved Nicky really, not him, but they still said he saved her first. If he hadn't held her up, she would have drowned, they said.

And then the thought came, it was his fault she fell in the first place, because he wouldn't climb, and he told them that. But they still seemed to think he did something special. *Him!* Roy hunched his shoulders under the bedclothes, in the private darkness, and thought about it, and it felt good.

The nightmares, of course, would come later.

Mr Nelson came to see Nicky and Roy, just for a minute, in the morning.

'You're supposed to be in school!' said Nicky, sternly. 'Taking Assembly.'

'I think the Office will forgive me,' said Mr Nelson. 'It was too late to get a train last night.'

'And your arthritis is worse! Just look, what you done to your arthritis!'

'I know,' said Mr Nelson. 'Very careless of me.'

'You should look after yourself better!' Nicky scolded him. 'You're getting to be quite a bit old now, you know.'

'I shall try to bear it in mind,' said Mr Nelson. 'All right, Roy?'

'Yes, Sir,' said Roy, turning his head shyly.

'Have you caught a cold as well, Mr Nelson?' said Nicky. 'Your voice has gone all funny.'

'It must be a cold, then,' said Mr Nelson.

'Do you know what I've been thinking, Sir?' said Nicky.

'No,' said Mr Nelson. 'I'm sure it's something interesting, though.'

'I've been thinking I'm not going to fight for Roy any more, in the playground.'

'I should think not indeed,' said Mr Nelson. 'He doesn't need it!'